ISBN-13: 978-1492753056
ISBN-10: 149275305X

Text Copyright © 2013 Angela Warwick

All Rights Reserved. No part of this publication may be reproduced, stored in a retrieval system or transmitted, in any form, or by any means, without the prior written permission of the author, nor be otherwise circulated in any form of binding or cover other than that in which it is published and without a similar condition being imposed on the purchaser.

Cover Art © 2018 Nick Warwick
All Rights Reserved

MOTH TO THE FLAME

The Story of Anne Boleyn

Angela Warwick

Also by Angela Warwick

Vyvyan's Vicarage

Return to Vyvyan's Vicarage

CONTENTS

1: Reality
2: Small Beginnings
3: Debut
4: To France
5: Maid of Honour
6: Life at the French Court
7: The Field of Cloth of Gold
8: A Lady of Fashion
9: Home Again
10: Life at Court
11: First Love
12: Shattered Dreams
13: Exile
14: Old Friends
15: The Return
16: Elevation
17: The Decision
18: Wolsey's Quest
19: Sweating Sickness
20: Back to Court
21: Slow Progress
22: Downfalls
23: Marquess of Pembroke
24: Secret Ceremony
25: Coronation
26: New Life
27: Hope and Despair
28: Seymour's Move
29: Diversions

30: Misery and Joy
31: Failure
32: Impending Doom
33: May Day
34: Trial By Peers
35: Condemned
Finality

Author's Note
Bibliography

REALITY

The setting sun slanted through the windows of the Lieutenant's lodgings, creating diamond shaped patterns upon the black velvet gown of the young woman who sat motionless in the window seat, one long slender arm resting along the buttoned back. She could not be still for long though; frequently she sprang to her feet and paced restlessly from window to bed and back again, clenched hands pressed to her mouth, before resuming her seat at the window for often just a matter of seconds.

Her mind was in turmoil, her eyes fixed unseeing somewhere in the middle distance. Only minutes before the news had come that the day was decided. She had known she was to die, but that it should be so soon, the next morning at eight o'clock! In her shock and distress she had shouted at them, tears springing to her eyes, "I am innocent. Innocent!"
All protestations were useless of course, she knew that. But how to accept a fate which was undeserved and unjust? She so desperately wanted to live her proper span, see her children grow up and enjoy a dignified old age. Her eyes fell to her clenched hands and she held them away from her, relaxed and extended, up to the light; narrow hands with long tapering fingers which were suffused with a rosy

glow from the window. She could see the fine tracery of veins, the smooth skin, all the signs of youth and health. Even the tiny blemish which had been the bane of her life seemed inconsequential; in a few short hours nothing would matter anymore. She had been a gentlewoman who had been raised far beyond her wildest imaginings but all was to count for nothing. It seemed to her that Henry, finding no further earthly honours with which to shower her now sought to endow her with a martyr's crown.

Anne Boleyn, her queenly estate stripped from her with the annulment of her marriage the previous day, rose to her feet once more and resumed her pacing. To a casual observer she may have seemed calm, but her serene countenance only masked her inner terror. Against her will her eyes strayed to the window and across the green towards the partially erected scaffold as she desperately tried to focus her mind on her present situation.

Realisation took hold of her "I should have guessed" she said aloud, more to herself than any other present. "Try as we may we have no control over our destinies; all is marked out for us from the moment of conception". She fell silent, her eyes closed, hands wringing together. Her mind would not focus, could not accept that life was almost done. Then without warning her eyes snapped open and she burst into cynical, hysterical laughter.

The women who had been sent to watch her and report her every word and action, exchanged meaningful glances. Her mind was obviously unhinged and hopefully she would soon let slip some snippet of information for which, suitably twisted, Master Cromwell would pay well. Condemned she may be, but nothing was to be spared in the effort to blacken her reputation still further, lest the fickle masses should see through the farce and rise in her favour.

However they were to be disappointed. Displaying the sudden change of mood for which she was legendary, their victim assuming calmness once again, climbed on to the pallet bed in the corner of the chamber and carefully arranged her skirts before laying back and closing her eyes.

Any hopes she might have had for restorative rest immediately dissipated. Instead of the dreamy blackness she craved, weird images flashed beneath her eyelids. The shapes were blurred and indistinct at first but would then come into sharp focus, each successive image bearing the smiling face of a dear friend; a friend no longer of this earth, all having met violent ends at the hands of the King's executioner. Despite the nightmarish qualities of the visions it seemed to Anne that each in his silent way was reassuring her that when her life too was brutally ended they would all be reunited in a far greater Kingdom.

Her thoughts turned to Elizabeth, her baby, her most treasured possession. When it became clear that the King no longer wanted her mother it was suggested that rather than be divorced she may prefer to admit a pre-contract with Percy of Northumberland. Thus her marriage to the King would be invalid and Elizabeth illegitimate. However she would still die, even though she could hardly be guilty of adultery if she was unmarried. Percy himself had sworn on the sacrament that no binding contract or public promise of marriage was ever exchanged between them, so she was mystified as to why so much pressure was brought to bear on her to admit such a thing. In the end though, she had said the words they demanded of her. Despite her best efforts her life was forfeit and the stigma of illegitimacy had fallen on her small daughter. Elizabeth was a Tudor and was born to rule; bred to rule.

Later, when she opened her eyes, the sun had gone leaving the room gloomy. And she was alone. Her women - or spies, as she knew they were – believing that she slept, had left her in peace on this, her last night on earth.

As ever totally alert the moment her eyes opened, Anne slid across the low bed and swung her legs to the floor. Once upright she smoothed the folds of the black velvet, thinking as she did so that the worn pile would need to warm her for little longer.

She found the gloom comforting, only brightened as it was by tiny flickers from the small fire. Even though it was May, spring had come late in this year of 1536 and although the days were bright and warm, the nights were cold and her room was chilly. The lodging house had been built but a few years previously and seemed as draughty to the prisoner as the lofty chambers of Greenwich and Windsor had seemed to the Queen.

Immersed in her thoughts she did not hear as the door softly opened and closed, admitting a cloaked figure. What she did hear was her name, a whispered question "Anne?"

She did not have to turn to know the identity of her visitor. "Margaret!" she cried. "I had not thought to see you again"

Margaret Wyatt, Lady Lee, pushed back the hood of her cloak and undid the clasp at her neck. "Why Anne" she said, infusing a false brightness into her tone. "All alone in the dark? That is not like you. Not on this…" Her voice faltered and trailed away. Anne finished the sentence for her "Not on this night of all nights?"

Returning to the door, Lady Lee threw her cloak on to a convenient chair then called for lights and wood for the fire.

A little later they sat together before the rejuvenated flames. Seeing Anne's face for the first time since her farcical trial Margaret noticed that apart from its paleness, in itself unremarkable for she was always so, there were few visible signs of the strain that she had been under since her brother and the others were arrested on May Day.

After a while Anne spoke "How did you managed to

gain entry Meg? I was not expecting to be so blessed". Margaret reached for the fire poker and shifted a chunk of wood in the heart of the fire, which fell into the cinders below emitting a shower of sparks. "I went to the King" she explained. "I begged him to allow me to come to you for these last hours and he agreed".

Anne fumbled for her friend's hand "It is good to have you here Meg. It will mean much to me tomorrow to have a friendly face beside me".
"I have seen Tom, Anne" Margaret lowered her voice. "He sends you his best love and urges you not to give up hope for a last minute reprieve'

Anne smiled at Margaret, her dearest friend since childhood and sister to Thomas Wyatt. "Bless him" she whispered. "I only thank God that he was not taken with the others".

Then there was silence, for between such friends words were not needed. The presence of each was comfort enough for the other.

Looking away from Margaret and in to the fire, Anne swallowed hard as she formulated the question she knew she had to ask. "Have you heard if he was sent for? The swordsman from France?"
"Even now he travels" replied her companion. "The King sent to Calais the moment Cranmer made known your wish to him".
"No doubt he considers it a last boon for a traitorous wife!" This was Anne the betrayed Queen speaking. Turning to Margaret she continued "And the

Seymour bitch, what of her?"

"Sent to Wolf Hall yesterday".

"I'm glad of it!" Anne exclaimed. "When my blood spills that's one little cat I would not wish within lapping distance. I wish Henry luck in his quest for sons. He'll not get a child on her with the health and beauty of my Elizabeth!"

Her voice, which had been rising close to the edge of hysteria, the edge over which she had toppled countless times, dropped low with misery. "Why didn't he give me another chance Meg? Why? I proved I could have a healthy child; I proved I could get boys. One more chance and I know I could have given Henry his heir and made myself safe for life".

"Don't think of it Anne" Margaret soothed, dropping to her knees beside the other's chair and taking both hands into hers. "It does no good now to brood. You cannot change what is past, only pray that when your time comes you can look the world in the eye and die with dignity".

"You do not believe there will be a reprieve?"

Margaret took a deep breath "To be truthful, no. The others are dead and he wants you dead too. He wants no impediment to his next marriage even though he must know in his heart that you never betrayed him with any man, except in your dreams".

"You know me so well, Meg. So well".

Leaning closer to her friend Anne whispered urgently "Take care of my daughter. Watch over her as she grows and when she is old enough, tell her I was innocent of all charges. Tell her that her mother loved her very much and was so proud of her; my sole crime in her father's eyes being that I did not provide her with a brother. Promise me you will do this!"

Burying her face in Anne's lap, Margaret sobbed out her promise. Seeing the other finally break down stirred in Anne something of her inner strength. "Meg, Meg, no more tears now". She lifted Margaret's chin until the tearful face was on a level with her own. "I thought you came here to cheer me, not to dampen my only gown with salt water!"

Anne's small attempt at gaiety was rewarded with a tremulous smile from her friend. Anne embraced her, glad of the human contact and whispered "Let us not think of tomorrow, but of the past. Long ago when life was simple and we were but children, at Hever.

Chapter 1

Small Beginnings

The ageless sounds of children at play floated across the Kentish garden. Sir Thomas Boleyn paused in his meditations as he caught sight of the five brightly dressed youngsters chasing across the grass, clustered around the very old, very small and exceedingly bad tempered pony which Sir Thomas had recently acquired for his daughter Anne.

Anne herself was mounted upon this steed, being led at a somewhat hurried trot by young Tom Wyatt whilst in close pursuit were Wyatt's sister Margaret and the other Boleyn children, Mary and George.

"Yet another game of damsels in distress!" Thomas Boleyn spoke his thoughts aloud as, hand stroking his beard, he watched them turn in to the copse at the edge of the park.

His train of thought totally disrupted, Boleyn resumed his walk towards the house; for although it had the impressive title of Hever Castle, it was little more than a moated manor house. Sir Thomas liked to think of it as a family home and was very proud of his little brood. He had his heir, young George, a bright, healthy little boy now ten years old. It was a great pity that neither of his two brothers had lived, but infant mortality was high and losses were both expected and accepted.

Then there was the elder of his two girls, Mary, the beauty of the family. Even at nine years old she was already displaying the softness and submissiveness which would no doubt endear her to many in later life. With such a nature coupled with her dark eyes and fashionably blonde hair, Thomas felt sure that she would attract the attention of a wealthy husband.

Thomas's eyes softened as he thought of the last of his children, six year old Anne. Not a conventional beauty by any means, not in an age when paleness of skin and hair was most admired. No, Anne could not even be considered as pretty, but then she was not one who would need to rely on mere looks to attain her desires. At so tender an age she already had the stirrings of a mysterious charm, a magnetism that drew every man into her snare, be he six or sixty. And what was more; she was always the damsel to be rescued in all the children's games. The others had to let her have her way unless they wanted a show of temper as black as her hair and eyes.

Reaching the castle, Sir Thomas entered by a side door then climbed a narrow stone spiral stairway to his writing chamber. Once seated with quill in hand, he set about penning a letter to the Archduchess

Margaret of Austria. "It has come to my notice" he wrote, "that your Highness's court is highly regarded as a moral and educational institution for the rearing of young ladies of good parentage…" Here he paused, quill poised, wondering if he had over exaggerated a little. No, he decided. Such compliments could only please the Archduchess and make her all the more likely to comply with his request. He went on to tell her that his daughters were greatly desirous of a place at the court of such an esteemed lady, then threw in a few more flowery phrases to further appease her Highness.

On reading through the finished article, Sir Thomas found himself deeply satisfied with his effort. He had managed to pen a letter of great admiration for the person of the Archduchess and the moral fibre of her court, whilst the main reason for his writing, in order to procure places as maids of honour for Mary and Anne, seemed incidental.

Sir Thomas sanded and sealed the letter with a flourish, then calling for one of the four messengers he kept on standby in case of urgent communications, immediately dispatched man and missive to Brussels with strict instructions to remain at the court until such time as an answer should be forthcoming.

Standing at the small casement window watching the messenger gallop on his way, Sir Thomas wondered idly whether to call the girls to him and let them know of his plans. After careful consideration, he decided against it for childhood was precious and short enough as it was. There would be plenty of time to prepare them once he had his answer.

Almost in response to his thoughts, Mary, Anne and Meg Wyatt shot into view, closely followed by Tom and George amid much shouting and screaming. Seeing them again brought Thomas's plans for his son to the forefront of his mind. George, he decided, must soon be sent away to some great house where he would learn all manly skills. As Sir Thomas firmly closed the casement to keep out the childish voices he decided that should the Archduchess decline Anne's services on account of her extreme youth, she could remain at home for a little longer, until another opportunity presented itself.

With a sigh he returned to his writing table laden with documents and correspondence to continue with his duties as King Henry VIII's Ambassador to the Court of Brussels, making up his mind to, in the course of his official duties, remind the Archduchess again of his modest request regarding his daughters, should the lady not immediately comply.

Chapter 2

Debut

The Boleyn girls had been barely twelve months at the court of Brussels before another more glorious opportunity arose for them.

The much talked-of alliance between England and France had finally materialised and Mary Tudor, the King's adored younger sister was to become the bride of the elderly Louis XII. It had taken careful and protracted negotiations, but Louis had finally agreed to take Mary because she was young, beautiful and enjoyed the excellent health required to produce the sons he needed to make his dynasty secure.

Thomas Boleyn managed to secure a place for Mary in the Princess's entourage and also a minor post for Anne. With George already safely placed elsewhere honing his skills as a gentleman, the ambitious father felt that his plans for his children were progressing satisfactorily.

Mary was now ten years old, very pretty and sure to be popular with the Princess. Anne was seven; young it was true, but displaying both manners and boldness well in advance of her years. Sir Thomas felt sure that his daughters would distinguish themselves since they were already in possession of valuable court experience and fluent in the French language. Lady Boleyn was less inclined to allow her girls, Anne in particular, to travel to yet another foreign court at such tender ages. Sir Thomas stressed to his wife that it was too good an opportunity to let slip and the girls would at least have each other for company. However the first priority was to persuade Margaret of Austria to release them from her service in Brussels.

Sir Thomas concocted a humble letter, emphasising that the Princess Mary herself had requested that his daughters accompany her to France. Not that such a statement was entirely true, but Sir Thomas was well versed in the diplomatic phrases which made it seem so. It was with great reluctance that the Archduchess Margaret released her youngest and most amusing maids of honour, who on arriving in England immediately travelled to London to take up their places with Mary Tudor.

So in the middle of September in the year 1514, a cavalcade of more than 1,500 headed by King Henry, Queen Catherine and the Princess Mary, left London and wound its way through the Kent countryside to the port of Dover. The conditions remained fine and they made good speed to the King's impressive fortress on the coast. However once they had arrived at the castle, the ever mercurial English weather changed for the worse and the King declared that he could not possibly risk his sister on such treacherous seas.

The only course of action was to wait it out. During those days, whilst the miniature court made merry at Dover, Anne had her first tastes of life in English royal service. Her sister Mary, having been in close attendance on the Princess for some weeks, was just a little superior towards her young sister and often during that Dover sojourn the sisters' voices were heard raised in anger. Invariably it was Mary who gave in first for besides being essentially peace-loving, she did not have the necessary sharpness of wit to better Anne, despite being the elder of the two.
"But it is so unfair Mary!" cried the youngest Boleyn. "This is the third time you have been asked to sing and play for the court and they haven't once asked for me!"
"It's because I'm more mature than you, my sweet" replied her sister with all the dignity of her ten years. "You are much too ambitious Anne, for such a little girl!"
"But I sing sweeter than you" whispered Anne slyly, rocking her small body gently from side to side in time with the melody running through her mind.
"So be it!" cried Mary, her placid nature for once stirred. "Come with me and I will set about presenting the smallest Boleyn, with the voice of an angel, to the court".

Although never dreaming for a moment that Mary would ever attempt to do such a thing, even ambitious Anne was slightly perturbed.

Mary, now thoroughly roused, grabbed her lute with one hand and her sister's wrist with the other, and propelled them both at speed through the gloomy passages. Anne dragged her feet rather, expecting that at any moment Mary would laugh and let her return to their chamber, saying that the whole caper was but a jest to teach her a lesson.

But Mary did no such thing. Anne was now conscious that at the end of the passage, which had now widened considerably, was the great hall, from which emitted bright flickering lights and the sounds of merriment.

The men-at-arms, standing slackly now because their sovereign lord had not yet appeared on the scene, did not trouble to hide their amusement at the sight of Anne, the miniature court lady, being hustled along by her sister. Already they had marked Mary down as worthy of closer scrutiny, perhaps in a few years.

Anne's eyes widened in disbelief as one of the men leaned forward and lightly slapped her small rump as Mary dragged her past him. Looking back over her shoulder she rewarded the guilty party with a scowl of such magnitude that the entire guard burst into delighted laughter.

However her indignation was quickly forgotten as she stood on the threshold of the great hall and beheld a scene which she felt must surely be paradise.

The banquet over, musicians were tuning their instruments, ladies and gentlemen were trying out dance steps in any available space and on the dais at the end of the great chamber sat the Princess Mary in conversation with her chief lady in waiting, Lady Jane Guildford.

As the light and colour danced before Anne's eyes, she was barely aware that her sister was once again moving her forward. Suddenly they stood before Mary Tudor, youngest daughter of King Henry VII, famous victor of Bosworth Field.

As etiquette demanded, Mary Boleyn stood silently, waiting for the Princess to finish her conversation and turn to herself and Anne. Anne's eyes were full of her royal patron, appreciating the small boned but shapely frame, the wonderfully animated expressions flitting across a perfect ivory skinned, heart shaped face, and oh, that glorious sunshine blonde hair contrasting with eyes the colour of a summer sky!

As the subject of her scrutiny turned to face her and her sister, Anne's eyes dropped swiftly to the floor. It was not good manners to stare, she knew, but where was the harm in doing so if one could avoid being caught in the act?

As the Boleyn girls sank gracefully into deep curtseys, a fanfare of trumpets heralded the arrival of the King and Queen. King Henry and Queen

Catherine had not presided over the banquet but had supped privately together in their chambers. The Queen was once again pregnant with the hoped-for heir and Henry, wishing to appease her every whim, had indulgently complied with her request that they eat alone.

However, nothing would stop him making merry with his court and his sister on possibly her last night in England, and Catherine knew better than to abandon her husband to the attentions of the court beauties. Whilst she sat and watched he would at least behave with decorum to avoid distressing her in her delicate condition. Catherine had long ago realised that to keep Henry in line she always had to be one step ahead of him. So far, she believed, she had achieved this and kept him faithful to her. Henry, as astute and crafty as his father and grandfather before him, was adept at covering his amorous tracks and keeping the Queen's suspicions allayed.

Princess Mary motioned the Boleyn sisters to their feet as the King and Queen made their way to the dais, the colourful glittering throng parting at their approach. "But he's so big!" an incredulous Anne whispered to her sister.
"Sssh!!" was Mary's reply.

But Anne, only having seen the royal personages from a distance, most lately from her place at the rear of the Princess's ladies, was quite overcome and lowered her eyes in confusion as the King approached. As the royal knees came into view,

Anne was aware of the Princess Mary rising from her seat in preparation for her deep obeisance to her brother. Taking their cue, the Boleyn sisters also curtseyed deeply, in perfect unison with their royal mistress.

"Well met, sister!" the great voice boomed, as scarcely taking in the presence of two of his sister's youngest ladies, the King handed his Queen up the two steps of the dais and into her chair, before sinking his bulk into the sturdier model beside her.

Once comfortable he swept his little eyes over the assembly whilst he waited for his sister to settle, mentally marking down the loveliest of the ladies for later dancing. And dalliance, he thought to himself, sneaking a crafty sidelong glance at the Queen. Catherine, as always, knew exactly the way in which his mind was working and she too was scanning the company, a fixed smile on her pale, slightly puffy face as she tried to locate the King's possible quarry.

Henry clapped his huge hands together and called jovially "Who is to start the entertainment? Come, let us make the Princess's last night in England something she will never forget!"

This was the opportunity for which Mary Boleyn had been waiting. Again she curtsied to the Princess, surreptitiously pulling Anne down with her, and on their rising addressed their mistress in a high clear voice "If it pleases your Royal Highnesses, my sister and I will sing and play for the court".

The Princess glanced sideways at her brother who had shuffled to the edge of his chair, one elbow resting on his knee, the hand propping up his huge face as he gazed closely at the sisters. "Who would say nay to such charming songbirds!" laughed the King, leaning suddenly back in his chair, disregarding its protesting creaks. He pointed to the carpeted steps of the dais "I pray you ladies be seated and set about entertaining this company with sweet melodies".

Anne, forgetting that she should wait for her sister to sit first, plumped thankfully down on the steps, her face turning as red as her new gown when she realised her error. The King's lips twitched as he suppressed his amusement. A merry child, he thought to himself. Please God Catherine will present me with such a daughter once she has birthed a Prince of Wales and a fine Duke of York.

Mary Boleyn, aware that the King's eyes had returned to her already budding figure said "I pray Your Grace forgive my sister Anne. She is but seven and unused to the ways of the court". She curtseyed again, colouring prettily.

The King's eyes softened as he gauged Mary's potential a few years hence. "She is forgiven" he said softly. "And doubly so, should she grow into such a beauty as yourself".

Mary inclined her head in acknowledgement of his compliment as she took her place beside Anne and began tuning her lute. Under cover of her bent head she said in a low voice "You sing, Anne, and I will accompany you".

Dumbly Anne nodded and it was only as Mary began to strum softly that she realised that she had forgotten to ask her sister which song she had selected. However further embarrassment was saved as she recognised Mary's playing as the introduction to the King's own latest composition. Of course, she thought, Mary would know what to choose to best please the King. Risking a quick glance at her sovereign she noticed that he was already well sprawled in his chair, fingers softly tapping the rhythm upon the carved arms.

As Mary finished her introduction and nodded her head to cue her sister's singing, Anne forgot her nerves, forgot that she was singing before the world's most glorious monarch; she was back in the rose garden at Hever, and Tom Wyatt was painstakingly teaching her all the latest court tunes, humming the melodies as she sang.

And so it was all the gaiety of youth and purity of innocence that she poured into her voice. The whole court listened, enthralled, as her clear voice, surprisingly deep and strong for one so young, soared to the very rafters.

As the song ended she was brought swiftly back to reality as appreciative applause filled the hall; even the King applauded, she noted. Anne felt so happy she feared she might burst with pride and treated the King to a huge bright smile so filled with gratitude that he, surprised, smiled back at her and thumped his meaty hands together all the harder.

As the applause died, and everyone naturally took their cue from the King and ceased clapping as he did, Henry rose to his feet, crossed the dais and stood in front of Anne. Again Anne found herself gazing at the royal knees, however this time a great jewelled hand was stretched out to her. Hesitantly she put out her little paw and he took it, raising her to her feet and motioning her up the two steps until she stood on his level. "We must congratulate our sister for choosing so rare a songbird to accompany her to France" he said, his eyes on Anne's small pointed face. He went on "For surely wherever Mistress Anne Boleyn travels, she will take a little of England with her". With that, he stooped and kissed the little hand he still held within his.

Anne, eyes dancing with merriment, loving being the centre of attention, dropped a cheeky little curtsey as he raised his lips from her hand. "I thank Your Grace" she breathed, then a little overcome as he released her, she backed down the steps and took her place next to Mary, who was already beginning to play the next melody.

The sisters performed three more songs before they were given the King's leave to retire, and so it was that at the tender age of seven years, Anne Boleyn felt herself well and truly arrived at court.

Chapter 3

To France

With all the excitement of the evening, Anne was well prepared to sleep soundly that night. And so she did, at least for the hours she was allowed, for as the Watch called out two of the morning, she was shaken awake by her sister Mary.

"It can't be time to get up already!" Anne's cross little face emerged from her crumpled sheets, her eyes immediately going to the window. "It is as black as pitch out there Mary" she hissed. "Whatever is the matter?"

Mary Boleyn did not attempt to offer any explanation until Anne had finished huffing and puffing. "The weather has calmed and the tide is right. Anne... are you listening? We must prepare to sail within the next few hours".

"Why didn't you say so before?" Anne demanded, swinging her legs over the side of the bed and wincing as her bare feet came into contact with the cold floor. "All this fuss! I'll never be ready!"

The sky was already lightening as the Princess and her entourage arrived on the quayside. All her gowns, plate, horses and personal possessions had been loaded on to several ships and now all that remained was for herself and her immediate household to board the largest of the fleet.

The King, his eyes even smaller and puffier than usual due to lack of sleep, had come down to take his last farewell of his sister. From the ship's deck, Anne and Mary watched as brother and sister embraced for the last time. There were tears on the Princess's cheeks; tears which Henry fondly imagined were the signs of her grief at leaving him.

He held her to him again and whispered "Queens do not weep in public you know".
"Well Princesses do!" she replied with a flash of typical Tudor defiance. Then, "Henry, you will not forget your promise. The promise you gave me last evening?"

With effort, Henry managed to recall the promise of which she spoke; the promise she had insistently wormed out of him. "I have not forgotten, sweetheart" he assured her, standing slightly away so that he could look down into her face. "But first you must keep your promise to me. You must be a Queen above reproach, and most of all do not stint in your efforts to become mother to a Dauphin".

Thinking of the old man who was to be her husband,

Mary's face assumed something of a grimace. However she did this away from her royal brother's gaze as he clasped her to him once more, angry in his way that this purest of Tudors had to be but a sacrificial pawn in Anglo French politics.

"It is a bargain then?" she asked, looking up into his face, fresh tears welling into her eyes.

"A bargain!" he affirmed, having rarely been able to resist any pretty woman who wept.

Her farewells over, the Princess Mary of England curtsied to her brother and then walked towards her ship, negotiating the walkway with grace and dignity. She had now left English soil and to all intents and purposes was now Queen Mary of France.

The small party stood on the quay, lit by torches and a sky streaked by a rising sun as the little fleet sailed from view. Henry lifted his arm in a final, silent salute, then abruptly turned on his heel and strode purposefully towards the castle, his gentlemen scurrying in close pursuit.

Out on the calm waters, the Princess Mary too turned away and went below, those of her ladies who had chosen to take a last glimpse of England close behind. The Princess selected about a dozen companions to sit with her for the duration of the voyage; Mary and Anne Boleyn were amongst those chosen, both for their amusement value and the fact that due to their youth and stature they took up very little space in the cramped quarters below deck.

They had been travelling for some time when all became aware that the gentle swaying of the ship had become a definite roll. As the Princess voiced this thought aloud, there came a knock on the cabin door. Lady Guildford answered the knock and spoke in hushed tones with the messenger. Returning to the Princess, Lady Guildford curtseyed and said "Your Highness, that was a message from the captain. It seems that we are sailing in to rough seas, but he bids you be of good cheer, for there is no danger".

"We shall all have to take turns at being seasick" replied the Princess, leaning forward to chuck a very apprehensive looking Anne Boleyn under the chin. "I suggest we carry on with our work ladies, and let the weather take its course". Smiling, she dropped her eyes to her embroidery and took up another skein of silk.

However within the hour, embroidery was forgotten as the Princess lay groaning on her bunk. Those ladies who were not affected with seasickness, and there were but two, took turns to administer to the Princess's needs and to the others in the cabin.

On the floor beside the Princess's bunk crouched Mary Boleyn, holding her sister tightly to her. Every time the ship tossed more wildly than before, Anne emitted a short, shrill shriek. At times it seemed as though the vessel was intent on somersaulting its way to France. "We shall all drown" moaned little Anne.

"Oh no. No, you're quite wrong Anne" said a voice from above them. The Princess had raised herself on to one elbow and was looking down at them. She continued "It took me nearly half of last evening to persuade Henry to promise me that should Louis die, I should be allowed to choose my next husband for myself. Ladies, I mean to marry Charles Brandon, and the sooner the better. I have been good and I have been devout; surely God would not seek to deny me my heart's desire by sending me to the bottom of the ocean!" Having said her piece, the Princess fell back on to her bunk, clutching her stomach, attended by a clucking Lady Guildford.

Anne, her queasiness momentarily forgotten, whispered hoarsely to her sister "Who is Charles Brandon?"
"The King's best friend" replied Mary. "You must have seen him last evening; almost as tall as the King himself, handsome, broad shouldered, black hair and beard?"
"Oh yes, I know who you mean" Stretching up to look at the supine Princess, then nestling back in to the protection of Mary's arms, Anne confided "But I much prefer the King".

Then almost as suddenly as the storm had started, the rocking motion of the ship ceased and far away up on deck, the queasy assembly heard the welcome cry "Land ahoy!"

"Oh dear God!" Mary Tudor sat up abruptly in her bunk and called for a mirror. "They have sighted France and just look at the state of me." Suddenly she laughed. "If Louis sees me looking like this he will send me straight back to England, and after this voyage, even French soil will be welcome!"

One by one the Princess's stricken ladies recovered their composure and set about repairing both their mistress's ravaged looks and their own. When eventually the captain knocked at her door, all within were almost themselves again, if a little rumpled. Looking slightly apprehensive at entering this female stronghold, the captain approached the Princess and bowed low "Highness, the storm scattered all your ships so I set for the first French port we sighted, to save you ladies any further distress". He finished his speech rather lamely, for casting his eyes around the cabin, he could see that the ladies looked not at all distressed.

The Princess rose somewhat unsteadily to her feet. "We thank you for your concern captain" she replied.
"So at which port are we?"
"Boulogne, Highness".
"Boulogne. And are we ready to go ashore?"
"The water is too shallow for us to sail right into the harbour, Highness. However, we have been sighted and recognised, so row boats will take us ashore".
Smiling, the Princess dismissed him, saying "In that case, we will make ready".

However, reaching the shore was not without complication. The sea, even close to the harbour walls, still churned relentlessly and no matter how hard the oarsmen tried, they could not manoeuvre the boat close enough to the jetty for their royal passenger to disembark without becoming soaked in sea water. After several fruitless attempts, one of Mary's attending gentlemen leapt gallantly into the water and lifted her to safety as the salt water lapped around his thighs and soaked her trailing skirts.

This method had to be adopted for all the ladies in the retinue, and there were no shortage of volunteers for the task. Mary and Anne Boleyn thought it huge fun to be bodily lifted over the churning water to safety; Mary in particular more than happy to find strong male arms wrapped around her.

Shortly afterwards, the Princess and all her ladies stood on French soil for the first time, their dignities somewhat ruffled by a landing almost as rough and uncertain as the voyage. They were immediately escorted to a nearby dwelling where they ate and rested, then progressed to the small town of Montreuil where Mary Tudor was able to finally discard her dishevelled travelling clothes and be reunited with the huge chest containing the gown in which she intended to greet her future husband.

Princess Mary soon recovered her high spirits. She was young, beautiful, and by the way the French had received her even in her bedraggled state, she was going to be popular with the people. With so many things in life going her way, she felt that she could overlook the handicap of bedding with an ancient husband.

Within three days the Princess felt able to continue with her journey, and so the procession formed, with her at its head, to proceed to the royal town of Abbeville, where the marriage would be celebrated.

Anne, riding pillion behind Mary about a quarter of

the way down the procession, was almost delirious with delight. It was all so unlike anything she had ever experienced before. There was colourful bunting and banners all along the route, musicians playing and hundreds upon hundreds of cheering, waving people.

About ten miles outside Abbeville, a party of horsemen were sighted galloping towards them. The Princess's French escort brought his horse alongside hers and said "The King approaches, Your Grace".

Frantically the Princess dusted off her clothing and tucked some stray strands of hair back beneath her hood. Then she straightened her back, lifted her chin, composed her features and prepared to meet the man who would shortly become her husband.

As the riders came closer, the Princess and her entourage halted. The small party stopped some distance away, and then a lone horse and rider detached themselves and approached her.

Louis XII of France, gorgeously attired in crimson and cloth of gold, pulled up alongside his English bride and swept his velvet cap from his thinning grey hair with a courtly flourish. "Welcome to France, Madame".
Mary, thinking that he looked a good deal older than she had even feared, smiled graciously, murmured her thanks and held out her hand for him to kiss. As he leaned closer she saw his pale wrinkled skin and tried not to wince as his dry lips brushed the back of her hand. As he straightened and looked into her

face, Mary diligently searched his features for some trace of the young man he had once been and finding nothing, mentally prayed for strength.

But now she must smile and be charming for he was presenting the other members of his party, mostly close relatives and friends. Mary was interested to meet the people who, up to now, had just been names on official documents. In particular Francis of Angouleme; for if Mary bore no heir to the throne, he would succeed to the crown. Mary suddenly thought how amusing it would be to provide Louis's heir and put Francis's extremely long nose out of joint. For Francis's part he was looking at her with open admiration. Truly a Tudor rose, he thought. If old Louis can stir himself to get a child on any woman, this is the one!

Louis explained to Mary that he had been on a hawking trip and that he had sighted her party quite by chance. Mary smiled prettily and expressed regret that he had been waylaid from his purpose, although she was in truth fully aware that the whole thing had been staged. After being introduced to the leading nobles of her party, the King continued on his way with his hawks, leaving Francis and a full company of Swiss guard and French nobility to escort his bride to the town of Abbeville, where the marriage would be celebrated the following day.

Within sight of Abbeville, Mary was able to change her gown ahead of the grand entry in a convenient tent erected for that purpose at the side of the road. Once attired in her gown of white and gold brocade, she emerged to be presented with Louis's gift of a beautiful white palfrey which stood waiting for her underneath a large white satin canopy embroidered with the arms of England and France, held aloft by four stout valets.

The enormous procession proceeded to Abbeville where the people gave their new Queen and her attendants a noisy and joyous welcome; marvelling at the rich apparel and jewels of the English nobility. After a mass of thanksgiving at the church of St Vulfran, the party joined the King for a state reception.

The very next day, Mary and Louis rode together in yet another procession, the most important yet, to the great cathedral to celebrate their marriage. There, amid great pomp and ceremony, the English Princess became the wife of the French King.

Other than witnessing the event, the Boleyn girls had no parts to play in any of the ceremonies. They watched as their Princess, sumptuously gowned in gold brocade trimmed with ermine, a coronet set with flashing colourful jewels confining her blonde hair as it rippled over her shoulders, played her part impeccably. As Louis clasped a costly ruby and pearl necklace about her neck as they stood before the altar, Anne wondered at her mistress's serene expression, realising how much her heart must be crying out for Charles Brandon to be beside her.

Expensive and impressive celebrations continued for the rest of the day and half the night, the King surprising his new wife and all those present by his energetic participation in the festivities. Finally the newly married pair were solemnly lighted to bed and as the chamber door closed, the last face Mary saw was that of an anguished Francis of Angouleme; he who feared to be cheated of his inheritance.

With great determination Mary turned over in the great bed to face Louis. Neither spoke as they lay looking into each other's eyes. After only a moment's hesitation, Mary held out her arms. It was time to do her duty.

Chapter 4

Maid of Honour

The wedding celebrations were barely over before Louis approached his new Queen and announced that he was sending all her English ladies home and replacing them with those of her adopted country.

Shocked and tearful the Queen begged him to allow her to keep at least Lady Guildford and a few other senior women, but Louis stood firm. He told her that he was not happy with the influence the older ladies had with her and felt that she should begin to renounce her English ways and settle to her new role as Queen of France.

So Lady Guildford and her contempories were packed home on the next ship, although to compensate his wife for the loss of her greatest friend Louis did allow a few of the younger maids to stay. Mary and Anne Boleyn were amongst those few, considered by Louis to be of no influence and little importance.

To cheer herself and take her thoughts away from what she felt was an unkind and thoughtless move by her husband, Mary absorbed herself with re-establishing the court of France as the brightest in Europe. Night after night she devised plays, masques, moonlight banquets and every other possible entertainment she could think of. She encouraged her husband to join in all the activities and was heard to remark wryly to her maids on more than one occasion that whilst he threw himself so wholeheartedly into day and evening pursuits there was little chance, if any, for the hoped-for heir.

Louis made no secret of his delight and contentment with his new wife, showering her daily with luxurious gifts and fine jewels; declaring loudly to any within earshot how marriage with his beautiful Queen had rejuvenated him. Francis tried to avoid being nearby on such occasions; it wasn't so much the revelations of what occurred behind the royal bed curtains which disturbed him, but the possible outcome of such passion.

The court began its progress towards Paris, stopping at St Denis so that the new Queen could be crowned on 5th November. Not only did ancient custom dictate that no monarch could officially enter Paris until crowned, Louis wanted all of France to know of his marital bliss and dedication to his bride. Unsurprisingly after all his efforts and exertions, not long after their arrival in Paris, Louis complained of feeling weak and unwell. However he encouraged his Queen to continue with her gaiety and on many occasions she found herself partnered in the frolics by Francis, the heir presumptive.

Francis had a reputation as a tireless womaniser, an expert in the chase and a connoisseur in the arts of love. Although only a little older than Mary herself, he was a man and therefore his behaviour was not only condoned, but expected. A woman who behaved openly thus, even at the liberal court of France, would be condemned as a whore.

One evening during the dance when Francis was holding her just a little more closely than etiquette demanded, Mary murmured "My Lord, I beg you release me a little lest my husband should become suspicious as to your intentions".

Making no attempt to relinquish his hold on her, in fact tightening it, he replied ardently "I would you were not the Queen for I feel you and I would complement each other perfectly in a little affaire"

They parted, she pirouetted twice as the dance demanded, then came back into his arms laughing lightly as she said, with an innocence which her seductive gaze belied "I am sure you are correct in your assumption my Lord, but think how galling it would be if you were denied the succession by your own son!"

He could not hide his look of horror as he bowed with a flourish at the end of the dance. She curtsied with the merest bob, refusing to meet his eyes, then walked sedately back to the dais and her husband.

The King was slumped in his chair, his face as grey as his hair, his trembling hands gripping the ornately carved arms with such force that his knuckles were white. She knelt beside him, at once full of genuine concern. "My Lord?" she whispered "You should retire to your chamber; you do no good by staying here. Come...."

Louis heaved himself to his feet with difficulty, then leaning on his Queen, shuffled across the banqueting hall towards their privy staircase. The assembled company swept bows and curtseys as the royal couple departed, a barely imperceptible nod of Mary's head summoning her ladies and the King's gentlemen to follow them.

During the night, the King's condition worsened. His physicians could not say exactly what it was which ailed him; although they did suggest hesitantly that his condition could have been brought on by undue exertion.

During the early hours of January 1st, the Queen was woken and summoned urgently to the King's bedside. His physicians explained in hushed voices that there was nothing more to be done for him and that he should receive the last rites. White faced, Mary nodded and with a single motion of her head indicated to the attending priest that he should set about his duty. Shortly afterwards, Louis lapsed into unconsciousness, slipping quietly away scarcely an hour later.

As she prayed with the priests for her husband's soul, Mary found herself weeping, although she was shocked to realise that her tears were more for the solemnity of the occasion than for her husband's passing.

After she had returned to her chamber leaving her husband's body for the embalmers to do their work, she found she had a visitor. Francis's mother, Louise of Savoy was waiting to see her, ostensibly to advise the Queen Dowager on her period of mourning. Mary knew that such advice was necessary as she was not yet fully familiar with the rituals of the French court, but was well aware also that the woman's eyes were furtively assessing her body, terrified that she sheltered a Dauphin within who would deny her Francis the throne.

As custom demanded, Mary retired to the Hotel de Cluny to mourn her husband for the statutory six weeks, dressed entirely in white. This period was calculated specifically to ascertain whether a posthumous heir was expected. During those six weeks Mary was allowed only to receive visits from her physicians and members of the royal family. Needless to say, Louise and Francis insisted on calling on her almost every day, officially to help her bear her grief, but using that excuse merely to reassure themselves of her true condition.

The mourning period was barely three weeks old when Francis one day visited without his overbearing mother. At his request Mary dismissed her attendants, for he said he wished to speak with her privately.

As the door closed behind the last of her maids, Mary, noticing the smug expression he wore upon his face, decided to give him the shock of his life. With a smile she advanced towards him, holding out her hands in greeting, then whilst still a few feet away suddenly stopped and closed her eyes. Putting a hand to her forehead, she swayed slightly.

In a trice he was at her side, ushering her to a chair and only leaving her briefly to pour a goblet of wine which he insisted she drink before even attempting to talk. Moments later, she managed a tremulous smile. "You are recovered Madame?" he asked.
"Yes, I think so" she replied in a weak voice, after a pause. "I think I must have caught a chill... this dizziness has assailed me several times over the past few days".
"Marry me Mary!" he said suddenly, desperately.

She was genuinely taken aback at his plea but assumed that he had been taken in by her little ruse and thought her with child. If he could marry her quickly enough, he could claim the child as his.

Tempting though it was to torture him for longer, she dropped her pretence. "I am not with child Francis, if that is what you think".
An expression of utter relief flashed across his face as he knelt by her chair. "Even so" he said quietly "I still want you for my wife. It was because I wished to ask you this that I came alone".
She hesitated, trying to wipe the thought of Charles

Brandon from her mind. As Francis's wife she would live a good life, her sons would rule and she would be revered as the mother of France. But Charles Brandon would not go away; neither would her thoughts of England, which she missed more than she had ever expected.

At length she looked into Francis's eyes and replied "I am sorry, I cannot marry you. There are many reasons; for one, I do not love you".

In answer he pulled her roughly to her feet and enfolded her in his arms. His face close to hers he whispered "Love will come, in time".
"No!" she struggled to free herself and amazed that he could not charm her, he let her go.
"Give me another reason!" he snarled.

Moving away from him, agitatedly smoothing her veil, she replied "You are betrothed to your cousin Claude".
"No problem. Betrothals can be broken just like that!" He snapped his fingers dismissively as he spoke.
"I love another".
His face betrayed his shock at her candid statement but before he could speak there was a knock at the door. Relieved, Mary called "Enter!"

Anne Boleyn, in her eighth year, dipped a sedate curtsey to Mary and made a deep obeisance to Francis, whom all France regarded as King even though he was yet to be proclaimed. She turned to Mary "Madame, a messenger from England has arrived and desires an audience".

Glad of the welcome interlude, Mary asked "His name?"

"Sir Charles Brandon, Madame".

At once, fresh colour flew into Mary's cheeks and she swayed once more, genuinely this time, and would have fallen were it not for Francis's fast reaction. "My rival no doubt" he said quietly, not without a spark of amusement.

Imperiously Mary turned to him. "I would be alone with my brother's messenger" she told him, giving him no option but to take his leave. Gracious to the end, even in defeat, Francis paused in the audience chamber and warmly greeted a surprised Brandon, the lucky man who was the object of Mary Tudor's affections.

Three weeks later, very early in the morning, Anne Boleyn as Mary's favourite maid of honour was sole attendant at her mistress's secret wedding with Charles Brandon, Duke of Suffolk. As the ceremony ended, Mary threw herself into Brandon's arms and declared "I fancy I much prefer to be Duchess of Suffolk than Queen of France!"

King Henry, unaware of his sister's remarriage, had to be told that she no longer considered herself a pawn in European politics, having wed herself to the man of her choice. This calamitous news was broken diplomatically to him by his most trusted advisor, Cardinal Wolsey. Henry ranted and raved for some time, threatening all kinds of retribution before graciously giving his sister and her new husband leave to return to England. The price was every jewel

Mary possessed and all Brandon's manors, lands and livings, save the one at Westhorpe.

Anne Boleyn, thinking to remain in the new Duchess's service, also made ready to return to England. However her preparations were interrupted by a summons from her father who was temporarily resident at the court of France.

Surprised, because her father had made no move to contact her upon his arrival in France some ten days earlier, her knock on his chamber door was somewhat timid. She entered at his command, closed the door and approached the ornate table where he was busily writing, quill skimming over parchment. He glanced up, then continued writing. "Ah, Anne. How are you my dear? You have grown taller I think in these past few months".
"Very well, thank you father. I think the French air suits me although no doubt I will do as well in England".
"England?"
"I am making ready to accompany the Duke and Duchess to their estate at Westhorpe".

With a sigh her father carefully laid down his quill before getting to his feet and moving round the table to stand before her. He put his hands on her shoulders and said gently "No Anne; Westhorpe is not for you. Do you think I could allow a daughter who has been such a success in service to the Queen of France to return to England and retirement with an out of favour Duke and his Duchess?"
"King Henry has forgiven them!" Anne burst out

hotly. "Who could not?" Then softly, "They are so much in love".

"My dear". Thomas Boleyn sank wearily into a nearby chair and pulled Anne on to his knee, as he had habitually done when she was very small. "You are one of the brightest rising stars at court. Why, Francis himself has asked for you to be a maid of honour to his Queen".

"Claude!" Anne spoke the name disdainfully. "What sort of life would I have in her service? She hardly ever speaks other than to pray and has no interests outside of religion".

"A far better life than as a poorly paid servant of the Duchess of Suffolk. Anne, King Henry has left them with barely a penny. They will live quietly out of necessity, rarely, if ever, going to court".

"I would happily serve her for just my keep!" Anne retorted, although a little less sure of herself now.

"Think of it Anne" Sir Thomas put his face close to hers and his voice dropped almost to a whisper. "You would be in the middle of the countryside with only servants for company and visiting tradesmen upon whom to sharpen your wit. And do you think she will have time to converse with you so freely once she is mistress of the estate and has babes in her nursery?"

He knew the best way to bend his daughter to his will. Anne had to admit to herself that she was one who thrived on the gaiety and stimulation only to be found at court. Already she loved to be at the centre of things and could not suppress the thrill of gratification she felt because Francis had asked for her to remain in France. She was mature for her age, for one could not long remain a child when living in the brightest and most immoral court in Europe. She fancied that the King of France most likely had some ulterior motive in wanting to keep her close. "What of my sister?" she asked.

"Mary too has been noticed" her father replied, and if Anne understood the inflection in his voice on the word 'noticed', she made no sign. "Mary will remain here with you, for now".

Chapter 5

Life at the French court

So began the formative years of Anne Boleyn's French education. As Anne had predicted to her father, life with Queen Claude was very different to that with Queen Mary. Anne and her sister were amongst some two hundred girls of similar age and breeding kept strictly under Claude's wing; their days consisted of church services, theological gatherings, and interminable embroidering of religious subjects together with their duties upon the Queen's person.

Within a very short time of the consummation of her marriage to Francis, Claude was dutifully pregnant. To the horror of her maids, particularly Anne, the forthcoming child drove Claude even deeper into her religion; the embroidering of religious subjects became obsessive.

Even Francis himself was slightly concerned by his wife's odd behaviour, particularly as she seemed not to realise that the making of garments for the child should now be taking precedence over all other needlework. Often he would come to pay his morning respects to his wife – he no longer shared her bed now that she was pregnant, rejoicing in the opportunity to take his pleasures elsewhere – and would jokingly ask of her priorities for the day, altar coverings or infant coverings. Such innuendo was completely wasted on Claude, who looked on disapprovingly at the bolder maids who dared titter in the presence of the King.

Amongst the many activities for young ladies upon which Claude frowned were music, singing, dancing and the company of men. Whilst she realised that every gently reared young lady should be able to play several musical instruments, sing sweetly and perform stately court dances, she felt that such pursuits were merely necessary accomplishments and should not be used in a frivolous manner at every opportunity.

Male company was especially to be avoided, at least until a suitable prospective husband had been chosen for a girl. However, most men of the French court nursed not the slightest inclination to marry any of the Queen's ladies. The seduction of the innocent was a favourite male pastime, more than encouraged by Francis himself.

Occasionally Claude allowed her ladies to attend a masque or banquet, purely in order that they should have experience in how to behave at such functions. If Francis and his friends had anything to do with it, often three of four of the young ladies had gained experience of a vastly more intimate nature by the end of the revels.

In this vein, life continued at the court of France for Anne Boleyn. She had quickly realised that as one of the Queen's two hundred and also as one of the youngest, she was unattainable to the accomplished court seducers. So at the end of a long and boring day she liked nothing better than to flirt with any court gallant who would take an interest in her. In this manner were gained some of Anne's most useful accomplishments; the art of leading on the victim until he is sure she will comply then repulsing him fiercely as he thinks to take his quarry; sensuous sidelong glances from devastatingly dark eyes, tempting many a lecherous male to know more of her immature body. All these characteristics and more were honed during those French years.

As time passed the Boleyn sisters grew further apart, Mary becoming quieter, more secretive, infuriating Anne with the secret knowledge in her eyes which she refused to share. However all was revealed to Anne one day, whilst she walked her wolfhound in the palace gardens. Without warning, she came upon her sister locked in a passionate embrace with a man whom she presumed to be a gentleman of the court. The man had his back to her and only turned once Mary had indicated her young sister's presence.

Anne's mouth dropped open with surprise as she recognised the gentleman as none other than the King himself. She stood, rooted to the spot, oblivious to the frantic barking of her dog and the consternation on the face of the King. She saw only Mary's angelic blushing face and realised in a flash the reason for the change in her sister.

Flaunting etiquette by making no attempt to acknowledge the presence of the King, Anne walked on, crimson faced. They did not follow her or call out after her, so Anne put what she judged to be a safe distance between them before sinking on to a convenient garden seat and pressing her palms to her burning face.

Mary the mistress of the King of France, if not already in deed then surely by intention. What would the court say? What would their father say? She sat quietly for some time, conflicting thoughts racing through her shocked brain. What should she do? Challenge Mary for prostituting herself and disgracing the family name? No, that would not be wise. By doing such a thing she could bring down the wrath of the King upon her family in both France and England. The best course of action seemed to be to try and forget the little scene she had come upon in all innocence and try to carry on as normal.

As the first bell for evening prayers sounded from the distant palace. Anne, all serene now the matter was thought through, stood up, brushed down her skirts, adjusted her veil and called her hound.

There was an answering bark from a nearby clump of manicured bushes. She called him again, but he did not come to her. Exasperated, she walked across to where she suspected him to be, thinking perhaps that he had found a rabbit burrow and was looking for an early supper. "Urian, where are you?" She parted the bushes and finding a little arbour she had not known existed, pushed her way in and looked about her for her dog.

A whimper came from her right and she swung round sharply. Urian sat close by, thumping his tail in greeting, and there was no mistaking the figure whose hand was restraining the dog, his long fingers looped through the hound's studded collar.

"Your Majesty!" Anne exclaimed, and this time remembering the respect due to the King, swept him a deep curtsey.

"Mistress Boleyn" he said, releasing the dog and moving closer to her. "I came to find you but instead found your dog. Now it seems I have both of you". As he finished speaking he covered the distance between them in a single stride and took her into his arms.

She did not panic or struggle, but it was with a cold expression in her black eyes that she quietly said "Release me, I beg of you Sire".

He laughed, amused at her calmness. "I am afraid I cannot release you sweet Nan; you must know how closely I have watched you of late? I have followed your every move for some months now and mean to have you for my own".

She put both hands on his chest, prising her body away from his as she answered "Then that is a great pity Sire for I do not reciprocate your desires. It seems that you must make do with just the one

Boleyn!"

"Sweet Nan" he repeated, tracing the smooth line of her cheek with his finger. "You would do well to emulate your sister and be kind to me for I swear I should be faithful to you and give up all others".

"Faithful!" she snorted. "With all due respect Sire, you do not know the meaning of the word, apart from which I am almost young enough to be your daughter!"

He made no answer, merely smiled and gathered her again to his chest. "Come Nan, no more excuses. You must be fifteen at the very least!"

"Then it seems that the court of France ages one faster than I had thought my Lord for I am but twelve years old".

If she had hoped her so few years would frighten him off, then she was to be disappointed. "No matter" he replied, casually attempting to draw her towards a convenient grassy bed. "The younger the virgin, the faster she learns".

A tiny worm of panic took root deep inside Anne's brain. Realising that her honour could soon be but another notch on the amorous King's bedpost, she played her last desperate card. "So be it my Lord". She shrugged, feigning surrender. "But I beg to inform Your Majesty that you will not be the first".

As she had calculated, he immediately let her go. "What do you mean?" he demanded.

"Exactly what I said" She was enjoying herself now, sensing victory. "If it pleases you to become one of many Sire, then carry on. We should just have time before prayers".

Her uncharacteristic coarseness caused a look of distaste to pass across his face. He pushed past her and snapped "I shall be interested to discover the guilty parties to your deception, Mademoiselle!" With a rustle of leaves, he was gone.

As the sound of his footsteps receded down the path, Anne laughed aloud and clapped her hands exultantly. She turned to Urian, who apparently bored by the whole proceedings had stretched out for his evening doze. "You bad dog" she admonished him lightly. He opened one eye and regarded her lazily. "You are supposed to leap to defend my honour, not ignore me in my perils!"

Urian thumped his tail apologetically and closed his eye. "Come, hound!" she cried gaily. "We must return to the palace lest the Queen suspects my tardiness to signify that I have truly lost my maidenhead!" Picking up her skirts with one hand and holding her cap in place with the other, she pushed through the bushes and sprinted down the path towards the palace, the huge hound nearly as big as she bounding by her side and barking delightedly at this new game.

At supper that night Anne amused herself by shooting Francis languishing looks from large mournful eyes whilst he regarded her suspiciously through narrowed ones, his gaze only leaving her face to stare equally suspiciously at those gentlemen whom he suspected may have cheated their monarch of his long awaited prize.

Despite her best intentions, Anne's lips began to twitch. The laughter was bubbling up inside her and her eyes were beginning to water with the sheer effort of keeping a straight face. Suddenly she could bear it no longer and the entire court immediately ceased eating and stared at her with amazement.

Then Francis himself began to guffaw with laughter; he had guessed the reason for Mademoiselle Anne's uncontrollable mirth and found himself admiring her for the way in which she had extricated herself from that most delicate situation in the gardens earlier.

Soon the entire court was laughing, although they did not know the reason for it. However, Mademoiselle Boleyn's peals of laughter were infectious and the King himself appeared to share her joke.

Wiping her streaming eyes, Anne's gaze fell upon Queen Claude, who ignoring the hilarity around her, sat poker faced solemnly continuing with her meal.

Chapter 6

A Sister's Shame

Once the meal was over and whilst the maids of honour were preparing to retire, having seen Queen Claude ceremoniously tucked up in the huge bed, Mary sought out her sister Anne feeling that as the elder, she should admonish her for her lack of self-control.

Anne stood staring in disbelief as Mary launched into her sisterly rebuke. "So you see Anne" she finished "You were extremely lucky that the King himself decided to pretend to share your mirth, to save you from the Queen's undoubted displeasure".
"The Queen's displeasure!" Anne snorted. Now it was her turn. "You prate to me of incurring the Queen's displeasure yet you sleep with her husband?"

Mary stared back at her, head held high with no trace of shame on her face. "The King has need of me" she stated simply. "Anyway who are you to know the desires of men? You are still a child".

"Woman enough for Francis to attempt to seduce me in the gardens this evening!"

Mary's face registered first horror and then disbelief. At last she spoke. "You're making it up. He told me he was going to seek you out, yes, but he said it was to explain the situation to you".

"Well he would hardly tell you that he had decided to play a quick seduction scene with me before prayers, would he?" Anne was amazed at her sister's naivety, for all her put-on worldly wise ways. "Anyway I told him that I was no innocent and that if he cared to join the queue I would be happy to accommodate him!" She began to laugh. "And that scared him off as surely as if I had pressed a dagger to his heart". She flung herself down on her bed, emitting more peals of laughter before making a supreme effort to control herself; looking back over her shoulder at Mary who remained rooted to the spot. "Don't you see Mary? That was the reason for all the hilarity at supper. He realised I had duped him and he appreciated the actress in me!"

Mary turned away, her eyes filling with tears. "He said he loved me" she whispered, more to herself than Anne. "He swore he would be faithful to me alone".

Anne stood up, solemn now, seeing her sister's very real distress. She approached Mary and took her gently by the hand. "He used similar words to me; no doubt he uses the same pretty little speech to all his would-be conquests. How could you be so simple Mary? You, a Boleyn; a King's whore!"

Suddenly Mary turned on her with more savagery in the lovely face than Anne had ever seen before. "Take care whom you condemn sister" she spat. "If he truly wanted you as you say, then think why that might be. It was because that in you he recognised similar desires to those he knows are in me. Never forget we share the same blood!" Avoiding Anne's outstretched hand, Mary ran for the door, slamming it behind her with all her might.

Anne remained staring at the closed door for some minutes after her sister's exit, mulling over her words. Then as the door opened once more, this time to admit the chattering throng of her room-mates, she sighed deeply, shrugged her shoulders and made ready for bed.

It was some hours later that Mary quietly slipped into the small bed she shared with Anne; once settled, she lay quietly, basking in self-satisfied warmth. After leaving Anne she had gone straight to Francis's chamber and on bursting in without bothering to knock, had found him enjoying the embraces of yet another lady. She had unleashed a temper she had never known she possessed and in no uncertain words had told him he would need to look elsewhere for an English mistress for she would sleep with him no more. Then, without so much as acknowledging the other woman's presence, she had left the room, slamming the door so hard that the draught created dislodged the sumptuous tapestry hanging in the passageway, which fell crumpled at her feet.
As she had leaned against the wall, breathless and

shaking with both fear and excitement, a French Duke to whom she had only once been introduced, emerged from the shadows and insisted that she accompany him to his chamber where she might take some wine and recover from her ordeal. He had heard all, he told her, and admired her spirit.

As he escorted her slowly along the passageway, arm solicitously around her waist, he complimented her constantly and told her how he had always admired her. When they finally reached his chamber door, Mary looked up into his eyes and read there exactly why he had waylaid her. She did not hesitate; she needed consolation after what she saw as Francis's betrayal and this man obviously desired the King's ex-mistress. She pressed her body against his and smiled invitingly then together they entered the chamber and barred the door.

However, once day dawned, Mary found that her French Duke's ardour had cooled somewhat and when another of Francis's friends tried to claim her for his own, she did not resist.

So began the pattern. She went from courtier to courtier, saying no to few and yes to many. If she hoped that she was hurting Francis by her blatant betrayal then she would have been immensely shocked and hurt had she known that her lovers frequently compared notes with their royal master.

If Anne knew what her sister was about, she made no comment. She had decided that she had finished with Mary, for Mary had dragged their family name through the dirt and had earned the nickname the 'English Mare'. Anne feared that if she continued to associate closely with Mary then she could be tarred with the same brush. Already a number of gentlemen had tried their luck with her, thinking that she would be as easy as her sister.

Eventually, when their father paid a brief visit to the French court, Francis summoned him and spoke with him at great length. When Thomas Boleyn emerged from that meeting he called Mary to him and ordered her to pack her possessions immediately and make ready to leave for England.

So when Anne, returning to their chamber one afternoon to fetch fresh ribbons for her lute, came upon Mary weeping on their bed, instead of leaving her to it, forgot her hurt pride and put her arms around her sister.

When eventually Mary controlled herself sufficiently to gulp out the news of her dismissal, Anne held her even more tightly and whispered "It had to come, Mary. Even here in France there is a certain moral code and you have overstepped it".

For answer Mary raised her tear stained face, still lovely even in distress and murmured "They needed me Anne, all of them, but I am guilty also for needing them".

Looking round at Mary's clothes scattered all over the bed, some thrust untidily into a trunk, Anne said "You will be able to make a clean start in England;

your reputation will not have reached the English court".

Mary nodded mutely and set about brushing her blonde hair with its beautiful auburn highlights that Anne had always so admired. Already she was more cheerful, her tears drying and a soft smile curving her generous mouth.

Watching her, Anne thought, she is but fifteen years old and has been mistress to half the French court. She is greatly cheered now by the thought of returning to England but is it because she truly wants a fresh start or is she dreaming of the conquests yet to be made? She may say she wants to change her ways but can any of us truly alter our basic nature? It is said that the English court is more moralistic, but will that help or hinder her? There can be no doubt that a soft, gentle female creature with beauty such as hers will always attract men and I fear that she will not be able to resist temptation.

A sixth sense told Mary something of Anne's unspoken thoughts which prompted her to say softly, without spite "Are you sure that your disapproval of me does not stem from jealousy Anne?" Anne opened her mouth to make a sharp retort, but Mary continued "After all, you may be very young, but already the gentlemen buzz around you like bees around a honeypot. Take very great care little one for it is all very well for a man to need you, but once he sees that you maybe need him more, it is over before it barely begins".
"My pride would never let me be used as you have".

Then in an attempt to change the subject "Come let us pack these gowns carefully. You will surely stun the English court with these wonderful Parisian creations. I will want to hear all about it so be sure to write often!"

It was with some regret that Anne Boleyn watched her sister and father ride away from Amboise a few days later. She was alone now; the sole representative of her family and it was up to her to restore some respect to that family name. She made up her mind that any man who wished to bed her would have to wait a very long time before he attained his desire, and even then, she would demand constant proof of his undying devotion. She had learned a very valuable lesson from her sister; that which men can attain with ease, they rapidly come to despise. It was not a mistake which Anne Boleyn ever planned to make.

Even without Mary Boleyn to keep the gentlemen amused, life at the French court went on much as before. At those court functions she was allowed to attend, Anne found herself repeatedly singled out by Francis, both as his dancing partner and for prominent roles in plays and masques. She flirted with him outrageously and just when the French courtiers were laying wagers on the imminent capitulation of Mademoiselle Boleyn, she would reject him and turn her attentions to another.

Francis, alternately exasperated and enthralled by her, took vast numbers of mistresses in an effort to make her jealous. He delighted in sending his friends to her with the most intimate details of his latest conquests. However she would merely laugh scornfully and turn her sparkling conversation and devastating wit to another, whirling with him in the dance and leaving the frustrated French King in her wake.

Chapter 7

The Field of Cloth of Gold

Shortly after her thirteenth birthday Anne heard that the long proposed meeting between Francis and Henry of England was finally to take place during the following month of June.

The whole French court was thrown into a whirl of excited preparations; Francis quite determined to show his English counterpart just how lavishly the French could celebrate, given cause.

Anne found herself in something of a quandary; she was not quite sure whose side she should be on. She was English by birth and yet had spent almost half her life in France speaking the language as well as any native. Indeed amongst her many friends she was not thought of as an English outsider, but French like themselves.

Anne was in attendance on Queen Claude when Francis broke the news to his Queen that she too would be expected to be present during the festivities. Claude was for once sufficiently roused to protest that as a Frenchwoman she had no love for Henry's Spanish Queen. Her husband retaliated by saying that Queen Catherine, being Spanish, would have no love for her either so that made them even! Having made his point, Francis retired, throwing a wicked wink in Anne's direction as he did so.

Once the arrangements were completed, the French court removed itself to Ardres, camping just outside the town boundaries in fabulously luxurious tents.

Meanwhile the English landed in France on schedule and made their way to Guisnes where a similarly constructed camp awaited them. Messengers rode feverishly back and forth between the two camps and at last, one warm June evening, the two Kings accompanied by their courts left their respective camps and drew up four hundred yards apart, face to face either side of a specially constructed valley.

Anne, seated on her palfrey amongst Queen Claude's maids, anxiously craned her neck and strained her eyes, futilely trying to locate members of her family in King Henry's retinue.

They made a gorgeous sight, those two courts. Their Kings were dressed in their finest; Francis mounted on a white charger, Henry on a black. The silence as they faced each other was broken only by the stamping of hooves and the jingling of harness. A gentle breeze shifted the cloaks and veils of the ladies, their sparkling jewels catching the fading sunlight and blazing like a kaleidoscope of fire.

The gentlemen, both French and English, sat tensely with their hands gripping the reins as though they expected to ride into battle. They too were elegantly attired, their doublets and hose as colourful as the silks and velvets of the ladies; lavishly embellished with costly jewels and their gold chains of rank.

All eyes were fixed on the two main characters in what was a virtual confrontation. Each slowly raised his hand in silent salute to the other before they eased their horses into a walk down the sides of the valley and towards the centre.

Henry, Anne noticed, sat his horse well. The beast was spirited but went kindly for him, recognising the hand of a master. On the other hand Francis, she noted indulgently, was capitalising on the opportunity to display his equally fine horsemanship, making his stallion prance and jig across the intervening space.

At last the two Kings drew alongside one another and embraced. They then dismounted, threw their reins to the pages who seemed to have appeared from nowhere, and arms slung casually over each other's shoulders, together entered the great tent made from cloth of gold which all but covered the bottom of the valley. It was this very tent which caused onlookers to dub the occasion 'The Field of Cloth of Gold'. Solemnly the two Queens performed a similar but more dignified ritual before they too entered the great tent.

That was the signal for the festivities to commence.

Seventeen long, long days with activities beginning shortly after dawn and continuing by torchlight far into the night.

The two kings spent most of their time trying to outdo each other in the athletic events, wrestling matches and jousts. They even held impromptu eating contests during the banquets. Whilst the first nights celebrations took place, the French and English servants had the mammoth task of moving each camp closer to the valley so that no time would be wasted travelling to and from the great golden tent.

It took Anne three days to track down her family amongst the English. Eventually she located their tent and burst joyfully in. Decorously she curtsied to her parents and then made haste to embrace the mother she could barely remember. "My little Anne" murmured Elizabeth Howard-Boleyn tenderly. "But you are no longer my little girl; you are an elegant lady of the French court!"
"I shall always be your little girl" replied Anne, revelling in the first maternal embrace she had experienced for six long years.

Finally releasing her mother, Anne looked around the tent and asked anxiously "Where is Mary and where is my brother? They did travel with you?"
"Yes, yes" soothed her father. "You will be reunited soon. At present they are with the King".

At once Anne's face hardened, casual remarks she had heard over the past few days finally falling into place. "So it is true then? Mary is the mistress of the English King?"

Her father drew her aside and looking surreptitiously about him said quietly "Hush Anne. What if she is? It is a great honour to be the King's favourite and already she is working to advance our family".

Angrily shaking off the paternal arm she snapped "So you would sell your daughter's honour for titles?"

Elizabeth butted in "She had precious little honour left when she came out of France, Anne. You know that".

Close to tears Anne retorted "She swore to me that she would turn over a new leaf; give up her loose ways and live modestly until she found a husband".

Whilst she spoke she had been unaware that another was listening closely. The stranger spoke "At least she has fulfilled one part of her promise to you. Let me introduce myself, I am Mary's husband William Carey". He moved into the torchlight from his seat in the shadows.

Not troubling to acknowledge his greeting, Anne at once turned on him "It does not bother you then, that your wife shares another's bed?"

Evenly, without meeting her eyes, he replied "In order to secure her hand in marriage I gave my undertaking to the King that I would not object to their union". Coming closer to Anne he sought her hand, raised it to his lips and kissed it, saying "I loved her you see and it was the only way I could get

her".
Anne snatched her hand away and hissed "Then you are a fool, like all men!"

The hostile silence which followed was unwittingly interrupted by George Boleyn, who not noticing Anne at first, had entered the tent and announced to his father "I have left Mary with the King". Then he turned towards Carey, saw her and exclaimed "Anne!"

She flew into his arms. Since she had last laid eyes on him her brother had grown from a sturdy engaging little boy into a tall handsome young man.

Extricating herself she looked him up and down and exclaimed "I scarcely recognised you brother, you have grown so tall. No doubt you have been setting all the female hearts a flutter since you went to court?"

"Maybe" he replied mysteriously, his face bearing a wide grin "But rest assured sweet Nan, I was but passing time until I could again converse with she whom I love best in the world. And you, I hear, are capturing as many French hearts as you can lay your pretty hands upon!"

Merely passing time brother" she retorted cheekily. "All men are but shadows in comparison with you!"

She exuded such coquetry through her last words that their mother angrily stepped between them. "Such words would be better coming from the lips of lovers!" she snapped.

"Tis but a game mother" George stooped to lovingly

kiss his mother's cheek. "You must remember that even as a child Anne loved to try out her charms on any available male. She but practices on me!"

The expression on Elizabeth's face was unfathomable. "I am sure it is as you say George" she said carefully. "But take care not to display such affections in public or little Anne may find herself causing more scandal than she fears her sister does as the King's mistress". Satisfied with her parting shot, Elizabeth swept regally from the tent.
"We must behave ourselves George" Anne waggled her finger at him in mock reprimand. "Else the world will believe we commit incest. Is that not an inane assumption?"
"Quite ridiculous sister; you're far too ugly for my tastes" he replied lightly as arm in arm they too left the tent, leaving their father and Carey staring after them dumbfounded.

Later, when Mary and Anne were reunited, Anne was so mellowed by the company of her brother that she had no heart to berate Mary for what she believed was her light behaviour. She saw by the hunted look in Mary's eyes that being the King's favourite was not as simple as many liked to think. Sensing that her sister needed to talk to one of her own, Anne waited for the opportunity to catch her alone.
Her intuition was correct, Mary desperately needed someone to confide in, for although she had many acquaintances she could not pour out her troubles to

them, lest seeking to discredit or replace her, they went to the King.

"It is so hard to keep his interest, Anne" Mary complained. "Every moment I am with him I must think of new ways to amuse him, different ways to rouse his interest in me. I am not witty and clever like you and it takes brains as well as beauty to engage a King's affections". She sighed deeply.
"Could you not just be content with your husband?" Anne suggested. "Give up the King".
"But I love him" Mary protested. "So how can I leave him? Poor William, he tries so hard to be a good husband to me but compared to Henry he is a mere mortal against a god. Being loved by a King is like no other earthly experience".

Anne took her sister's hand. "Whatever happens" she said "And you know that he will not love you forever; but remember that I will always be ready to help you if I can. Perhaps as we grow older we can be closer than we have been of late years. I would like that".
"I value your friendship deeply" Mary replied gravely. "So you forgive my transgressions? You do not condemn my behaviour as you once did?"
After a pause, "No, Mary, I cannot pretend that I relish your current position, unlike our parents! But you are what you are, it is in your nature and I realise that now. I have grown up enough to understand that none of us can help being what we are".

Chapter 8

A Lady of Fashion

On 20th June 1520, Henry and Francis embraced for the last time with a great show of affection. Henry even managed to conjure up a few crocodile tears; for effect, Francis guessed.

The two Queens also took an affectionate leave of each other; each having displayed such dignity through the proceedings that the other could not fail to be impressed. It was said by many that a genuine friendship had sprung up between the two, far surpassing the show of faux amity staged by their husbands.

Yet again the young Anne Boleyn said her farewells to her family and watched as they set sail for England.

As the French court resumed its normality, on taking stock of her situation, Anne realised that there were in fact two courts operating simultaneously under the same roof. The first was that of her royal mistress

Queen Claude, where life was still rigorously dictated by religious pomp. The other was that of Marguerite, Francis's sister; it was to Marguerite's circle that the younger courtiers were attracted and it was there that Francis preferred to spend his time.

One evening, whilst performing in a play before the whole court, it being one of the rare occasions when the two intermingled, Anne became aware of Francis and his sister watching her closely, inclining their heads to speak together without taking their eyes from her. Therefore once the play was finished and the players had taken their applause, she was not surprised when Francis intercepted her on her way back to the Queen.

"Dearest Anne" Francis pressed her hand to his lips and gazed deeply into her eyes, as was his way. "How would you like to escape my dear wife's tedious little court and go into service with my sister?"

It was the chance for which Anne had been hoping, but she knew that to seize the opportunity with unbecoming eagerness was not what Francis expected of her. She did not disappoint him. Instead of following her impulse to shout yes, yes gladly! She flashed him a flirtatious little look from her talking eyes and answered demurely "The Queen is an excellent mistress, Sire, devout and kind".

Francis's eyes twinkled; he was enjoying the game hugely. He said nothing and she continued "Yes, Queen Claude is a great lady" then moving her head closer to his and lowering her voice murmured "But oh so very dull". She raised her eyes to his, a smile playing about her lips, and then they laughed together as Francis led her by the hand to meet his beloved sister.

Within hours a rapport had sprung up between the Duchess Marguerite and Anne Boleyn. With Marguerite, Anne was able to drop the pretentious court manners, except in public, and be herself.

Soon after meeting, Marguerite who was always direct, sometimes painfully so, told Anne that many considered her beautiful but felt that her complexion was marred by the small mole upon her neck. Before Anne had time to retort or take offence, Marguerite produced the ultimate disguise, one of her own pearl encrusted chokers.

Anne received it gratefully and by the time she had worn it but a few times, a number of other ladies noticing how well it became her, had similar collars made to emulate the little Boleyn, who was becoming something of a leader of fashion. Together in private, Marguerite and Anne laughed, for something that had been utilised to hide a small fault had quickly become an essential accessory for fashion-conscious ladies.

Another day Marguerite decided that at almost fourteen years of age, it was time little Anne discarded her velvet cap and tiny veil in favour of a hood, so she produced for Anne several of the French style hoods which she told the girl would suit her oval face with its determined chin far more than the cumbersome gable hood customarily worn by English ladies.

There was however one tiny remaining fault which in Anne's eyes constituted a major disfigurement. This she could not bear to reveal to anyone, even Marguerite. It was a tiny deformity on the little finger of her left hand; at the extreme outside edge, the nail was split, forming a small horny growth. When she had been younger her brother had teased her that it was the beginnings of a sixth finger and that she would grow up to be a witch.

She had grown up to be nothing of the kind but the tiny growth bothered her and she was always afraid it would be noticed and commented upon. Frequently she clipped it off, for the scrap of nail covering it grew at the same rate as its larger neighbour, but it only grew back and to her anxious eyes seemed bigger and more unsightly each time.

So, with her keen eye for fashion developing all the time, she devised something to draw the eye away and also to partly disguise her problem; an ingenious hanging sleeve which turned back from an under cuff at the wrist and fell almost to the floor. She immediately had this design made in several colours to co-ordinate or match with all her gowns and the Boleyn sleeve, as it became known, was an instant success and every lady copied it.

Anne's supreme moment of glory came one day when Marguerite herself appeared at a state occasion wearing the fashion created by her young maid of honour.

As she approached her fifteenth birthday it was common knowledge that the Anglo-French relations which had been so good two years earlier at the Field of Cloth of Gold, were fast decaying. Within months the clouds of war were looming and France prepared to go into conflict against England.

Minor skirmishes had been taking place for some weeks when Anne received a letter from her father informing her that due to the state of relations between the two countries, he had been instructed by King Henry to withdraw her from the French court. George was on his way to France and would escort her back to England.

Anne was stunned by the news. The thought of uprooting from the country where she had been so happy and had learned so much, appalled her. She took the letter to both Francis and Marguerite but they told that regretfully there was nothing they could do. King Henry was recalling all English nationals.

All too soon Anne found herself standing one morning with her brother on the deck of an English ship, watching as the coastline of her beloved France receded into the mist. George, looking down at her white, strained face, turned her to face him. Pulling the folds of her woollen cloak more closely about her he asked gently "What ails you Nan?"

Her eyes turned again to the French coast before she looked into her brother's face. "I suppose I am afraid George" she said frankly. "It is just like all those years ago when I left England for France. I was leaving home and going to live in a foreign country. That is how I feel now; it is France which I consider as home and England is the foreign land".

She moved away from him and stood, her hands on the rail, staring back at the land she loved whilst the angry wind pulled her headdress awry and played havoc with her long hair.

George moved to stand behind her and putting his hands on her shoulders whispered "Let us go below now sister. I swear I shall repeat so many hilarious tales of the English court that you will not be able to wait to get there and see it all for yourself".

Gratefully, and with a smile on her face, she turned to him and as they went below deck murmured "You always cheer me up George. Whatever should I do without you?"

He kept his promise. Soon the mingled laughter of brother and sister could be heard coming from her cabin and as he prophesied, Anne found herself longing for the day when she would take her place amongst her own English people at the court of King Henry VIII.

Chapter 9

Home Again

As Anne and her brother rode along the leafy Kentish lanes on their journey home, she was aware of a great sense of peace. Taking deep breaths of the clean air she turned to George and told him "England smells different to France".

He raised his eyebrows cynically "Worse or better?" he enquired.

Playfully she swished her riding whip at him "You know what I mean George, stop teasing me. Although, on the whole, I do believe that England smells fresher".

"Perhaps the English wash themselves more frequently than the French" he suggested, swiping his hand at a diving insect.

Exasperated she glared at him. He was out of reach of her whip, so she could not give him a sisterly poke in the ribs.

"Race?" he asked, dropping his horse back into step with hers.

"Oh yes! Just one little thing though; I don't

remember the way!"

"No problem sweet sister" he laughed, making ready for the off. "You won't win anyway, so you can follow me home!" With that, he spurred his horse lightly and galloped off. Indignant at his inference that her horsemanship was inferior to his, she shortened her reins and sped off in his tracks.

They dismounted at the stables, a short distance from the castle. As the grooms took charge of the horses, Anne, a little stiff from the long ride from Dover, walked awkwardly along the path until she stood in front of her childhood home.

Enraptured she stood and stared. The mellow honey coloured stone was turning to gold in the softening rays of the setting sun, the mullioned windows sparkled with the dancing reflections from the moat. Carried on the light breeze towards her was the scent of the newly seasoned wood of the drawbridge and portcullis. It was quite unlike anything Anne had seen for many years. Walking slowly towards it she breathed "I never remembered it to be as beautiful as this. It looks just like a fairy tale castle from a romantic fable".

"It could just be that you never appreciated it when you were little" George decided, having slid to a half in front of her amid a flurry of stones. "Anyway, when you have finished gushing over the family seat, how about some refreshment? We've been riding for hours and I smell roasting beef!"

Anne's elegant little nose sampled the air in consideration. "Brother I do believe you speak truth!" she exclaimed, and together they walked over the little drawbridge, beneath the raised portcullis, through the inner courtyard and into the castle itself, both shivering a little in the chill of the entrance hall.

During the days which followed, Anne enjoyed spending her time re-acquainting herself with the castle and the surrounding countryside. When the weather was warm and fine she walked in the grounds and rode along the lanes. If the weather was inclement she spent her time in the long gallery; a charming room which boasted window seats overlooking the moat and gardens.

However, so valuable a commodity was not to be allowed to idle away her time for long. One evening as the family - with the exception of Mary who was at court – were enjoying a quiet supper, Thomas Boleyn announced to his son that he was to return to court on the morrow. "And you" he turned triumphantly to his daughter, "are to go with him. Queen Catherine has graciously accepted you as one of her ladies".

Anne dropped her spoon and clapped her hands with delight. Then, clasping her hands beneath her chin and raising her eyes heavenwards, she exclaimed to the ceiling "I am so lucky!"

The next day, a chill January morning with the sun glinting palely between the clouds, Anne Boleyn left her enchanted castle to grace far larger, grander establishments. As they rode away she turned in her saddle for one last look at Hever. "I shall always feel safe and happy there" she stated gravely to no-one in particular. "Whatever the circumstance".

They travelled on horseback for most of the journey, and then completed the final stage by barge. As they glided up to the landing stage, Anne eagerly skipped on to the wooden boards, courteously assisted by her brother. They collected their own light hand baggage then together climbed a flight of stone steps to a large paved terrace. From there, lying across well-kept gardens and stone pathways, brother and sister were treated to an uninterrupted view of Greenwich Palace.

Used to exotic French architecture, in which she had taken a great interest, Anne regarded Henry's red bricked T-shaped palace with great appreciation, noting the huge windows gracing the galleries and the impressive courtyards.

It's a lovely building" Anne pronounced, as George conducted her through the maze of passageways towards the Queen's apartments. "Although quite small by French standards".
"Don't let King Henry hear you say that" George warned. "He is extremely sensitive regarding all things French since the war began and quite apart from that, Greenwich is his favourite residence. He was born here".
"Oh dear" Anne shrugged her shoulders and spread her hands wide. "If he is against all things French then he won't like me very much!" As she spoke she glanced down at her French gown with its fashionable hanging sleeves, quite unlike anything

seen in England, and put her hand apologetically to her French hood, the perfect frame for her face.

"Don't worry overmuch" George assured. "Just be yourself. The King never could resist a pretty face and a sharp wit, although it may be politic to disguise the French accent a little, if you can".

George enquired of a passing page the whereabouts of the court and was told that it was assembled in the great hall, the banquet finished and the dancing under way. On George's advice, Anne left her cloak and bag in a small ante chamber for later retrieval and readied herself for her entrance.

"Stay close to me" whispered George. "It will be crowded in there and we must first pay our respects to the King and Queen if we are not to incur instant displeasure!"

The heavy oak doors swung wide to admit them and immediately Anne's senses were assailed by the strong odours of food, wine, grease from the torches and five hundred perspiring bodies. She wrinkled her nose, and George, expecting such a reaction whispered reassuringly "Don't worry, you'll soon get used to it. Surely even the French have to sweat?"

"No-one would ever admit to it" Anne laughingly told him. "Even base bodily functions are achieved with a certain elegance and panache in France!"

For a moment they stood on the threshold at the top of the wide steps gazing down at the colourful capering company. The King and Queen were seated at the far end, on the customary dais; Anne noticed that the Queen looked tired and ill and the King overfed and bored. At once she thought of elegant Marguerite and her select court and sighed regretfully.

Obediently she followed her brother through the milling throng. Here and there they were forced to pause as someone recognised George and greeted him, or slapped him on the back and called his name. Perceptive Anne noted that many of the young ladies coloured delicately as he passed by. Sister-like she stored the knowledge, to make use of for future jesting.

At last they broke through the inner ring of courtiers, the type who always hung about persons of importance, and stood before their monarchs.
"Your Grace" George bowed deeply to the King, then turned to bow to the Queen. "I beg your leave to present my sister Anne". The King's piggy eyes flickered over her.
"Lately arrived from the court of France, Your Grace" she said carefully, only a slight accent betraying her as she sank into her obeisance.

For a moment Henry's eyes narrowed as he looked down at her bent head, then as she raised her eyes to his face he broke into a grin and rising from his chair, extended his hand to assist her to her feet.
"Your Grace is too kind" she said meekly. "I have long awaited this honour".

Ever susceptible to flattery, the King's grin grew wider. He addressed George "Why, your sister has turned into a little French lady" he observed, "for only the French can speak such a pretty compliment and appear to mean every word!" Delighted at his own joke he roared with laughter, slapping his thigh in his merriment. His courtiers obediently tittered.

Anne became aware of George whispering in her ear "You are obviously going to be able to manage quite well without me". Then excusing himself to his sovereigns, he turned and melted into the throng.

Anne watched him go with barely concealed surprise before turning to the King and saying clearly "Evidently my brother believes I can take good care of myself for I have only been at court for five minutes and already he has abandoned me!"
"Rest assured that your King will not forsake you Mistress Boleyn". The King stood beside her, offering his arm for the dance. Gracefully she accepted and they took to the floor.

Eager to try out her powers of attraction on this great bull of a man, Anne was at her most engaging, wasting no time in complimenting the King on his grace and lightness in the dance for so well built a man. The King beamed; he found himself very glad that she had come to court and felt sure that she would bring some sorely needed sparkle into his life. "I well remember you as a child, singing for us at Dover" he told her. "I thought then that maturity would render you into a uniquely talented person of note".
Anne inclined her head to acknowledge his compliment, delighted to know that he had not

forgotten her court debut. "Your Grace has a remarkable memory" she told him. "It is many years now since I left England to make France my home".
"We have you back now, Mistress Anne" the King told her, as they touched hands and circled each other as the dance demanded. "And we wish to keep such as you in our court".

The dance ended, she thanked the King for the honour and curtseyed. Gallantly he replied that it was he who should be grateful to her, then chuckling to himself he made his way back to the dais where his plump Spanish Queen awaited him, looking even more dowdy he decided, beside Mistress Anne's elegance. Catherine said nothing, but she had watched them both closely, missing not a single smile or gesture.

The King was barely seated before a young man, speaking Anne's name, took her hand and bowed. For a moment her brow creased as she tried to place his face, then suddenly she knew. "Tom Wyatt!" she cried delightedly, before placing her hands on his shoulders and kissing him on both cheeks, French style.

Wyatt, quite overcome by her enthusiastic greeting, glanced sidelong at the dais, aware that the King had straightened his back and was craning his neck over the many heads in order to see just who Mistress Boleyn embraced so gladly.

The pair danced together for a while, then during a lull in the proceedings he drew her aside in order to talk with her privately. "I have thought about you many times Anne" he told her, pressing her hand ardently, "I have longed for this day".

"I too have thought of you Thomas" Anne confided truthfully, "but those days when we were childhood companions seem so long ago now".

"Indeed" he agreed sadly. "Did you know that I asked your father for your hand in marriage?"

"But no!" she was genuinely surprised, never having guessed that his regard went beyond their childhood attachment. "And his reply?"

"He refused me without a second thought" the poet's mouth twisted regretfully. "And before I could set about persuading him to change his mind I found that my own father had betrothed me to Elizabeth Brooke". He paused and looked at her, her eyes wide, and in answer to her unspoken question, finished "I married her some years ago. We have a son".

"You are happy?"

"I thought I was, but now seeing you again has reminded me all too sharply of what I have lost".

"Oh Tom" Anne squeezed his arm in a small attempt at consolation. "I never guessed, never realised that your feelings for me ran so deep. I would have been glad to take you for as a child I loved you truly. You and George were the dashing princes rescuing me from the dragon's very jaws!" She began to laugh at the memories, then seeing his serious expression, stopped abruptly.

She held out her hand "Come, Tom. Let us not mope over what might have been. We must make merry for tonight is my first ever appearance at the English court. And in tribute to our long friendship, I shall dance with no man but you" she finished generously.

She kept her word.

Chapter 10

Life at Court

She had been at court for little more than six weeks when one day the King's master of revels drew her aside and informed her that the King had asked that she be given a prominent part in the following night's entertainment.

She accepted delightedly, full of confidence that she would further impress all by her success. At it happened, she gave a sparkling performance, prompting the King to declare that he wanted no other as his leading lady.

Sensing her monarch was quite captivated by her, Anne set about entertaining herself by spinning her little web about him. Poor Henry, he was not over-bright in such matters; he could not understand why she would not immediately melt for him the moment he crooked his finger. On the odd occasion he managed to get her alone she would raise her voice in anger to him should he attempt to take what she believed were liberties, as though he were any common courtier. His intentions were not honourable, she told him.

She was not easy prey, and Henry failed to grasp that this was not just coquetry; this was the essence of the woman herself. He, ever relishing a chase be it of woman or beast, threw himself into her pursuit with great amusement and enjoyment, feeling sure that his overwhelming charm and manly beauty would have her capitulation within weeks, if not days.

Anne made sure she kept just out of his reach, relishing her power but seeing it as no more than a game; one which she had played many times before when in France. It added a little spice to her daily duties in the Queen's chambers.

Her life of carefree gaiety was brought to an abrupt halt one afternoon when her father sidled up to her whilst she was observing an archery contest. "Father!" she exclaimed, "I have seen little of you since I came to court".
"Business, my dear" he answered, "for only business commitments could keep me from so charming a daughter".

She narrowed her eyes suspiciously and swivelled her gaze to his face. Judging by his expression she gathered that he had news to impart to her; news which gave him great pleasure. "What is it that you wish to say father?" she asked innocently, turning again to the butts and giving every outward sign of being fully absorbed in the contest before her.
"I have at last arranged a very advantageous

marriage for you, my dear" he announced triumphantly.

"Oh yes?" she answered indifferently, "and who then is chosen to be my husband?"

"James Butler, eldest son of my kinsman Sir Piers Butler".

Not removing her eyes from the contest before her she replied in a calm, unemotional tone "I will not have him".

Thomas Boleyn was immediately angered by his ungrateful daughter. "You will obey me, girl!" he thundered, causing several onlookers to turn their heads in amazement.

"So then, I spent eight years of my life learning to be an elegant court lady in France merely to moulder away the rest of my years in an isolated Irish castle with a bunch of savages?" she hissed, finally turning from the contest to lock flashing black eyes on to his. "Is this the alliance you planned for me all those years? Delightful, I must say!"

"Nevertheless" blustered Boleyn, slightly crushed by the force of her verbal onslaught, "it is arranged and you will go!"

She turned her head back to the archery and applauded an excellent shot. "I think not father" she commented pleasantly. "I shall pick my own husband, as Mary did".

"The only reason your sister was allowed to do such a thing was because she had behaved as little more than a whore and no nobleman would have her!" he burst out.

Even the contestants on the green raised their heads

at that profound observation. Anne coloured hotly, then rose and walked away; her father followed. Once they were a safe distance away from curious ears she swung round to face him. "So she was a whore was she? I thought it was a great honour to be a King's mistress – your words father, not mine! You twist the truth to suit yourself. I tell you I will not marry James Butler!"

Turning on her heel she walked as quickly away from her father as dignity and heavy court clothing would allow. Boleyn stood and gaped after her. Such spirit, he reasoned was akin to his own. She had ambition did little Anne so maybe she was right; maybe Butler was not good enough for her. Perhaps it would be worth his while to look higher for his youngest daughter.

Meanwhile Anne, cheeks still burning with indignation, was striding purposefully through the inner courtyard when a small man suddenly appeared in front of her. "Out of my way sir, if you please" she demanded imperiously.

He came nearer and she noticed with distaste that his garments were some twenty years behind the times. His person was also most displeasing, he had a scar which extended from his right temple to the side of his mouth and a good deal of the ear on that side was also missing. The apparition spoke "James Butler at your service, Mistress". He swept her an arthritic little bow. "No doubt your father has acquainted you with the news that we are to be married?"

She gazed at him in disbelief and then broke into nervous laughter. So this was her future husband. This miserable deformed little creature was the man her father would tie her to. She hoped for his sake that he had a mother who loved him for she knew that she most certainly would not.

Controlling her mirth she looked sternly down at him, for he was a full three inches shorter than she. "Forgive me sir, but I fear you are mistaken. I am betrothed to no-one. I do not wish for a husband at this time and when I do, I shall choose him for myself!"

Butler put out his hands in an attempt to catch hold of her but she neatly sidestepped him and ran into the palace. Hearing his footsteps close behind her worried her not at all; she knew the palace well and that she would be able to shake him off was not in doubt. But first, she decided, she would lead him a merry dance.

So she hid in alcoves, suppressing her giggles as he hurried past, believing her to be ahead of him, then made sure that he caught just a glimpse of her skirts as she turned the corner and ran back the way she had come. Over and over, she gave him the slip.

Eventually James tired of her childish games and from her hiding place she saw him stride out through the main door to the courtyard where as luck would have it, he met with her father. There was evidently an angry exchange between the two, small James shaking his fist and her father stepping hurriedly back out of range. She smiled, guessing that James was telling her father that nothing on earth would induce him to take her now. Her goal attained, she returned merrily to her archery contest by a different route.

Later that evening, wicked Anne lost no time in acquainting her friends of her father's wish that she should marry Butler and their roars of delighted laughter when she described in graphic detail how she had led her prospective husband a merry dance through the bowels of the palace, drew the King to her circle like a magnet.

"Why all this hilarity?" he growled, his twinkling eyes belying his gruff tone. Anne immediately acquainted him with the essence of the story and soon he was laughing as heartily as the rest. "I would not have allowed the marriage" he pronounced. "I could not allow the most scintillating personage at my court to marry with such a man".

Curtseying demurely, Anne ventured "Surely such a title belongs to Your Grace? I cannot compete with such dazzling wit or profound knowledge".
"Maybe not" he countered, "but you are surely by far the prettier!"

The little company broke into fresh laughter, whilst on her dais Queen Catherine noted that again her husband was drawn to the younger Boleyn girl, a frivolous wench who should be watched closely, she decided.

Suddenly the King held up his hand. Immediately his young friends ceased their chatter and fixed their eyes upon him. "Listen!" he exclaimed. "Can you not hear a lute sadly out of tune?" His keen ear for true melody distressed, he scanned the musicians' gallery where its occupants, oblivious of their royal master's scrutiny, continued to play. "You!" roared the King suddenly, pointing an accusing finger at the offender. "Can you not hear when your instrument is badly tuned sir?"

All playing ceased abruptly and the guilty party grew visibly pale. King Henry pointed to the floor in front of him and said sternly "Here!" as though he were speaking to a dog.

The little face immediately disappeared from the gallery and soon the object of the King's displeasure scampered across the floor and fell at his master's feet. Seeing that he was only a boy, Henry immediately softened. "You are new to court?" he asked, in something approaching his normal voice.
"I arrived this morning, Your Grace" the musician stammered. "So enthralled was I by Your Grace's presence that I knew not what I was doing"
"Rise, you are forgiven" the King spoke kindly now. "It is not your fault, the fault lies with the master of the King's musicians" He raised his eyes to the gallery as he spoke, where the apologetic master stood looking down on the scene.

Turning his attention again to the lute player, Henry although professing no spectacular skill on that particular instrument, could not resist taking the lute from the lad and tuning it himself before beginning to play a song of his own composition. A stool was brought for the King and he sat absentmindedly, absorbed in his music. Anne and her friends signed silently to pages to bring them cushions before settling on the floor at the feet of their King.

As the sweet melody filled the hall, Anne found herself seeing the King in a new light; seeing a sensitive part of his nature that she had not known existed. Nodding her head in time to the cadence, she began to sing softly, stimulated as always by good music.

The King looked up, still playing and rewarded her with a smile before returning his attention to the instrument. As the song finished, Anne and the King were loudly applauded by the entire court who had by now gathered around the group.

In the best of tempers now, Henry handed the lute back to his owner telling him that it was a fine instrument with good tone. Overcome with awe that the King of England should deign to tune and play his lute, the lad stammered his thanks before bowing and scraping his way from the hall.

The King, his eyes on Anne's face, huskily called for his harp. "We are weary of dancing and capering" he explained to his court. "This night we would prefer to sit quietly and play our harp with Mistress Anne's voice as accompaniment.

The King was an expert on the harp and the court,

knowing they were in for a treat, settled nearby in every available space and waited expectantly.

It was a Welsh harp and had belonged to his paternal grandmother Margaret Beaufort. Henry was proud of his Welsh roots and cherished the instrument, only rarely bringing it out in public. He extended his arm and indicated to Anne that he wished her to move closer. Only when she was settled to his satisfaction did he begin to play. Anne had never before heard a Welsh harp and listened transfixed as he began with a purely instrumental piece. When he would have started on a tune to which she could sing, she begged him to play another instrumental melody so that she could listen for longer. It mattered not to her that he was the King of England, only that here was a skilful player who could pluck either a poignant melody or flood the hall with full blooded music. .

It was a night to remember for Anne Boleyn; the night the King singled her out above all others, for rarely would he play an instrument and allow anyone to sing with it but himself.

Least of all, the harp of his forefathers.

Chapter 11

First Love

With the question of the Butler marriage safely avoided, things went on much as before, with Anne reigning over her own little court of friends and admirers and the King joining them when he could.

Cardinal Wolsey journeyed by barge to the court from his fine houses at York Place or Hampton Court on an average of three times each week to speak with the King. He and his retinue had lately arrived at Westminster one morning and the Privy Council was in session with the King and Cardinal in attendance. The Queen was resting in her chamber, troubled by one of her incessant headaches and Anne for once had absolutely nothing to occupy her.

She could not imagine where everyone had disappeared to. The tilt yard was empty, so too was the tennis court apart from a few players with whom she was not closely acquainted. More from habit than desire she found her feet leading her towards the great hall. The doors were wide open and the lofty room empty, except for the long trestle tables placed in readiness for the banquet which would not start until at least three o'clock. She had only ever been in the great hall when it was crowded and noisy; empty, it was distinctly eerie, cold and uninviting despite the profusion of light from the pair of enormous windows overlooking the river.

However, the great hall at Westminster did boast a particularly fine hammer beam roof and it was this which commanded her attention. Her hands clasped behind her back, she gazed up in awe at the magnificent structure and it was as she was stepping backwards to where she expected to find the wall, neck still craned upwards, that her hands came into contact with human flesh.

Startled, she sprang forward and whirled around. Standing beside the wall was a tall, handsome young man with reddish hair and soft brown eyes. He was dressed in the manner of a soldier rather than a courtier, not sporting amongst other things the latest male fashion for beards.
"I'm sorry" he held out his hand in apology. "I did not mean to frighten you; it seems we were both admiring the architecture and each was unaware of the other".

She put her hand in his, thinking to herself how handsome he was and admiring his trim figure and the manly breadth of his shoulders. Placing her other hand on her heart, she laughed, in a manner that the young man found quite delicious, and said "I am quite recovered now, thank you, but oh my, you did

give me a shock! Did I step on you?"
"No" he replied, "not that the weight of one as delicate as you would cause me too much pain. You are a lady of the court?"
"Yes" she replied, "and you are…?"
"I am of the Cardinal's retinue, his ward until such time as I inherit my father's titles and lands. Forgive me, I am most rude, I should have introduced myself before now. I am Henry Percy".
"I am Anne Boleyn". She was totally stunned by him and could not tear her eyes from his face. And the wonderful thing was that he too seemed similarly affected by her.

Coming closer, he gently placed the palms of his hands on either side of her face and tilted it up towards him. "If you will forgive the manners of a rough borderer, mistress, may I say that you are the loveliest thing I have ever seen?"

There was silence as they gazed at each other, then Harry Percy bent his head and kissed her gently, lingeringly on the lips. It might not have been the thing for a well brought up lady to do, but she closed her eyes and blissfully gave herself willingly into his embrace. When they finally parted she sighed softly "I have waited all my life for this".

His hands slid from her face and locked around her waist. Drawing her to him he murmured "Then you feel as I do? I did not realise that such powerful feelings could be both instantaneous and mutual!"

She laughed again, then raising her eyes to the roof,

said "I shall always remember you, hammer beam roof, for you brought me the man I have always dreamed of"

She lowered her eyes again to his face, drinking in every detail of him. Reluctantly drawing away she said "Come my love, let us walk in the gardens privately together, for soon this place will be teeming with servants making ready for the banquet".

He nodded his agreement, his eyes also on her face, and then hand in hand they walked out into the bright sunshine.

Happily for Anne and her new love, the Council meeting far overran its allotted time, thus the Cardinal and his followers stayed for the banquet.

For all her scheming, Anne could not procure a place for Harry Percy at her table so they both had to content themselves with gazing at each other across the great chamber, moving their heads and craning their necks on occasion to maintain eye contact as other courtiers moved across their line of sight. Several people intercepted their burning glances and turned to their neighbours with raised eyebrows, all whispering the same thing. What would the King say when he found out?

But it seemed that for once the King was unaware of Mistress Anne and her business; matters of state had evidently spilled from the council chamber to the banqueting table.

The eating of the forty courses took up almost four and a half hours, every long minute a torture for Anne and Harry who only wished to be in each other's arms. However at last the company finished the huge meal and the trestles were pushed aside in order that the entertainments might begin after a suitable interval for the digestion process.

Having been in love for just a few short hours, Anne and Harry did not care who guessed their secret. She danced with him every time she took to the floor and in between exertions they found that they could not stop talking. They desperately needed to know every detail of each other's lives so that their love could take root and flourish strongly.

Whilst she and Harry were recovering their breath after a particularly energetic galliard, her brother and Tom Wyatt appeared at her side. Still breathless, her hand on her rapidly beating heart she gasped "George, Tom, I am glad you are here; I want you to meet Harry Percy".

The three men greeted each other courteously, then George, who knew her better than any, drew her aside from the other two saying in a low voice "Anne, you are in love with this man?"

"Does it show that much?" she asked, exchanging a little smile with Harry over her brother's shoulder.

"How long has it been going on?" George demanded.

"But a few hours. Why George, are you jealous?" Anne giggled softly.

"You realise who he is?"

"Lord Henry Percy".

"He is Northumberland's heir, sister, and what is more, he has been betrothed to the Lady Mary Talbot these last six months to my knowledge!"

She screwed up her face, remembering "Someone once told me that a betrothal could be broken like a snap of the fingers…yes, I think it was Princess Mary. Francis said that to her when he asked her to marry him after Louis died".

"Oh Anne!" George sighed. "You are possessed of the sharpest wit at court and yet still you do not see. Mary Talbot will bring much gold to Northumberland's rapidly emptying coffers for she is the daughter of the Earl of Shrewsbury. In comparison, our father is a nobody!"

"My breeding is as good as any!" she flashed, finally moved to anger.

Henry Percy, in deep conversation with Wyatt, looked up at the sound of her raised voice. Her angry expression caused his gentle face to crease with consternation.

She glanced apologetically at him, then voice lowered, turned back to George. "Am I not related to the Earls of Ormonde through our father and the powerful Howards through our mother? Why, but very recently I was considered an acceptable bride for Ormonde's heir".

"Yes, yes. But whether such connections will placate mighty Northumberland, only time will tell. I think the issue here is as much to do with riches as breeding".

Thus it was a much chastened Anne who returned to her beloved's side minutes later. She decided that at the earliest opportunity she and Percy must slip away from the court and find somewhere private where they could talk. As luck would have it, her chance came sooner than expected, when the King ordered that the floor be cleared for wrestling.

Signing to her brother to say nothing, she seized Harry's hand and together they backed out of the great hall unobserved, or so she hoped. Besides George only one other noticed their going and that person sat on his dais watching them slip away with narrowed eyes and pursed mouth. That person was the King.

Hand in hand they raced down deserted passageways and did not slow until Anne pulled up outside a small ante chamber which she knew to be rarely used. However, she opened the door slowly and checked that the room was indeed empty before she pulled Harry in behind her and closed the door.

Once inside, they both began to giggle crazily for neither had thought to bring a torch, and with the door shut the room was in almost total darkness. There was a faint glimmer of moonlight from the tiny window and it was towards this that Anne stumbled, pulling Harry with her.

Finally they stood in each other's arms, both desperately trying to make out the features of the other's face in the dim light.

"I can barely see you my love" Anne whispered.

"No matter my sweet" he replied. "For if the sense of sight is missing there is only one other worth using".

Mentally Anne began to run through the five senses, then as his lips came down on hers, she knew just what he meant. "Touch!" she murmured.

Once the kiss was ended, Anne broached the subject which had been uppermost in her mind since her conversation with her brother. "Harry, are you truly betrothed to Shrewsbury's daughter?"

"Regrettably yes" he affirmed. "But maybe when I tell my father of our love he will reconsider".

Hope sprang into her heart "You really believe he would break the alliance?"

"He is a hard man" admitted Harry, "although there are times when he is approachable. I may be able to persuade him if I can catch him in a mellow mood".

"I do believe you are proposing to me, Harry Percy!" Having said what she hoped was in his heart, Anne caught her breath and looked searchingly into the dimmed features.

"Did you ever doubt my intentions?" he cried. "Did you think that I meant to treat you as a mere light o' love?"

"No…" she admitted slowly, "although a girl does like to be acquainted with her man's hopes and desires".

"All my hopes and desires are caught up in you" he told her earnestly. "I love you more than life; would you do me the honour of consenting to be my wife?"

"Well…" she pretended to consider, then backing away a little dropped a cheeky curtsey and said demurely "I should be greatly honoured to accept, my Lord!" and threw herself again into his arms. "Promise me you will settle the matter with your father as soon as you can?"

"As soon as he comes to court" he promised, holding her tightly.

So caught up in each other were they, that it took a little time for them both to become aware of the tramp of many feet passing their hiding place. "The court is preparing to retire" she told him. "Do not worry, no-one will come in here but we must take our leave now, separately, before we are missed".

They indulged in one last lingering kiss, then she, after listening at the door to ensure nobody was near, slipped out into the passageway, blowing him one last kiss as she gently closed the door.

For a long time after she had left, Henry Percy stood by the window staring into the night. But it was not the beauty of the moonlit gardens which so absorbed him, more how to break the news to his father that he wished to reject his intended bride.

Chapter 12

Shattered Dreams

Similar ante chambers in all the King's palaces became secret meeting places for the lovers. After that first wild and indiscreet evening, they had come to realise that it was necessary to keep their true feelings for the moments when they were hidden from prying eyes. They feared that to bring their innocent love to the attention of the King or Cardinal would bring about instant separation.

In public they were careful never to be seen alone together, always remaining within the circle of their friends. Since that first heady night of their love, they had not danced with one another exclusively.

Meanwhile the King was playing his own little game; that of observing those who thought themselves unobserved. It would do no harm, he decided, for their friendship to continue for a little longer. Perhaps when Mistress Anne tired of the boy she would look to a more mature man for her security. The King sat in his chair, these thoughts coursing through his head, puffing out his chest in mute pride as he thought of Anne comparing the worldliness of his thirty two years to the awkwardness and inexperience of a mere seventeen year old.

Anne's friends, with the exception of Wyatt, were delighted that she was at last experiencing true love. Wyatt, whilst glad for her in a way, found it hard to keep his jealousy under control, although he had to admit that he liked Percy.

Love itself had a miraculous effect on Anne. Gone were her flirtatious ways with others, her somewhat cynical outlook on life. All her hardness had melted away, leaving her soft, loving and very vulnerable. George, still keeping a close brotherly eye on her, compared this new Anne to their sister Mary. Anne had acquired all of Mary's gentleness and submissiveness but thankfully not her morals.

Mary herself, still clinging to her position as the King's favourite, had little time with which to associate with her sister, but she too noticed the change.

Sadly Anne's pure innocent love was doomed. The King came in to the great hall one night in a foul mood; his privy council had dared to cross him over some small matter and Henry was a man who hated to be crossed.

His smouldering eyes alighted on Anne and Harry executing one of the newer dances straight from France which involved the partners exchanging courtesy kisses, the merest brushing of lips, during certain parts of the dance.

The King noticed jealously that Percy kissed Anne just a little more heartily, his lips lingering on hers just a little longer that convention demanded. With a barely stifled roar the King leapt to his feet and stamped out of the hall, calling for the Cardinal to follow him as he cast a murderous glance in Percy's direction.

Once alone with the Cardinal the King made some trifling excuse for his bad temper, then as the Cardinal prepared to leave said casually "Lord Henry Percy; he is betrothed to Shrewsbury's girl is he not?"
The Cardinal's shrewd blue eyes immediately flew to the King's face as he affirmed "Indeed he is, Your Grace".
The King did not flinch from his gaze as he said lightly, "then maybe it is time the boy married her, before he commits some indiscretion with one of the Queen's ladies".

The Cardinal's mind worked quickly. Just who had Percy been dallying with of late? Ah yes, Anne Boleyn. Backing from his Sovereign's presence with a series of bows the Cardinal murmured "Rest assured Your Grace that I will waste no time in acquainting the Earl and his heir with your observations".
Henry allowed himself a self-satisfied smile "Then see to it!" he muttered.

It so happened that the conversation between the

King and Cardinal had been inadvertently overheard by Wolsey's gentleman usher, Cavendish. He had been sent by the Queen to deliver a message to the Cardinal, but as soon as he had gleaned the nature of the King's instructions, message forgotten, he returned swiftly to the great hall.

The dance which had so inflamed the King long finished, Harry and Anne stood talking with her brother. "A word in your ear my friend" whispered Cavendish, laying his hand on Percy's shoulder and drawing the surprised young man aside. "You and Mistress Anne are found out! Even now the King is instructing Wolsey to summon your father and arrange the marriage to Mary Talbot without delay".
"It is what I feared might happen" Percy admitted sadly, "but I thank you for the warning my friend".
"Now I must take my leave Harry, for I am supposed to be delivering a message from the Queen to the Cardinal. If she spies me talking here, you will not be the only member of the Cardinal's household to incur royal displeasure!" Quickly George Cavendish left the great hall in search of his master.

As Percy stared unhappily after his departing friend, he felt a hand on his arm and heard Anne asking "You are deeply troubled, my love?"
Closing his hand over hers, Harry gently told her of Cavendish's warning. "There is no hope for us now, Anne" he told her sadly. "My father will be greatly angered that I have incurred the displeasure of the King and have caused him to travel down from Northumberland. At best he will disinherit me, at worst, marry me immediately to Mary Talbot".

"But there is still a way Harry". Anne's dark eyes were full of love as she gazed appealingly at him.

He frowned as his eyes met hers. "You do not mean…. Anne, I would not have you bear the shame!"

Standing on tiptoe, her lips close to his ear, she said softly "There is no shame in bearing a child to one's husband. Whatever happens, there need be no shame. If I conceive your child, they must let us marry. If I do not, then no-one need know. Quickly, we must leave this place before the Cardinal thinks to part us!"

Their minds whirling, they somehow found themselves in the chamber they had lately been using to meet whilst the court was at Greenwich. Anne barred the door, then leaned against it facing Harry, wishing that her heart would not pound so furiously. Gently he took her into his arms. "You are quite sure you want this?" he asked, tilting her earnest little face up to his. "And if you do not conceive what then?"

"Then we must find another way to win your father over to our cause, but should our child leap into being this night then all our wishes will be granted!"

And so it happened that on a dusty floor in a locked chamber somewhere in the heart of Greenwich Palace, Anne Boleyn gave herself utterly, body and soul, to the only man she believed that she would ever want to marry.

It was well into the small hours before he could bring himself to leave her. Helping her to her feet he gently brushed the dust and cobwebs from her hair and helped her rearrange her disordered clothing. She did the same for him, her fingers lingering lovingly over his body, until eventually they stood before one another in some sense of sartorial order and prepared to say goodbye.

Not wishing to take the risk of meeting a guard whilst creeping around the silent palace at such an hour, Harry elected to climb out through the little window and return to the Cardinal's lodgings by way of the gardens.

One last kiss, then he climbed nimbly through the small casement and dropped the few feet to the ground. As he raced silently across the gardens, he paused to turn and wave several times, aware that he would carry the image of her framed in that moonlit window, her hand raised in farewell, in his heart for the rest of his life.

When at last he had disappeared from sight, Anne shut the window and heaved a great sigh. Then gazing at the dusty floor with a secret smile curving her lips, she relived their love. Folding her arms about her body she closed her eyes and tried to will the spark of life within her to blossom. If they had not succeeded in their endeavours, then it was not for the want of trying!

As she basked in the warmth of their delicious secret, she was not to know that it would be many long years before they would meet again.

It was George who brought the news to her. As she watched his approach, his face betraying his compassion, her heart sank.

It had been some days since the consummation of her love and she had heard that the Earl of Northumberland had already arrived at Hampton Court, purple in the face with rage, in response to the Cardinal's summons.

"Wolsey sent for Harry early this morning" began George. "Harry tried to tell him that you and he were committed to each other and that your bloodline was every bit as good as his, but the Cardinal would have none of it".
Her great eyes mournful, Anne whispered, "and?"
"The Cardinal went on to say that Harry should not so lower himself by aspiring to marry the daughter of a paltry knight, whatever her lineage. Then the Earl appeared and there ensued a mighty row, the upshot being that even now Harry and his father ride north".

Tears spilled from her eyes as she buried her face in her brother's doublet and sobbed "He is gone then, without even saying goodbye?"
"Believe me he tried to get to you, but the Cardinal has had him under virtual house arrest since he discovered the attachment".
She was aware of some small relief at her brother's use of the word 'attachment'. At least Harry had not revealed the extent of their love. All that was left for her now was to wait and hope.
"And" George continued, "I am afraid there is still

one more piece of news I have to impart".

Anne raised her head and drying her tears with the back of her hand, asked "Which is?"

"On the King's command you are banished from court for your indiscretion in seeking to entangle yourself with Northumberland's heir".

Shocked, she gasped "For how long?"

"I do not know, but I hope to God the King misses you sorely!" George exclaimed furiously. As one of the gentlemen closest to the King, he knew how much Henry relied on Anne for his amusement.

"This is surely the Cardinal's doing!" she burst out. "I truly believe that the King would not seek to part true lovers".

"But Anne, surely the King could overrule the Cardinal should he so desire? More likely the King is behind this because he did not want Percy to have you".

She shook her head. "No, not the King. Why should he be jealous of Harry? You're wrong George; it's all the fault of that red-cloaked imbecile!"

In vain George tried to calm her, but she was determined to give full vent to her anger. "As God is my witness, I hope one day that it will lie within my power to destroy his life as he has surely destroyed mine!"

George put his arm around her shoulders. "Come" he said gently, "I will help you pack; it is Hever for you sweet sister. Remember you once said that the place would always make you feel happy and safe? Mary is there at present, so you will have some company".

However Anne was not listening to George's soothing words as he propelled her swiftly to her chamber. She was already mentally plotting her revenge on the Cardinal, whom she believed had cruelly shattered all her dreams.

Chapter 13

Exile

It was a much subdued Anne who again set eyes on the Kentish castle over which she had so joyously exclaimed only twelve months earlier.

Before she had left the court, her father had sent for her and admonished her for daring to bring down the King's displeasure on the family name. Thomas Boleyn had been further angered by the fact that Anne had made no attempt to defend herself or justify her actions. Indeed, she had seemed almost bereft of life as she listened to him rant, staring dully at the floor before her.

As she stumbled into Hever supported by her mother and sister, she seemed as though in a trance. Even the warm spiced wine her mother called for did little to revive her. It brought some colour to her white face but could not restore the spirit behind her eyes.

When eventually she spoke, it was only to request

solitude. So, after helping her to her room, they left her. Only then, lying on the bed that she had used since early childhood, did the hot tears force their way from beneath her closed eyelids, running through her tangled hair on to the coverlet.

As the days passed it seemed that nothing could rouse her from her melancholy. The only company should would tolerate was that of her wolfhound Urian, who had come home with her from France. Long past his playful puppy stage, he would sit gravely beside her with his head in her lap, closing his eyes in ecstasy when she, grateful for his sympathetic and undemanding presence, would absentmindedly fondle his ears.

Only several weeks later when spring's freshness forced its way through her chamber window, did she at last venture outside the castle, walking slowly through the gardens accompanied by the faithful Urian.

Also with the coming of spring, her melancholy developed into bitter resentment, If Percy had loved her so desperately, why had he not flouted his father's wishes and come for her? But the bitterest pill of all was that she now knew for sure that there was to be no child of their brief union.

With that knowledge, her last slender thread of hope was gone. When the news that Harry had married Mary Talbot finally filtered through to Kent, she received it silently, shocking herself with the realisation that all hope had so long since left her, she no longer really cared.

Now there was no reason to mourn further for her lost love. Gradually, hesitantly, she began to emerge from her silent world. She turned first to her music, then to her family and friends. She began to take an interest in herself, a pride in her appearance. Her mother Elizabeth permitted herself a huge sigh of relief for she had feared that the child would die of a broken heart or at the very least send herself mad. The family had tried everything they could think of to rouse her, but all had failed. Nature was a wonderful thing, Elizabeth thought, for it had succeeded where silent company, sympathy and support could not.

Anne was almost herself again when one evening, whilst gathering rose petals with her sister in order to make sweet scents and lotions, Anne observed a distinct roundness to Mary's body and an added bloom to her cheeks. Even at her tender age Anne was well aware of the portent of such changes.

Sufficient petals having been collected, Anne drew Mary to a favourite seat beside the sun dial, surrounded by fragrant rose bushes. As they sat, enjoying the warm evening, Anne turned to face her sister and said softly "You are with child Mary. I wonder I did not notice before".

Sighing deeply, Mary admitted that it was true. When Anne asked when the child would be born and how her husband had reacted to the happy news, Mary fell silent for a time.

Eventually she said "The child will come in August, but it is the King's child, not Will's".

Anne was not surprised. "But how can you be sure?" she asked. "Surely there is just as much chance that it could be William's?"

Mary shook her head. "There is no doubt that it is the King's" she replied "For when the King shares my bed, my husband shuns me. We have not truly been man and wife these past twelve months".

Her face pensive, Anne got to her feet and began gathering a few of the early blooms for her bedchamber. "You make yourself too available Mary" she scolded. "He must have picked you up and cast you down countless times these past four years. Is he really worth it?" Anne looked down at her sister as she finished speaking and was struck by her contented, dreamy expression.

"It will be worth everything once I have the child" Mary replied, "and as for the King, he is like no other man. What woman would ever want to tell him no?"

Anne's expression said it all, although she chose not to voice her opinion.

"I have always wanted to give Henry a son" Mary continued, her hand resting on her swollen body, "and very soon, I will".

Anne laughed with delight. "You bear the King a son sister and you will be the most celebrated woman since Bessie Blount. And more than likely the Queen will never speak to you again!" Then she suddenly became serious. "You are not afraid?"

"Afraid of what? Childbirth? No, the pain is but fleeting and soon forgotten once the child is delivered".

"But what if it all becomes too much?" Anne continued urgently. "Is it not possible that you may resent the child when it is born for causing you so much suffering?"

Mary laughed and rose clumsily to her feet "The pain will but double my joy in the infant" she replied. "Believe me Nan, when you too have the experience of nurturing a child within you for so many long months, you will understand why I shall welcome the pains which herald the birth".

Together, arm in arm, they walked slowly back to the castle through the fading sunshine. "It will be a great joy to have my body to myself again Nan" Mary confided. Then she added "If only to be rid of this infernal backache!"

Laughing together they made for the still-room, where they would press their petals before the delicate perfume should begin to fade.

As Mary had predicted, her pains began one sunny August afternoon. In the first stage of her labours, when the pain was only slight, Mary asked that Anne might sit with her. Observing her young sister's anxious face, the mother-to-be could not help but laugh, even though the movement sent her labouring body into yet another spasm. "Really Anne, can you not cheer up a little? I am but in the process of producing a new life, not preparing to depart my own!"

"Does it hurt?" Anne enquired with concern, as she watched Mary wince and alter her position slightly.

"Only a little, but becoming more intense by the moment. If you would please call our mother, I think the time has come to take to my bed".

With Anne's assistance, Mary rose awkwardly and made her way towards the bed, prepared in readiness.

Within hours, Anne was embroiled within a strange new world she had not known existed, as she assisted her mother and the midwife at Mary's confinement. She sat at the head of the bed, mopping her sister's face with a cool damp cloth and tenderly brushing back the thick tendrils of hair which stuck to Mary's perspiring face as she thrashed her head from side to side at the height of her agony.

When at last the child, crying lustily, was propelled into the world by Mary's exhausted, sweat-drenched body, Anne experienced a relief so great that it was almost as if it were she who had given birth.

Elizabeth approached the bed and knelt beside the inert body of her eldest daughter. "You have done well Mary; you have birthed a fine red-haired boy".

Before exhaustion overwhelmed her, Mary asked for the child to be brought to her. He was placed in her arms, still yelling his disapproval and wriggling strongly. Mary gazed at him adoringly and planted a kiss on his nose, at the same time saying to her mother "You will notify the King?"

"The messenger is already on his way" her mother told her, stooping to lift the baby. "Now rest, Mary".

Mary was only too glad to obey her mother and when hours later she opened her eyes, she smiled to see Anne still seated beside her bed, rocking the infant in a family cradle which had last sheltered Anne herself. Seeing her sister awake, Anne leaned towards her "How do you feel?"

"Marvellous" replied the new mother. "The child?"

"Very beautiful, but oh so noisy! You were so brave Mary; I wouldn't have missed it for all the world, although I'm not sure that I look forward to experiencing it all for myself!"

Feeling herself drifting back to her slumber, Mary put out her hand and squeezed Anne's. "I am glad you were with me and when one day your time comes, I shall be with you also".

Mary quickly recovered from her ordeal and soon she and Anne were again seated in the gardens, this time with the baby beside them. Mary had proudly named him Henry after his sire and indeed he was the living image of his Tudor father.

The King had been at Westminster when news reached him of the boy's birth and he had immediately announced his intention to travel to Hever to visit mother and child as soon as matters of state would allow.

Thus it happened that on a blustery afternoon in late September Henry Tudor, resplendent in new hunting garb of green and gold, led his small entourage over the ancient stone bridge which spanned the River Eden close to Hever Castle. The occupants of the castle, who had not been informed in advance of his visit, were taken entirely by surprise, just as Henry had intended.

Elizabeth Boleyn, clothed most suitably in the russet velvet which she had hastily donned as soon as the King's party had been sighted riding along the banks of the river, stood in the small cobbled courtyard whilst her husband greeted the King, mentally calculating the state of her kitchens. As the King had brought only a few gentlemen, she estimated that there would be just enough food to go round. Even before the russet velvet had left the clothes press, her message to set about preparing a modest banquet had reached the kitchens. No need to ask the King if he were hungry, Elizabeth remembered enough of him to know that he was always ready to do a meal justice.

The King had turned from her husband and was approaching her. Although it had been a good while since she was court, Elizabeth could still execute an elegant curtsey with the best of them. Spreading her skirts about her she sank gracefully down to the cobblestones, head bent in reverence. "Why Elizabeth!" the great voice boomed, "rise my dear; let me look at you".

Obedient to the royal command, Elizabeth rose and looked into the face of her sovereign. With a sinking heart she studied his face, the puffy pink flesh almost obscuring the vision of his hard, small eyes; the aristocratic roman nose and small pursed mouth. All in all, she could see little trace of the Henry she had once loved.

Henry, looking closely at the woman few knew had been his mistress, albeit briefly, thought to himself how lovely she still was, how comely her figure even after five children. He suppressed a chuckle as he remembered that the Howards always did breed fine looking women.

Taking the King's proffered arm, Elizabeth escorted him into the castle, thinking to herself as they walked that not for anything would she want to be in Mary's place.

Once the King and his gentlemen were safely settled in what passed at Hever for a great hall, with refreshments to hand, Elizabeth excused herself and made for the herb garden to the rear of the castle where she expected to find her daughters and grandson. Turning a corner briskly, she suddenly came upon them by the fountain. Anne was holding the baby, whilst Mary dabbled her fingertips in the water spray, making the child start with delight as the tiny droplets sparkled in the sunlight. As Elizabeth's shadow fell across them, Mary looked up expectantly, having heard some of the commotion of the royal party's arrival. "The King is here" her mother confirmed. "No doubt he wishes to make the acquaintance of his son at the earliest possible opportunity".

Mary nodded, dried her hands on her apron and

held out her arms for the child. "Come my little one" she cooed to the infant. "Come and meet your royal father".

Her mother fell into step beside her as Mary began to walk along the path towards the castle, the pair only stopping when they realised that Anne was not with them. Mary turned, calling "Do you not wish to see the King Anne?"
"No I do not" replied her sister moodily, pointedly turning her back on them. "Neither will he wish to see me since he has banished me from his court. I will remain out of sight for the duration of his visit".
Elizabeth and Mary exchanged bemused glances, then resumed their walk to the castle.

Left alone, Anne pictured in her mind the fat King's delight when presented with his tiny, chubby replica. Sighing discontentedly she began to walk towards one of her favourite spots by the river, the ever present Urian at her heels. As she walked she allowed herself to lapse into one of her frequent daydreams about her life in France, the memories heightened by the sounds of music and laughter drifting from the castle.

Within a few minutes, she reached where she wanted to be; a shady little nook hidden from the castle by a clump of trees. The river widened and deepened considerably at that point, both banks dotted with small trees and bushes.

For some while she stood looking down at her reflection in the clear water, lost in thought. Looking about her for a stone, she found one and dropped it into the river, watching with fascination as the angry ripples distorted her reflection before the waters became still once more. She dropped in another, a bigger one. This time the water was slow to clear, but when it did, there was another reflection beside her own staring back at her.

She recognised the other face immediately but said nothing, merely straightening her back, setting her jaw and tilting her chin in the air, a fraction higher than normal as she waited.

The apparition spoke "No obeisance for your sovereign? Treason Mistress Anne, treason!"

Sighing loudly, purposefully so he would hear, she turned and dropped a curtsey as scanty in respect as it was in elegance. Not meeting his eyes she complained "I came here to be alone; Mary and the child have gone inside, you must have missed them".

He laughed, remembering his son. "I have seen them" he stated proudly. "He is a most beautiful child and your sister the epitome of motherhood".
"Then I suggest you return and spend some time with them" she retorted sarcastically. "For he will be a man soon enough".

Not in the least abashed, he came closer to her, his expression conciliatory and his arms outstretched. Her means of escape cut off by the river, Anne could do nothing but allow him to loop his arms around her shoulders. "I also came here to be alone" he told her. "Alone with you".

She sniffed disinterestedly and looked out across the river. "I have missed you Anne" he continued. "How would you like to return to court?"

She raised her eyes to his then stiffened as he drew closer. Her expression disdainful, she told him "No, on both counts!"

Angered by her attitude he barked "And your meaning?"

"No, I do not wish to return to court and no I will not surrender my body to you!" Shaking off his arms she slipped nimbly past him.

"You are not still in love with that fool Percy?"

"No".

Exasperated he cried "Can you say nothing other than no?"

Coolly she looked him up and down. He was the King of England yet standing as he was before her with the blood rushing to his face and his fists clenched in anger, he looked for all the world like a large, thwarted child.

She resisted the impulse to laugh and instead smiled mysteriously, advancing towards him until her face was only inches from his. "I have many words in my vocabulary" she whispered seductively, "but the word you wish to hear is one I intend to keep close until I am in the arms of my husband!"

He drew back, blinking rapidly. He was not used to being spoken to in such a way.

"Remember that my Lord King" she continued, "and when you have realised that I will never mould to your will, then, and only then, shall I be glad to come to court!"

He stood speechless as she gathered up her skirts and sprinted away from him, across the grass and into the woods. Shaking his head in disbelief he would have followed her, but found his way barred by her immense dog, teeth bared menacingly whilst a warning growl rumbled from his throat.

Annoyed that she had thoroughly outwitted him, Henry made up his mind to linger at Hever for as long as possible that day. Something may yet be salvaged for surely she would later wish to seek him out and apologise. He smirked to himself as he imagined their reunion; her repentant and he all magnanimous forgiveness.

Again, he was quite wrong in his assessment of her. When at last he and his gentlemen were forced by the advancing twilight to leave Hever for the long ride back to London, Anne still had not made an appearance.

Thus it was a much disgruntled Henry Tudor who rode homewards; his pleasure in the elder sister's child much diminished by the younger sister's refusal to have anything to do with him.

Chapter 14

Old Friends

After the Christmas celebrations, Mary Boleyn returned to court, taking her child with her. At first Anne missed her sister's company greatly and wished she had swallowed her pride and gone back with her, but soon her attentions were diverted by a frequent visitor.

Her neighbour Thomas Wyatt, when on temporary leave from court, delighted in spending much of his free time at Hever with his childhood friend. Anne, now aware of his deep regard for her, tried to treat him gently and with the respect his feelings for her deserved, but she found it difficult. As Thomas was almost the only male of her own age and station that she ever saw, she would often flirt mercilessly with him, testing that her strange power over men was still potent. For Thomas's part he had to admit that he enjoyed being with her for he never knew if she would treat him as a brother or a lover from one day to the next.

However it was as a brother that she spoke to him one day. "Tom, how do you manage to escape from court so often? Poor George always seems to be in attendance upon the King!"

Thomas, smiling ruefully, lowered himself to the rustic bench where she sat. "I keep telling the King I have family problems" he admitted. "So whenever he feels that I do not seem as merry as I should, he packs me off to Allington and tells me to forget my differences with my wife and set about getting more sons".

She listened sympathetically. "And do you truly have differences with your wife?"

"Sadly yes" he told her. "She seems uninterested in me and lives only for our son, choosing to forget just how he came to be born in the first place"

"No doubt her feelings towards you are not helped by the fact that you spend so much time here with me". Anne, her sisterly feelings temporarily banished, threw Thomas a flirtatious sidelong glance.

Thomas, usually more than keen to respond to such banter, seemed not to notice. "No, Elizabeth shows no jealousy at all" he continued, "In fact she and I now lead quite separate lives. Whenever I arrive at Allington she removes herself to the other side of the castle and makes no attempt to speak with me. It's been that way for so long that her behaviour no longer bothers me. I only return to Kent to see my son… and you".

"Oh Tom" she whispered, shaking her head sadly, "I do so understand how you must feel. It is a terrible thing to be spurned by someone you love; someone who you thought loved you too".

It seemed only natural for him to take her into his

arms and she went gladly. "Don't think of him" he whispered, lips against her hair. "Waste no thoughts on a man who deserted such as you because he feared the wrath of his father and Wolsey".

She lifted her head and gazed into his clear green eyes. "It is not Harry the man that I mourn" she began, "it is just the fact that his love for me must have been so shallow for him to give up without a fight. I suppose my pride is bruised, that's the truth of it".
"If it is any consolation, rumour has it that his marriage is miserable; Mary Talbot hates him and he her".
She hung her head. "I feel desperately sorry for them; they are both victims of Northumberland's greed. But they no longer affect my life, the past is past. It is the future I fear, for with Harry, it was mapped out. Now I can see nothing to look forward to".
"It is not like you to wallow in self-pity" he told her teasingly, trying to raise a smile.
"I know" she answered, not picking up on his lighter tone. "I am also being very selfish. You are the one with the very real heartache. Poor Tom, so much love to give and Elizabeth not wanting to know you". She raised her eyes to his face and whispered "She must be a fool".

Wyatt suddenly jumped to his feet. "I must take my leave now" he told her, "before I do something we may both live to regret".
Surprised, she caught hold of his wrist "Such as?" she demanded. After a pause she stood up, still holding him captive, her eyes on his face.

"I think you know well" he said softly. "You tempt me sorely Anne, you know you do. Were I free, I would offer you marriage and to hell with your father's objections. Were you yourself married, perhaps you would be my mistress. But much as I want you, I would not so compromise a single woman. For honour's sake we must give up these private meetings for I am but a weak man with strong desires". Courteously kissing her hand in farewell, he moved through the trees to where their horses were tethered.

Anne followed him, her heart pounding. She came upon him untying his horse, his back towards her. Walking up to him she put her arms around his waist and rested her head against his back. In a whisper so low that he had to strain his ears to hear her, she said "Am I to assume that you love me, Master Wyatt?"

At first he made no reply, merely dropped his forehead to his horse's neck whilst he fought with his emotions. Finally, pushed to his limits he spun around and let his lips give her his answer.

At length, when their lips parted, he kissed the tip of her nose and told her "I have always loved you and I always will. Even in your darkest moments you can remember that".

Slowly, reluctantly he let her go and mounted his horse. Loath to leave her, he leaned down to her and asked "May I dare hope that my feelings are reciprocated?"
Raising her hand to caress the side of his face she

replied softly "With all my heart Tom. Always".

With her free hand she groped amongst the folds of her skirt until it closed about the little jewelled tablet which hung from her girdle. Detaching it, she lovingly presented it to him, seeing his eyes light up at this tangible expression of her affection. It bore her initials, picked out in precious stones. He kissed it reverently and slipped it inside his shirt. "I will carry it always" he told her, then turned his horse towards Allington, blowing her a kiss as he turned from sight.

By mutual agreement Anne and Thomas continued to spend much time in each other's company, but only rarely would they be alone. Thomas spent a good deal of his time with her repeating all the latest court gossip and tutoring her in the newest songs and dances so that she would be well prepared for the King's summons; when and if it came.

It was almost a year to the day since his last visit, when the King again arrived unannounced. Anne had become bored with her exile for Tom had not been able to see her much of late and she found too much of her own company extremely tedious.

The King was delighted to find her attitude to him much less hostile, and upon his suggestion, Anne agreed to accompany him on a short walk around the gardens.
"Your Grace does me much honour by walking with me" she told him demurely, "I greatly feared that after your last visit you would put me completely from your mind. I much regret the manner in which I

treated Your Grace".

He was quite delighted by her humility. Composing his features into a stern expression, he looked down on her as they walked. "You are forgiven, Mistress" he said benignly. "By your tone and repentance am I to take it that you are ready to return to court?"

Still keeping her voice demure and her eyes downcast, she replied "Only if Your Grace still desires my presence".

Henry was weary of word games and made a grab at her. Springing out of his reach like a frightened doe she gasped "But my terms still stand. Do not seek to read submission in my repentance".

Quick to anger, Henry glared at her. "Do you mean to say you still refuse your King?"

"Only that which I have a right to refuse you!" she flared. Then seeing that he was truly angered, thinking fast, she changed her tactics. Approaching him she seized the royal hand and knelt at his feet. "Your Grace, I am but a humble maid. I will have little in the way of dowry and the greatest gift I can bestow upon my future husband is my honour".

Henry's small pursed mouth broke into a wide grin. To save face he jovially cried "Mistress your King was but teasing you. We do not wish to place immoral women in our court and now we see that you will be a credit to us with your modest behaviour. Return to us soon, we beg you".

Lowering his voice to a more intimate tone and drawing her up from her knees and closer to him, he said "I have missed you Nan. My court is a sadder place without your gaiety and beauty to grace it".

Sensing he was fishing for a compliment she replied with as much sincerity as she could muster. "And I have sorely missed Your Grace. My life has little meaning when I am denied the company of my King". She was both surprised and appalled at how easily the lies flowed from her lips.

But it was just what he wanted to hear. Beaming hugely he put his huge hands around her waist and lifted her off the ground until her face was on a level with his own. "Then we are friends again sweetheart?" he enquired urgently. "As we were before?"
"Better than before" she told him, smiling despite herself at his boyish enthusiasm.
"You have made me very happy Nan!" he cried, impulsively kissing her mouth before setting her gently down.

They resumed their walk, her hand on his arm. Every so often he would pat the back of her hand with his spare paw and beam at her conspiratorially. Looking up at him she marvelled that she could manage him so deftly. He was so easy to read and even though she did not know him well, she could tell by the expression on his face the answers he wanted to hear.

Walking companionably with her King that afternoon, Anne felt that at last the future was looking brighter than it had for some time.

Although she had intended to humour the King's

whim and return to court almost immediately, winter set in early, making the roads impossible to travel with safety. When she did not arrive as promised, the King sent a letter asking if she had changed her mind for some reason, and if so, begging her to reconsider.

He went on to tell her how dull it was without her and how badly he desired to again converse with her. Reading between the lines Anne sensed a barely contained passion, a passion which filled her with contempt for she did not so feel for him as he evidently did for her.

Reading the letter again in the privacy of her bedchamber, its meaning became crystal clear. He still had intentions of making her his mistress, despite her many refusals. Certainly should she ever forget herself enough to surrender, she could expect him to soon tire of her and drop her as he had her sister.

"Then I must not surrender!" she said aloud, fanning herself gently with the King's letter. "I must keep his passion on the boil yet always manage to evade capture". She put her head on one side, deep in thought, then smiled wickedly. "It would be quite an achievement to have my sovereign dancing to my tune and quite a novelty for him to find himself denied what he desperately craves".

Still smiling mischievously, she sat at her table and penned a curt little note to her royal admirer, pointing out that the weather had prevented her making the journey and promising that she would travel as soon as the roads were fit. Then she added one or two lines to which his eager eyes would infer much and promise little. Satisfied she sealed the letter and sent it downstairs to the royal messenger.

The man had obviously received instructions to await her reply then return to London with all speed, for minutes later she observed his departure, galloping away as though pursued by the devil himself.

Anne retired early to bed that night for she had much to mull over. The King's letter lay where she had left it, before her mirror. As she brushed her hair, she scanned the neat script yet again, eager to glean every possible scrap of information from the indiscretions of its royal author. She knew that once she returned to court she would be virtually at the King's mercy and would need all her wits about her to repulse his attentions and yet retain his regard. It would be a great challenge; a light hearted game, she decided. The ultimate triumph would be to restore her family's good name and maybe even wreak some small revenge on Cardinal Wolsey.

Anne Boleyn had made her choice. She was about to embark on a career that would change the course of English history.

Chapter 15

The Return

Her re-emergence into court circles was to say the least, spectacular. Assisted by her brother and his friends she slipped unnoticed into Greenwich Palace one January day; the object of all the secrecy was to surprise the King and with her she had brought the tools she needed.

She had designed a fabulous gown composed of many colours in a spangled pattern. Her usual hanging sleeves were omitted for once lest they betray her identity; she had substituted tight sleeves of pink satin, finishing in a frill at the wrist. The neckline of the dress was, even by Tudor standards, daring, edged with black fur. The last item of costume was a full faced golden mask which she planned to wear until her little masquerade was completely played out.

Throughout the evenings feasting she had remained hidden in a small chamber only yards from the great hall. Her door was locked and only her brother had the key. She readied herself and waited patiently.

George let himself silently into the chamber at just after nine o'clock. Dressed in her strange garb she turned slowly to face him. He surveyed her in astonishment, shaking his head as if he could not believe his eyes. "Nan, is that really you? You look like a strange being from another land!"

"Then I have achieved my aim brother" she replied flippantly. "Is it time?"

"There is a distinct lull in the proceedings, if that is what you mean" he replied. "The Queen has recently retired and the King is slumped in his chair heaving great sighs".

"Good". Moving to the mirror, she turned first one way, then the other, checking that her disguise was complete. Pushing back a lock of heavy dark hair she asked "You don't think my hair will give me away? I would prefer to leave it loose and uncovered so that it may add to the air of mystery. What think you?"

Head on one side, he considered. "No, I do not think it will give you away, if that is your worry. After all, the King has never seen your hair thus, has he?"

"So you think I will command his attention?"

"You would command any man's attention dressed as you are; indeed sometimes I almost regret that I am your brother!"

Alarmed she placed her fingers on his mouth to prevent him saying more. "Be silent George" she pleaded. "You are but a man and I would guess that any woman dressed such as I would stir your senses, but I beg you have a care; there will always be talk regarding the nature of the relationship between a brother and sister as close as we. When I was in

France I remember hearing all kinds of stories about Francis and Marguerite. Rumours sprout from malicious tongues and we do not want to run the risk of ruining your court career, or mine!" Settling the garb more comfortably on her shoulders, she tied her mask securely and made for the door.

"Before you go, Nan".

Impatiently she whirled round to face him. "Yes?"

"Tell me the true purpose of this masquerade".

"I wish to surprise the King" she said carefully. "Also to bring home to him his foolishness in allowing the Cardinal to banish me in his royal name. Maybe by the end of this night I will have taken the first steps towards my goal".

George's face turned deathly white. "Which is?"

"To destroy the Cardinal!" she exclaimed with vehemence. "The only way I can pay him out for his treatment of Harry Percy and me is to sever his influence with the King".

"So you seek to turn the King's affections from the Cardinal to yourself?"

"Absolutely!" she confirmed. "And at the same time, by denying the King my body, which he already desperately desires, I am sweetly punishing him for his treatment of our sister! Now do you see George? Something inside me is driving me to this; something which is a mixture of ambition and hatred draws me to the King like…" she cast about in her mind for the phrase she sought, "like a moth to the flame. I cannot now alter my course".

"Take care Nan" he begged, taking her hand in his. "Remember what happens to that moth. It is destroyed!"

"Have no fear brother" she replied gaily, moving

away from him and opening the door a chink to ascertain the passageway was empty before she stepped out. "If I secure the King's affections, I cannot be destroyed, maybe just get my wings a little scorched!"

Beckoning to him to follow, she closed the door behind him and bade him go to the King and inform him that a lady from a foreign land begged leave to entertain the mighty King of England.
"What entertainment do you plan to provide?" he asked, his hand on the door of the great hall, preparatory to pushing it open.
"I shall dance at first" she told him. "Tom Wyatt has written some strange haunting music which the musicians will start to play when I give the signal. Then I shall sit at the King's feet and sing seductively to the same tune. Finally I will invite the King to dance with me. Hurry George, before someone comes!"

She was left alone in the passageway with only the two sentries for company. They stared lustfully at her whilst she threw them coquettish glances, turning her head this way and that, so they could see the moistness of her parted lips and the glitter of her eyes through the slits in her mask.

Suddenly the huge double doors were thrown open and she heard herself announced as the Princes Tashka. Confidently she stepped over the threshold and arrogantly surveyed her audience. Then, head held high, she looked directly at the King.

Her appearance had certainly made him sit up and take notice; she felt the little eyes sweeping her body as though he were undressing her with his mind. She shivered involuntarily then ran lightly down the steps and across the floor until she stood before him. With exaggerated elegance she curtsied low, the neckline of her gown leaving little to his imagination. Henry cleared his throat and said in an intimate tone "Welcome Princess. We look forward to your entertainment".

She said nothing as she rose from the floor; only the slightest inclination of her head acknowledged his greeting. The King cleared his throat again and shifted awkwardly in his chair.

Signalling to the minstrels' gallery, she stood in the middle of the floor, hands on hips, slowly rotating her lower body in time to the rhythm they struck up. Then she began her strange dance. She had not practised any steps in advance, preferring to trust to her imagination and as the strange melody swirled around the hall she swayed and twisted her body, her light skirts fluttering so high that a good deal of smooth bare skin was revealed to the ogling crowd. As the music progressed and the rhythm quickened she was reminded of a troupe of Moorish dancers who used to regularly entertain the French court and swiftly incorporated many of their sensuous arm and body movements.

At the climax of the dance the music became wilder and more abandoned; she spun round and round on the spot, arms outstretched, head bent back and the black hair flying. As the music ended she fell to the floor on her knees, her head bent to her thighs and her hands reaching out towards the King.

There was a stunned silence before applause swept the hall, the King himself clapping louder than any. He rose from his chair and started forward to raise her from the floor but before he could reach her she sprang up. Advancing towards him she planted her palms on his chest and pushed him none too gently back into his chair, her black eyes glittering through her golden mask.

She knelt at his feet and then twisted so that her back rested against his legs, and lifting her hair high, let it drop so that it spread across his jewelled codpiece. Once settled, and amused at the tenseness she could feel in the King's body, she began to sing. The words were equally as strange as the music; even the King, master of many languages could not identify the tongue in which she sang. Nor could anyone, for it was something else she had plucked from her imagination. The song ended and as the applause died, she seized the King's hand and mimed to him that she wished them to dance.

He was only too glad to agree, desperate to get closer to her and discover her identity, although he felt it perfectly feasible that she was indeed from a foreign land.

The dance was totally unlike anything he had ever executed before; she took the lead and he followed her steps as best he could, impressing her with his adeptness. Instead of her upper body remaining stiff and erect as in usual formal dances, he found himself with his hands spanning her waist whilst she swayed to and from him and from side to side, like a branch in the wind. As the last notes of the melody melted away, the musicians struck up a galliard and the rest of the court took to the floor.

Hands still locked around her waist, Henry steered her to a curtained alcove away from curious eyes. They regarded each other in silence for several moments then, her voice heavily disguised; she asked "You do not know me Sire?"
"I must confess you have me both intrigued and baffled" he admitted, after pause for thought. "Will you show me your face?"
"You are sure you truly desire to know my identity?" she countered. "Should Your Grace so wish, I could remain masked and entertain the court on another occasion".

Henry grimaced, running a finger between his bull neck and his shirt collar. "Your entertainment was delightful Madam" he told her, "but by the saints, another evening of your sensuous dancing in such scanty costume would be more than us hot-blooded Englishmen could bear!"

Seductively she entwined her arms around his neck, standing on tiptoe to bring her masked face close to his. "So the mighty King of this island has passion coursing through his veins?" she whispered, glad that he could not see just how hard she was struggling to keep a straight face at his discomfited expression.

With his florid complexion several shades paler than normal, he replied "I admit that I was... moved .... by your performance".

She moved even closer, then rubbing her head against his shoulder like a playful kitten murmured "Then Your Majesty is not the god I had thought him to be but a mere mortal?" She was enjoying herself immensely; for a man who so enjoyed the hunt he seemed terrified by the predatory female she portrayed. The power was exquisite.

"Even gods must multiply Madam" he told her, firmly disentangling her arms from his neck. Then unable to resist touching her, he extended his hand to tilt the masked face upwards, moving it from side to side whilst muttering "You have me completely fooled for I have no inkling of who you might be. Release me from this torment, I beg you!"

She knew her game was played out so she bowed her head graciously and murmured "As Your Grace pleases" before turning her back and lifting her arms to untie the strings which secured the mask.

Henry Tudor shuffled his feet and licked his lips impatiently. At last she held the mask in her outstretched right hand, her back still towards him. As he watched, fascinated, with her left hand she drew some of her hair across her left shoulder before turning slowly to face him. All he could see of her face was a high smooth forehead and a pair of sparkling dark eyes, for she had drawn her hair across the lower part of her face.

Slowly, strand by strand, she allowed the heavy hair to fall until her face was fully revealed to his incredulous gaze. Then a great smile illuminated his heavy features "Anne Boleyn!" he exclaimed, and before she could protest he had seized her and kissed her heartily.
"You Grace is pleased to see me?" she asked demurely.
"You have no need to ask me that!" he replied enthusiastically. "You have made me a happy man tonight!" Then his voice dropped to an urgent whisper as pulling her close he murmured "and you could make me even happier".

Exasperated, she closed her eyes, dropped her head and banged her two small fists against his massive shoulders. "Why must you spoil everything?" she sighed. "I have told you no so many times and I cannot, will not, change my mind!"
"But why, sweetheart" he cajoled. "You have shown yourself tonight as a sensuous woman, full of desire. Why deny the joys we could share?"
She did not answer immediately and for a blissful moment Henry Tudor thought that she was at last on the point of surrendering.

She pulled away from him and too exhausted from her journey and the excitement of the evening to infuse any real anger into her voice, told him "As I said at Hever, I intend to keep myself for my husband. What you have seen tonight may well be an expression of my inner being, but that is not for you. I cannot be your wife because you have one already and anyway, I am not worthy. But I am too good to be your mistress and I will not so lower myself!"

Dropping her mask to the floor, she pushed the curtain aside and was immediately lost in the throng, not for the first time leaving Henry Tudor gaping after her like a fish stranded on a river bank.

Chapter 16

Elevation

Now that she was back at last, Henry could hardly bear for her to be out of his sight. At first he tried to keep his adoration a secret from the Queen, but eventually he could not restrain himself from selecting her for his dancing partner on every occasion, playing dice and card games with her and above all, making music with her, whether the Queen was present or not. In their private moments together, he bade Anne to drop all protocol and call him Henry.

He was touching in his little attempts to please her. Once he overheard her talking to Margaret Wyatt, bewailing the fact that most of the court looked down on her for she was merely Mistress Boleyn and not even of sufficient rank to call herself "Lady".

Almost immediately the King gave instructions that the necessary documents be drawn up to render her complaint void. Within hours her father was created Viscount Rochford; her brother heir to the title thus a

Lord, whilst she and her sister Mary both bore the title of Lady Rochford.

Anne was astounded when she heard the news and impulsively ran to find the King. As soon as they were alone she approached him and allowed him to put his arms around her. "I have just heard of my family's elevation" she told him. "My most grateful thanks; you are so kind to me!"
"I would be kinder…." he began
"….if I were to give myself to you" she finished for him. "Don't say it Henry; don't spoil this moment". She paused and drew a ring from her middle finger. "Take this a token of my regard for you". Henry gleefully pushed the ring on to his little finger as far as it would go and kissed her soundly in gratitude.

Separating his greedy lips from hers with some effort, she reminded him of the bowls match he had promised to play. "There will be four players divided into two teams" she told him. "Your Grace with Henry Norris on one side, my brother and Tom Wyatt on the other. Come Sire, make yourself ready for soon I must be in attendance on the Queen and I would not wish to miss any of your casts".

Always one to take the opportunity to show off to his lady love, Henry Tudor allowed her to call in a groom of the bedchamber who at once helped his master into more sporting garb whilst the Lady Anne Rochford waited in the audience chamber.

When the King was ready, arm in arm they made their way down to the green. The Queen not being present, Anne was directed to sit in the place of honour. It was not a game she was particularly fond of, but Henry had explained the rules to her so at least she had an understanding of the procedure. However she was also aware, without any tutoring, of the difference between a good shot and a bad one. Whenever he made a cast Henry looked towards her for her reaction. If it was good she clapped her hands and smiled at him; if it was not good she made a little grimace and shrugged her shoulders, making him determined that his next cast would win her smile of approval.

Midway through the game Henry noticed that she clapped particularly enthusiastically whenever Wyatt made a cast, whether it was good or indifferent. After she had done this several times Henry threw down his bowl in a fit of temper and strode over to where she sat.

"Why is it Madam" he thundered, "that whenever the captain of the opposing team makes his cast you applaud it wholeheartedly?"

Her mind working swiftly she leaned towards him in what she hoped he would take to be a conspiratorial manner. Keeping her voice low she replied "It is merely a strategy I have adopted, Your Grace".

Intrigued, he squatted on his heels before her, listening intently. "By applauding the oppositions' every shot I hope to lull them into a sense of false security" she told him. "From their positions at the top of the green and by my enthusiastic applause, they believe that their every shot is true. With your casting my love…" she paused and extended a dainty forefinger which she moved in a caressing fashion around his face, "by appearing not to approve of some of your shots I am merely conveying to you that the next cast must be even better".

For a moment he seemed mollified, then he stood up abruptly pulling away from her hand, his face betraying his sudden suspicion "You would have us cheat Madam?" he asked.
No, no Your Grace" she replied hurriedly, her brain racing round in circles to find a plausible explanation. With her hand she motioned him closer yet again. "By my poor efforts I attempt to assist Your Grace in making your already incredible skills even greater".

With bated breath she scanned his face anxiously, waiting for his reaction. To her relief he straightened and smiled at her, then taking her hand, kissed it in leaving, whispering "I should have guessed that my Nan had only my best interests at heart. Forgive my rough manners sweetheart". She smiled graciously and he strode back to the game, not seeing Anne's breath puff out her cheeks or her relieved expression as she relaxed back into her chair, rapidly fanning her face with her hand.

Meg Wyatt leaned closer "You extricated yourself from a tricky situation remarkably well there Anne" she commented. "But is it wise to show your affection for my brother so openly?"

Anne turned to Meg and patted her hand "I try not to, Meg" she admitted "but apart from my love for him, he is a much better bowls player than the King!"

She met Margaret's eyes as she finished speaking and both had to smother their giggles, looking anxiously towards the players on the green. Thankfully they were far too absorbed with their game to notice.

The climax of the game approached. Due to considerable skills on both sides the lead changed hands after almost every shot; there only remained the two captains' casts to be made and the game could be won by either.

Wyatt was the first to step up. Holding the bowl under his chin with both hands, his face a study of concentration, he calculated the distance, stooped and released his final shot. Sweetly it sped over the springy turf slowing as it approached the jack eventually coming to rest only a few inches away. "Good shot Tom!" Anne called. Henry too congratulated Wyatt, but the look he threw Anne clearly said, now watch me better him.

Anne rose from her seat and walked to join the other three competitors at the jack end of the green. Silently they watched the King go through his pre-cast ritual of balancing the bowl on his palm and sighting the jack. Then he rocked backwards and forwards from right to left foot three times before finally stooping with left hand on left knee to send the bowl on its way.

As it rolled swiftly towards them Anne's mind was busy calculating how best to react whether he lost or won. Fascinated she watched the bowl slow as if caught by an invisible hand, finally coming to rest in front of the jack. There was a shout of delight from the other end; Henry evidently thought it was a winner. Sneaking a glance at the others, Anne could tell by their silence and blank expressions that they considered Wyatt's cast the nearer.

By now Henry was puffing his way down the green towards them, surprised that the applause and cheering he had anticipated was not forthcoming. On reaching them he scanned each face in turn then dropped on one knee beside the offending items. Eventually he straightened and faced them "Surely there is no doubt that my cast is the nearer?" he demanded. No-one was prepared to meet his eyes and through the increasing mists of rage he saw Anne and Wyatt exchange glances.

Reaching out he clamped a heavy hand on Wyatt's shoulder and jerked him roughly closer. Then pointing with his little finger, the finger upon which Anne's ring was jammed, he said in a dangerously quiet voice "Wyatt, I tell you it is mine!"

Suddenly the object of the fracas had turned from a bowls game to the love of Anne Boleyn. She sensed it, the other players sensed it and the watching courtiers certainly sensed it.

Wyatt gazed expressionlessly at the ring, then his eyes flickered to Anne's white face before returning to the King's now purple countenance. "I will measure it Your Grace" he decided. "By your leave". The King's nod was barely discernible as all watched closely whilst Wyatt unclasped a chain from his neck, upon which was a small tablet bearing the initials AB. Holding it in front of the King's face so the sunlight glinted on its precious stones and highlighted the identity of its former owner, Wyatt said "I will measure it with this Your Grace, for I have hopes that the prize may still be mine".

The watching assembly waited, holding its collective breath, as Wyatt carefully measured the two casts. At last he stood up. "Mine is the nearer by several links, Your Grace" he told his King.

Henry was by now in a state of extreme anger, glaring at Wyatt from beneath thunderous brows, his chin almost resting on his doublet and his jaw dangerously jutting. He realised all were waiting for him to speak. Angrily he kicked the offending jack as far as possible into the ogling crowd muttering "If it is as you say, then I am deceived!" Throwing a venomous glance at Anne, he strode from the scene, his mind unable to distinguish which was Wyatt's greater transgression; that he knew Anne so well he could recognise her smallest possession or the fact that he too wore her token.

Anne, whose hands had flown to her face the second Wyatt had produced the tablet, felt her legs begin to buckle beneath her. Dreadfully distressed and fearful for both herself and Wyatt, she was helped from the green and conveyed to her apartments at the palace where she lay on her bed for several hours, her mind too dazed to even begin to formulate the explanation she knew the King would shortly demand.

Margaret Wyatt came to her bedside. "Anne, should you not go to the King and tell him the whole episode was but a misunderstanding?"

Anne, by now a little recovered, raised herself on one elbow and regarded her friend with consideration. "I do not think that it should be I who go to him" she said at last. "He would soon tire of a weak creature who ran to apologise for every little thing. No, I will bide my time and let him stew in his own juice".

Her reaction concerned Margaret. "But what of Tom? If the King believes you care more for my brother than you do for him there is no saying what he might do in a fit of jealousy".
"Be calm Meg and trust me. I shall be able to win the King round and keep Tom safe. I still do not believe that the King really loves me, but if he does then he will come here".

Meanwhile, the King in his chamber was thinking along the same lines. If she truly loved him then she would come to offer her explanation. However by the time supper was called, neither had made a move towards the other.

Still deeply put out, Henry took supper privately with the Queen, something he avoided whenever possible although as yet there was no open breach between them. Catherine, who after seventeen years of marriage could tell the state of his temper at a glance, diplomatically kept silent.

Having eaten little, Henry stared moodily into the

depths of his wine, seeing the afternoons drama reflected therein. Then without warning he leapt to his feet, flung the goblet wine and all hard against the fireplace and stamped from the chamber. Catherine continued with her meal, the only sign that she had witnessed anything out of the ordinary was one eyebrow slightly raised.

The King went straight to Anne's apartments and without observing any of the niceties, flung open the door of her bedchamber. As her ladies scampered from the room, he barely waited for the door to close before thundering "Well?"

Anne cowered against a wall, white and shaking. He was agreeably surprised at this for he had expected to find her hard faced and arrogant. As he took a few steps towards her, she flinched, as though expecting a blow. In a trice he was beside her, gathering her small body to his massive chest and smoothing her tumbled hair with his great hands. "You should know that I would never strike you" he soothed. "I have upset you with my unsporting behaviour this afternoon; please forgive me!"

Crushed uncomfortably against him, her face suffering from the sharp edged gems which studded his surcoat, Anne's lips twitched into a smile. This was going better that she had even dared hope; perhaps with Henry, attack was not always the best form of defence. Another valuable lesson learned.

As he released her slightly to look down into her face, she resumed her terrified expression. "I feared to lose Your Grace's regard" she whispered appealingly.

"Nay" he told her, tickling her under the chin and being rewarded with a tiny smile. "It will take more than Wyatt's clowning to make me forsake you".

"Then you are not angry with me anymore?"

"I was never angry with you" then his voice hardened "I am however greatly displeased with Wyatt". He looked carefully at her as he spoke to judge her reaction to his words.

Frantically she forced her almost paralysed facial muscles to assume a light hearted devil may care expression, knowing that if he were to guess how deeply she cared for Thomas, her poet would quickly find himself in the Tower on some trumped up charge.

"How does he come to have your token Anne?" There it was, the forthright question she had been dreading. A question to which he had every right to demand an answer.

"Well?" He was waiting.

Hoping that he would not see the lie in her eyes, she forced herself to meet his gaze. "I did not actually give it to him" she began, "it was whilst I was at Hever last year. When I came to retire one evening I noticed that the tablet no longer hung from its cord at my girdle. I assumed I had dropped it somewhere in the gardens but no doubt Wyatt filched it merely to tease me. However when I made no mention of the loss, perhaps he kept it to save face". Pleased with her explanation, off the cuff as it was, she looked up at him hopefully.

Not entirely convinced, the King said slowly "But that does not alter the fact that instead of keeping it amongst his possessions, he wore it next to his skin".

Truthfully she replied "I do not know why he chose to wear it thus. Maybe to surprise me he had it put on a gold chain to replace my meagre silken cord and was set to return it to me after the game". It did not sound overly convincing, even to her ears, but Henry broke into a smile. Anne felt herself begin to relax a little and tried to mirror his doting expression as he said "Then your distress when Wyatt produced the thing was because you did not know he possessed it rather than fear that an attachment to him was revealed through a love token?"

Her insides felt as though they were melting and her knees began to shake but she forced herself to look him squarely in the eye and say in the most determined voice she could muster "Of course!"

The relief on his face was obvious. "Then all is right between us again. Whilst there is no doubt that Wyatt thinks highly of you I should remember that you grew up together and no doubt he looks on you as a sister".

Again she had escaped with grace from a seemingly impossible situation; however as she looked into her monarch's benign, smiling face, she asked herself for how much longer would he be so anxious to believe her every story?

Chapter 17

The Decision

The King's restlessness at having no male heirs was escalating. Worse still, the physicians had told him that it was unlikely Catherine would be able to have more children. His sole legitimate heir was his daughter, eleven year old Princess Mary.

He confided his worries to Cardinal Wolsey during one of their thrice weekly conferences and concluded lamely "I wish there was a solution to this problem!"

Had the King but known it, Wolsey had been aware for some months that the matter was playing on his sovereign's mind and had been racking his fine statesman's brain in order to produce a solution. And he had found one.

Sidling up to the King, his red silk robes rustling like a lady's skirt he said "No doubt Your Grace has already considered the grave fact that your marriage to the Queen could be invalid?" As Henry's mouth dropped open in surprise, Wolsey continued smoothly, "invalid because Queen Catherine was first the wife of your brother, the late lamented Prince Arthur".

"Ah!" exclaimed the King. He turned away from Wolsey and walked to the great window, forefinger caught between his teeth, his thoughts racing. Looking down he saw several of the Queen's ladies playing with bats and ball beneath his window. Anne was there; she saw him and waved. Snatching his hand from his mouth, he waved back, then turned back to the room and saw Wolsey waiting patiently. Uncomfortably Henry cleared his throat and dragged to mind the very exciting possibilities which were opening up before him. "Ah!" he repeated.

Having given his King a few moments to mull over the portent of his words, Wolsey continued "As Your Grace well knows, the bible clearly forbids any man to take his brother's widow to wife…"
"Or else they be childless!" the King finished for him gleefully. Then clapping his elder statesman so hard on the back that Wolsey feared for his internal organs, cried "You have hit the nail on the head, my friend! God frowns on our marriage which is why we have no son! We have been living in sin" he finished piously.

One matter however stuck out a mile and Wolsey felt obliged to bring it to the King's attention. "There is of course the Princess Mary" he began hesitantly, "she is undoubtedly a child of the marriage".

But the King had seen a glimmer of hope and was

undaunted "She is sickly" he reminded Wolsey. "Although she has survived babyhood, she may not outlive me. Our union would therefore be childless". The King regarded Wolsey expectantly and Wolsey was instinctively aware of the words for which the King waited.

Clearing his throat, he addressed his sovereign in his most pompous tones "As a member of Your Grace's privy council I beseech you to consider putting aside our dearly loved Queen with whom you have enjoyed an incestuous relationship for many years and choose a successor who will bear legitimate male heirs". Here Wolsey paused, then as Anne Boleyn's abandoned laughter floated in through the open window, continued hastily "preferably a princess of the blood royal who will bring Your Grace a handsome dowry".

Delighted at the thought of a new wife, Henry asked "Is there such a princess?"
Wolsey thought carefully. "Princess Renee of France would be eminently suitable, Your Grace; and it may be that at the same time we could also marry Princess Mary into France". Feeling Henry's eyes boring into him, he added hastily "should she live to a marriageable age, that is".

Wolsey winced as a jubilant Henry gave him yet another clap on the back. "Commence discreet enquiries Thomas", the King was saying. "Let me know as soon as you have news".

Once alone Henry rubbed his hands together

gleefully, thinking of a comely French wife and the strong sons she would give him, not to mention the piles of French gold which would top up his coffers. A gentle tap on the door startled him from his reverie "Come!" he cried.

Anne's head appeared round the door. "Come in Nan" he told her. "How is the bat and ball coming along?"
She curtsied to him, replying "Very badly, I fear. I was hoping that Your Grace might find time to give us ladies some tuition. Your tennis prowess would prove invaluable. You are not busy?" she peered around the chamber as she spoke.
"I cannot think of anything I would rather do" he told her, taking her hands and squeezing them gently, "however I would talk with you first".

Her face was alive with interest as they sat together upon the window seat. "It must be good news" she commented lightly. "I have not seen you so happy after a meeting with the Cardinal for months".

Unable to keep it to himself any longer, Henry burst out "Wolsey is working for a divorce between me and Catherine!"
"A divorce?" she repeated incredulously. "To what end?"
"In order to procure for me a rich French bride!" he told her joyfully.
At once, her face hardened. "Another foreigner!" she spat. Henry drew back, amazed by her reaction.
"I thought you'd be pleased" he said in a small voice.
"Pleased?" she exclaimed. "Pleased? Mother of

God!"

"Such oaths do not become you Anne" he told her primly, "and anyway, why should you of all people have any objection to a French queen? You are all but French yourself!"

Her temper thoroughly roused, she leaned towards him and with venom on her tongue replied "I had a French education certainly, but I am English born. I would have you remember that; English born! And why, pray, should I be pleased to welcome your French wife? She will no doubt be younger than I, more beautiful and more accomplished. Once you have a young wife to take to your bed, your much talked of, much professed love for me will be forgotten. I thank God I never yielded to you, tempted though I was, for you would have dropped me as soon as the marriage contract was signed!" Exhausted from her furious outburst, she tore away from his restraining arms and turned her back on him, one hand resting on her pounding heart.

"Had I known it would so upset you, I would not have told you of it" he said sadly.

"No doubt you would have carried on the negotiations behind my back!" she snapped, still facing away from him. "If you want more girl children to go with that half-Spanish daughter of yours, you are going the right way about it!"

"Anne. Sweetheart". Gently he turned her to face him. "What else would you have me do?"

"You want sons?"

"Most certainly!"

"Then take an English wife!"

He thought for a moment, face creased in

concentration. "But there are no English princesses available".

"And why must she be a princess?" she countered. "Think back to your maternal grandfather Edward IV and Elizabeth Woodville. He married that English girl for love and she bore him fine sons".

"And a lot more daughters" he reminded her.

"But she was fruitful and most of her children were born strong and lived" Anne argued.

She was beginning to win him over to her way of thinking. "Perhaps you are right sweetheart", he said slowly, making her more than a little suspicious by the way he looked at her, as though assessing a brood mare. "After all, then my son would be wholly English, like me!" He tapped himself proudly on the chest as he spoke.

"You are half-Welsh" she reminded him teasingly.

He looked at her and laughed. "It seems I can never win when I argue with you!"

Her dark eyes were warm as she disentangled herself from his arms and made for the door. "You will never get the better of me" she told him proudly. Then, a little anxiously "You do not think I have too much spirit Henry?"

Crossing to her, he slapped her lightly on the buttocks and cried "Not you! I like a woman to have spirit!" Then the smile left his face as he formulated his thoughts and looked searchingly at her. Softly he asked "Will you be my Elizabeth Woodville, Nan?"

It seemed as though the question hung in the air between them. Silently she looked at him, trying to read the thoughts hidden behind his intense expression.

"You are actually asking me to marry you?" she voiced the hitherto unspoken words a little timidly.

"Yes".

Confused, she ran her fingers through her unbound hair, for she was hoodless due to her energetic tennis play. "I don't know what to say!" For once she found herself truly speechless for never in her wildest dreams had she expected a serious proposal of marriage from the King of England. She didn't even like him that much, did she? Covertly she looked at him from beneath downcast lashes, playing for time. She had certainly done her best to dislike him; to use him. But despite everything, there was something about him; something about the power he exuded. She could suddenly see why her sister Mary had been so loath to give up her position as King's favourite.

He interrupted her thoughts, referring to her last spoken words. "How about just saying yes?" he suggested, a half smile about his lips.

What was there to lose? "Yes!" she cried, flinging herself into his arms. He caught her around the waist and swung her round like a child in his jubilation.

When they had calmed down a little, she said "But Wolsey would never work for a divorce if he knew you wanted to marry me. He despises me. He believes your love for me to be mere infatuation".

"Infatuation!" exclaimed her husband-to-be. "He wouldn't know true love if it were to punch him on the nose. What does a priest know of love?"

Casting her mind back to a recent rumour that Wolsey had lived secretly with a common law wife for many years, she murmured cynically "What indeed?"

However she was immediately forced to return her attention to the King, whom she decided was caressing her just a little too urgently. "Do I really tempt you Nan? Is it true what you said earlier, that you find it hard to resist me?"

"I would be a cold creature indeed if I were oblivious to your nearness" she retorted. Then seeing his whole expression smacked of lust, warned "And although I have agreed to marry you, I will not anticipate our wedding vows!"

His face dropped and assumed a sullen expression. Knowing she had to divert him before he fell into a rage, she whispered "Think of our son, Henry. He must be unquestionably legitimate; we must be married before he is born. It is not worth the risk my love; the divorce could take many, many months".

"You are right sweetheart" he concluded reluctantly. Then, grimacing "I shall respect your honour, although God knows it will be difficult!"

"Good!" she kissed him gratefully. "Now, I think my fellow ladies may be becoming a little impatient at our continued absence!"

Chapter 18

Wolsey's Quest

As much as they were inclined to shout it from the rooftops, Henry and Anne had to keep the news that they intended to marry, a secret. For one thing, the Queen was unaware that they intended to make their liaison permanent; for another, Henry like Anne, believed that Wolsey may not work so diligently for the divorce if he knew in advance that Henry had chosen a commoner for his future wife.

Wolsey had announced his intention to travel to France to have talks with the French King about the proposed marriage alliance. From France he intended to send messengers to the Pope, explaining the English King's dilemma and requesting the divorce.

Anne was deeply concerned over Wolsey's activities. "This document Wolsey hopes to persuade the Pope to sign, what if it has the French princess's name on it?" Anne asked Henry one evening.
Henry was perplexed. "What do you mean, sweetheart?"

"What if Wolsey presents the annulment papers to the Pope and they state that once the annulment is granted, you will marry the Princess Renee? Surely if Clement signs such a document then you will be obliged to take her to wife because the terms will not permit your marriage to any other?"

The King regarded her thoughtfully. "Do you think that it is Wolsey's plan to force me in to this French alliance?"

"I would not put such a thing past him!" she replied vehemently. "Securing a successful contract with Francis will no doubt line his coffers a little more and he has always seemed hell bent on moulding you to his priestly will".

Inferring to Henry that he was easily led, which on occasion he could be, was as deadly as waving a red cloth at a bull. Rapidly his lowered eyes flickered back and forth as though he were reading a document at speed; Anne knew it meant he was thinking quickly.

"I have it!" he exclaimed at last. "Once Wolsey is safely in France, amusing himself at court, we shall send another envoy to him, supposedly to assist his messengers in reaching the Pope. In reality this envoy will carry a paper signed by me, countermanding Wolsey's orders. We will provide the envoy with an annulment paper to present to the Pope which will give me the right to marry any woman I choose. Even one who is related to me by the first degree of affinity. There sweetheart! What think you of my plan?"

"Excellent!" she clapped her hands joyfully. "But why the affinity clause?"

"It is necessary because I am related to you thus as your sister was my mistress" he told her comfortably. Her face expressionless, she replied, "Oh, yes".

Later that same evening, whilst Wyatt was partnering her in the dance, he suddenly informed her "I have the chance to travel to Italy on a mission with Sir John Russell".

"Oh Tom!" she exclaimed, almost missing her steps in her dismay. "You will go?"

"I would rather stay near you" he told her passionately. "But in view of the King's interest in you, it may be better for me to be abroad. He regards me as a rival, no matter what he says, and he can be a dangerous opponent".

"You are right" she conceded sadly. "It would be safer for you to be away from the court, especially now…." Her voice trailed away.

"Especially now what?" Wyatt hissed, suddenly angry. "You have not become his mistress?"

"Oh no" she reassured him quickly. "It is just… oh…I may as well tell you, if you promise to keep it to yourself".

The dance ended and he stood looking at her expectantly. Motioning him closer, she whispered "The King has asked me to marry him. He is obtaining a divorce from the Queen".

"Oh, Nan!" Tom shook his head in disbelief. "Is this what you really want?"

"Of course not!" she retorted petulantly. "If I had been seriously looking for a husband I would have married you years ago". Looking into his troubled green eyes, she continued. "Wish me luck Tom. A fickle suitor makes an even more fickle husband, no doubt".

"I do wish you luck" Wyatt told her ardently. "You will certainly need it, but the thought of you in his bed makes me want to …. !" Sensibly he stilled his words, but his very stance, with body tensed and face flushed, spoke far louder than the treasonable words he had so nearly uttered.

Seeing his agitation, Anne said gently. "We must part now Tom, before the King sees. God speed, my love". Then she was gone, slipping through the crowd towards the royal dais. He watched her out of sight and then without a word to any, left the great hall to prepare for his journey.

Despite her assumed gaiety, Anne's heart was heavy that night. Panic periodically assailed her as she wondered how she would bear her royal suitor's caresses from day to day without sight of that face she loved so dearly.

Anne and Henry were supping privately in her chamber one evening when a hot, dusty messenger was ushered into their presence. The date was 1st June 1527; Anne knew she would always remember it.

Although exhausted, the messenger managed to gasp out that the Imperial troops of the Queen's nephew, the Emperor Charles V had mercilessly sacked Rome. The Pope, in fear of his life, had fled to the Castel St

Angelo overlooking the city, and was virtually a prisoner.

As the man was escorted to the kitchens for rest and refreshment, Anne looked into Henry's shocked face and said dully "this then is the end of our hopes. The Emperor will never allow the Pope to declare his aunt an incestuous wife".

Henry heaved a great sigh for he believed her to be right. "We will not give up!" he shouted suddenly, banging his fist on the table as he spoke. "Somehow Wolsey must reach the Pope; I will order him to travel immediately!"

Within two days Anne and Henry stood on the water steps at Hampton Court watching the pretentious prelate preparing to leave by barge on the first stage of his journey. His was a sumptuous retinue for he was determined to travel in style and comfort. As the barges began to pull away, Wolsey and the King exchanged glances, and in that moment Wolsey knew that it would be the worse for him if he did not succeed in his mission. Later, as Anne and the King were exploring Wolsey's great house, like two children whose mother has gone out, Henry told Anne that he would need to leave her to her own devices for a while as he had to see the Queen. "Why?" she burst out indignantly.

"No need for hysterics Nan" he reproved her gently. "I just feel that the time has come to inform Catherine of my intentions. I wish to be fair to her".

Dumbly Anne nodded and watched him go, her heart singing.

The approaching interview with Catherine had been preying on his mind for days and he was glad that he had finally steeled himself to do it. She and her ladies were quietly sewing when he walked in on them unannounced and became uncomfortably aware of many eyes regarding him with amazement; it was so long since he had ventured near. Catherine held his gaze for a few moments; her expression stony, before saying to her ladies in her deep, still heavily accented voice, "leave us, ladies. The King and I would speak alone".

As the door closed on the last of her waiting women, she looked at him with reproachful eyes. "It is many weeks since you last visited me Henry".
"I know" he blustered, "affairs of state, you know … "

She did not reply, keeping her eyes fixed on him. He stared back, trying to hide the distaste he now felt for her; she was only forty-two but looked so much older. Yes, she had experienced many sorrows in her life but she still had no right to look so dowdy! There were many women he knew who were her age and older, yet they had kept their looks. The one who immediately sprang to mind was Elizabeth Boleyn; she was close in age to Catherine yet looked a good ten years younger. He hoped Anne would look as lovely as her mother in later life.

Catherine spoke, startling him from his musings. "Do you wish to speak to me or merely stare at me?"
Thrust back into reality, he immediately began to speak his mind. "We have no living sons Catherine" he began.

"And is that my fault?" she interjected. "I have given birth to four male children; we cannot question God's right to call them out of this world".

Glaring at her, he continued. "The bible states that no man may marry his brother's wife and have issue. So therefore … ".

She cut in again. "We have Mary".

"She may die any day!" he snapped, his patience fast disappearing. "Kindly do not interrupt your King, Madam!" Taking a deep breath, he continued. "For some months my conscience has been troubled by this matter. God has not smiled on us Catherine, for we have done a great wrong. The only remedy is for us to separate; you must leave court and choose a house in which to spend your retirement". His speech had gone well, he decided, as he turned to Catherine expectantly.

She had pulled her embroidery frame to her and was calmly continuing with her sewing. Without meeting his eyes she said "I have been expecting something of this nature for some time. So it is official; you wish to put me away in order to take a new young wife to your bed". She paused and turned reproachful Spanish eyes to his. "But it is not your conscience which is aroused my Lord, merely your lusts! This is a cock and bull story which you have concocted in order to be rid of me and deny our daughter her right to the throne!" Her point made, she returned her attention to her work. Whilst Henry alternately sighed and stamped his way around the chamber she threw in her final barb. "Some weeks ago I wrote to my nephew informing him that I believed you wished to be rid of me, possibly by divorce … "

Henry wheeled round on her "You did what?" he thundered.

"I believe you heard me the first time Henry" she continued calmly. "The Emperor my nephew will have received my despatch before the sack of Rome. Perhaps it is what prompted him to take the eternal city and imprison the Pope.

Horrified, Henry clapped his hands to his eyes. That the Queen may be behind the Emperor's actions had not occurred to him or Anne. However, upsetting Catherine would only make her all the more obstinate, so he quickly changed tactics.

His voice gentle, he said "Catherine?" She looked up at him in surprise and he continued. "Catherine, agree to a divorce and retire from here. You may choose where you wish to live and you can take Mary with you. I give you my word that the pair of you will want for nothing".

She listened to him, open mouthed. He had not changed; he still refused to listen to things which did not please him. All her proud Spanish royal blood arose in her and she sprang to her feet, knocking aside her embroidery frame in her violence, her eyes shining with conviction. In a voice as loud and powerful as his, she cried, "nothing shall induce me to give up my position as Queen of this realm. I am your true wedded wife and Mary is your heir. You may disown me if you choose, but I shall fight for my daughter until the day I die!"

For a moment, Henry's courage failed him; all the

spirit of her dead mother, the redoubtable warrior Queen Isabella looked from Catherine's eyes. Without a word, without even changing his expression, he left the room.

Alone again, Catherine sat down in her chair with a bump. Her heart broken by this cruel betrayal she stared wordlessly at the door through which he had passed; stared until the picture became hopelessly blurred as she, a proud daughter of Spain, collapsed in tragic, bitter tears.

Some weeks later, Henry received that for which he had long been waiting; a letter from Cardinal Wolsey. Excitedly he read it, and then sent a page to ask the Lady Anne Rochford to join him immediately.

Minutes later, she entered the chamber. "This is our chance, sweetheart" he told her, handing over Wolsey's despatch.

Quickly she scanned it, reading one part aloud "… with Your Grace's approval I am sending three of my retinue to bribe their way into the Pope's presence. They will persuade him to hand over the administration of the Catholic Church for the duration of his imprisonment to myself and a select group of Cardinals". She tapped the letter with her other hand, her eyes shining. "You mean this is our chance to send Doctor Knight on the real mission?
"The ideal opportunity!" Henry told her gleefully. "I

have already drawn up the annulment papers; they now require only the Pope's signature before we can be married. Doctor Knight will be riding for Dover within the hour!"

Chapter 19

Sweating Sickness

The weeks following Doctor Knight's departure were fraught with tension for Henry and Anne. They had expected word to come from Wolsey once the envoy reached him, but although they looked at all hours every day for messengers from abroad, none came.

One autumn night, Henry and Anne were holding one of their frequent musical evenings with about a dozen friends, when a page appeared at Henry's side. "Cardinal Wolsey has arrived from France" he whispered. "He wishes to know where Your Grace will speak with him".

Before the King could answer, Anne rose to her feet and said coldly "Tell him he must come where the King is. Bid him enter".

Unceremoniously, the Cardinal was ushered into the music room. He was dusty and travel stained and held himself as though he were a very old man, looking ill and tired. The King was all bluff heartiness. "What brings you home so quickly Thomas?"

The Cardinal replied, "I felt I had done all I could Your Grace. I have left your envoy Doctor Knight working in my stead".

"Is there any news?" Anne interjected.

"None that I know of" Wolsey replied, failing to hide his look of dislike as he met her eyes. "Although I do have some matters of a private nature to discuss with the King".

Imperiously Anne waved her hand, addressing the onlookers. "It seems our music must be at an end for this evening my friends. I pray you leave the King and myself for we would speak privately with the Cardinal".

One by one the assembly gathered up cushions, music and instruments and left the chamber.

"Well?" asked Henry eagerly, turning to Wolsey. "What news?"

"Francis has agreed to a double alliance" Wolsey replied, "although I am now given to understand that Your Grace never intended taking the French princess to wife". Lips pursed, he fixed a cold glance on the king and saw him exchange glances with Anne.

Pompously Henry stated "I have decided that my subjects would not be inclined to tolerate another foreign alliance due to the failure of the present Queen to produce a male heir".

Wolsey kept his gaze fixed on the King's face. "In which case …" he prompted.

Henry continued eagerly. "In which case I have decided to select my future bride from amongst my own people; the English"

At this, Wolsey switched his gaze to Anne, who stared stonily back, a small triumphant smile curving her lips. Wolsey barked "You Grace has made his choice?"

Smiling, Henry reached for Anne's hand and held it to his lips, and then drawing her closer to Wolsey said "I believe there is no other more suited to queenship than my Lady Anne Rochford".

Wolsey's eyes swept her contemptuously. "None indeed" he agreed reluctantly.

Aware that her power over the Cardinal was complete, Anne felt that she was living her finest hour. "You will work to place me on the throne?" she asked.

Watching the pair of them, Wolsey grudgingly replied that he would do all within his power to bring the matter of the divorce to a speedy conclusion, fully cognisant of the fact that he had little choice.

"Good". Satisfied, Anne flashed the Cardinal a brief smile. "The King and I are agreed that you should remain here in England and liaise with Doctor Knight, who should by now be in Rome".

Wolsey inclined his head in acknowledgement, then begged leave to retire and rest after his long journey. The King dismissed him thankfully; maybe now with Wolsey on their side things would begin to happen at last.

As the door closed behind the crestfallen Wolsey, Henry turned to Anne and said gently, "were you not a little hard on him sweetheart?"

"Maybe" she admitted apologetically. "But he must be made to see that we are truly set on our course, Henry. The way that he looked at me just then; he still believes me to be just a passing fancy. I am sure that he will delay the divorce if he can, hoping that in the meantime you will tire of me".

The King took her into his arms. "We must trust him Nan" he told her. "But by God should he try any delaying tactics, or rouse my anger by not paying you the deference due to you as my future wife, he will find himself tumbled from his high estate and lodged in the Tower!"

Christmas that year was a joyous affair; the first letters had been received from Doctor Knight in Rome and it looked as though everything was going to plan. Shortly after the New Year's Day revels, Wolsey begged, and was granted, an audience with the King.

"Problems, Thomas?" the King asked, noting the Cardinal's troubled expression.

"Of a kind, Your Grace" he admitted. "I have today received a communication from the Pope. Clement says that he would be able to see his way clear to granting your divorce were he in happier circumstances. However, still being under the power of the Emperor, he fears for his life should he grant your desire.

Henry sighed wearily. "I knew things were going a little too smoothly. What now, Thomas?"

Confidently, Wolsey continued. "I suggest we reply to Clement and ask him to send a representative from the Vatican in order that we may try the case in England. Obviously this legate should be empowered to grant the divorce, should he be satisfied as to the grounds".

"You think Clement would agree?" Henry's voice was full of hope.

Wolsey shrugged his shoulders. "I can think of no reason why he should not. The selected legate could sanction the divorce thus relieving Clement of the responsibility".

"Excellent!" Henry leapt to his feet and prepared to terminate the interview. "Petition the Pope to send his legate and do all within your power to bring him to England with all speed. I must away now to acquaint the Lady Anne of these new developments".

The Cardinal watched him go; heaving a sigh for the old days when he had held full sway over his monarch; when there had been no scheming female to impose such a strain on their relationship. The Lady Anne Rochford was proving to be an adversary indeed, and the Cardinal wondered if he had the stomach for the upcoming battle for control over the King.

June 1528 was said to be the hottest in living memory. The court was at Greenwich, grateful for the cool breezes which came off the river, but ever watchful for the pestilence which never failed to raise its head in such conditions. On 14th June came the news which all dreaded, but expected; the sweating sickness had arrived in London and was fast tightening its grip on the population.

The King tried to suppress his panic at the news. His greatest dread was, and always had been, that some disease would carry him off leaving his country without a prince to succeed him. His physicians however felt that for the time being, the court was safe. The disease so far was confined to an area of the city far from Greenwich.

But as was its way, overnight the disease crept into the palace, attacking several of the kitchen skivvies. No person close to the King was afflicted, but Anne woke up to find one of her maids well within its grip and fighting for her life.

On the King's orders, the court had been making ready to remove itself well away from danger; to Waltham in Essex. Anne however knew that Waltham was not for her. She was well aware of the unwritten court rule that any person who had been in contact with a dangerous disease was to keep from the King and leave the court without delay. There was no alternative; she prepared to leave for Hever.

Again she wandered her home's quiet, peaceful surroundings; thankful in a way to be away from the chaos and intrigue of the court in order to relax and recharge herself. The divorce was still some months away, she calculated, therefore she would need to continue to hold the King in thrall until she could achieve her ultimate ambition.

Her sister Mary and brother George arrived at Hever only a few days after her own arrival. The news from court was bad; many had died and Mary's husband William Carey was among the latest to be afflicted. Mary had brought her son with her in an effort to escape infection.

A few days later, Anne and George were preparing to go hawking together, a sport which both enjoyed immensely. Anne had just led her horse away from the stables and was preparing to mount, when she suddenly felt all strength leave her body and slumped against her horse for support.

"Anne!" cried her brother in alarm.

"I feel so strange George" she muttered. "My head is pounding and I feel so weak and dizzy; and so hot!" Then realisation dawned on her. "God help me; it is the sickness!"

Greatly concerned, George threw the reins of his horse to a groom, picked her up and carried her hastily back to the castle. There, he handed her over to his mother and Mary, neither of whom needed any explanation about what ailed her. As they unceremoniously half lifted, half dragged her up the spiral staircase to her chamber, George, feeling suddenly very weary, dropped himself on to a convenient seat and called "Mother! As soon as she is abed, bring me news of her condition. I must inform the King immediately".

Sometime later when Elizabeth Boleyn returned to tell George that his sister was gravely ill with the sickness, she found her son sprawled on the floor. Gently she turned him over on to his back, knowing in her heart that he too had succumbed. There was no need for her to feel his forehead, for his face was covered with beads of sweat and even through his clothes she could feel his body's heat.

With a sinking heart she called for servants to put her son to bed, then sighing deeply, she sat down at a table to pen a brief message to the King.

Less than a day later the King eagerly tore open the letter from Hever. He had expected a cheery note from Anne; instead it was a tragic message from her mother informing him that both his favourite gentleman of the bedchamber and his future Queen lay dangerously ill with the sweating sickness.

Although it was late in the evening and the court but recently retired, Henry immediately called for one of his physicians. It was his second physician Doctor Butts who answered the call; his most favoured, Doctor Linacre, apparently not in the palace. Swiftly the King instructed him to set out for Hever with all speed where his dearly beloved Lady Rochford and her brother lay ill of the sweat. Doctor Butts agreed to leave immediately and as he prepared to take his leave of the King, Henry whispered menacingly "Do not let her die, for if you do, I will not be responsible for my actions".

He had made himself abundantly clear; should the Lady Anne die, then Doctor Butts knew he would most likely pay for her death with his own life.

When eventually a flustered Doctor Butts hurried in to Hever's entrance hall, he found himself met by a subdued Lady Boleyn. "I think my son is improving" she told him, "but I greatly fear for the life of my daughter". Her words sent Butts scurrying to Anne's chamber, where he found her conscious and able to speak of her symptoms.

"I feel racking pains all over my body" she whispered weakly. "One minute I burn with the fever, the next I shiver with cold. I find it hard to draw enough breath as my chest feels as though a great weight sits upon it and my head swims with constant pain. I know not whether I am living or dead and I no longer care for surely even Hell cannot hold such evil as this?"

After quickly examining her, Butts drew her mother to one side. "She is approaching the crisis point" he whispered. "Has she shown signs of delirium?"
Elizabeth nodded. "Some, yes. She slips in and out of it. She spent a terrible night, raving of things beyond my comprehension".
Butts nodded gravely. "I feared as much. If she survives until morning, she may well recover. If she should lapse into unconsciousness and we cannot rouse her to give her water, her body will give up the

fight and she will die". Butts rubbed the back of his neck thoughtfully, mindful of his sovereign's parting words. "We must see that she does not sleep during the next few hours".

Elizabeth nodded, her face pale with strain and worry. Butts gripped her arms. "What of you?" he questioned anxiously. "Have you developed any symptoms? What of the rest of the household?"

"I am well" she told him. "So far as I know, it is only Anne and George who have become ill. Their sister Mary and her child seem untouched at present, as do all the servants".

"I am relieved to hear it" breathed Butts. "As you and your elder daughter have not succumbed I think we can safely assume that you and she have some kind of immunity. We can only pray that your other two children have a similarly strong constitution and will be able to throw off the disease. Kindly conduct me to your son's room Lady Boleyn, I must examine him too".

They found George quite cheerful; conscious, and in full possession of his faculties. "My son reached the crisis point during the night" Lady Boleyn said, gazing lovingly at the bedridden figure whilst she tucked the coverlet more securely about him. "He tossed and turned and cried out in his agony then suddenly fell silent. I feared he was dead, but found him to be sleeping peacefully, all trace of the fever gone".

Butts performed a perfunctory examination. "You are well on the way to recovery, Lord Rochford" he pronounced at last. "However I advise you to stay in bed for a few more days. The rest will help you regain your strength and keep you safe from re-infection".

"How is Anne?" George asked. "Will she live?"

"I cannot say as yet" the physician replied. "She will approach her own crisis soon. If she is strong enough for the fight, she too will recover. All that remains for you to do my Lord is pray for her".

As Butts had predicted, soon after darkness fell, Anne's condition worsened dramatically. On the King's instructions, messengers were dispatched from Hever every three hours with news of her condition. They returned only hours later, bearing letters for the Lady Anne in which the King told her of his great love and the agony he was experiencing whilst she fought for her life. Elizabeth dutifully read the letters aloud to her daughter, but as midnight approached, Anne was aware of nothing but her pain and delirium.

Elizabeth watched her daughter with sad eyes for she seemed far worse than her brother had been. She raved incessantly, but thankfully her words were garbled and senseless. At times she seemed possessed of such strength that as she tossed, her writhing body caused the bed covers to slip to the floor. Patiently her mother tucked the blankets securely around her daughter yet again, and tenderly stroked her face.

After several hours, her condition had not changed. Close to tears, Elizabeth looked towards Doctor Butts and whispered "How much longer can this go on?

She is fast losing her strength!"

As she spoke, Anne writhed even more strongly and the physician rose from his seat to help her mother hold her down. "I have done all I can Lady Boleyn" he said. "Her fate is in God's hands now".

Seconds after he finished speaking, Anne half rose from the bed emitted a final agonised shriek and fell back amongst her pillows. Rooted to the spot, Elizabeth waited; fists pressed to her mouth as Doctor Butts bent over Anne, felt her forehead and put his ear to her chest. After a seemingly endless time, he raised his head and looked at Elizabeth. "The King should be told at once" he announced. "The Lady Anne will live".

Chapter 20

Back To Court

It was August before Anne felt sufficiently recovered to return to court. Having become used to the slow country life during her convalescence, the hectic pace of the court was not something to which she looked forward with any enthusiasm.

The King wrote to her almost constantly; reminding her of the great love he bore her, telling her that as the Almighty had spared her, surely He had given His divine approval to their proposed marriage.

Anne answered some of the King's letters, but not all of them. She reasoned that her enforced absence would likely increase his desire, so she determined not to hurry back to her King's arms.

When at last the King had word from Doctor Butts that she was fully recovered, he wrote eagerly to Hever asking when he might expect her. Anne replied airily that she had a mind to stay where she was indefinitely, for she was weary of the insults constantly hurled at her by the Queen's faction.

Upon receiving this reply, the King alternatively wept and raged, then immediately set about acquiring a separate house for her which would enable her to live her own life away from the Queen's service whilst remaining close to court. He decided on Durham House; its gardens sloped away to the river which would enable her to reach most of the palaces within a short time. Delighted with his scheme, he lost no time in informing her.

She was overjoyed; his actions were tantamount to declaring to the world that he intended to make her his wife. Durham House had been the lodging of Queen Catherine prior to her marriage with Henry, whilst she still bore the title of Dowager Princess of Wales. The omens were good, Anne decided, and immediately set out for court.

Henry received her with boyish enthusiasm, much in the way that a faithful dog might greet a long lost master, Anne thought with a smile. The morning following her arrival, they went together by barge to Durham House, for he insisted on personally guiding her around it.

Anne had expected a sizeable but modest house and when she saw the splendour of Durham she was quite overwhelmed. "It is so grand!" she exclaimed to a delighted Henry. "It is a miniature palace!"
Fondly he informed her "You are right. It IS a miniature palace, and you shall reign over it until you are able to take your place beside me as my

Queen".

Suddenly a thought came to her. "Surely this house belongs to the Cardinal?"

"Indeed" the King confirmed. "But when I informed him that I needed a suitable house for you, he was pleased to offer this". Henry diplomatically left out that fact that he himself had informed the Cardinal that he required the use of the house, leaving Wolsey no option but to agree.

Anne absorbed his statement with amazement. She fully believed that the Cardinal had fallen so low and was so in fear of her that he had offered one of his own houses in order to please her. This was power indeed!

That evening, at a banquet arranged specifically to celebrate her return; Anne turned to Henry and said sadly "I see the sweating sickness took its toll upon the court".

The King paused in the act of stuffing a capon leg into his mouth and replied thickly "Every gentleman of the privy chamber caught it; it killed three of them".

Anne sighed. "Poor Zouche. Whenever I write a note to you I always expect to see him bring the reply. He was so trustworthy".

Henry nodded, chewing thoughtfully. Then carefully scrutinising the leg bone to ascertain he had taken every last shred of meat, he said "You remember Sir William Compton? He died. So did your sister's husband, Carey".

"I never liked him" Anne admitted, "but I know he truly loved and cared for her and she mourns him sincerely".

Henry's eyes gleamed at the thought of his buxom ex-mistress. "We shall soon find her another husband. Once we are married sweetheart, the suitors will be queuing up for the hand of the Queen's sister. Your father must support her in the meantime". Then he remembered his son and wiping his mouth with the back of his hand, leaned towards her and asked in a low voice "How does the boy?"

"Bonny and growing fast" replied the proud aunt. "Whenever I see him I am reminded of how Your Grace must have looked at a similar age".

Henry puffed out his chest with pride, boasting "I have two sons now!"

"Both illegitimate" Anne reminded him quietly.

The contented smile left his face and he glared at her. "You never lose an opportunity to remind me that you will not give in before marriage, do you? I am well aware of that so kindly do not persist in raising the issue!"

Not a good start, Anne thought to herself, angering him so soon after their reunion. Quickly she said "I did not mean to imply that. I merely wished to remind Your Grace that as you have sired such healthy sons outside marriage and without God's blessing, surely the royal nurseries will be bursting with princes in the years to come!"

He liked that, as she knew he would. He grasped her chin, planted a great greasy kiss on her lips then loudly called for more capon.

Meanwhile, Henry's London subjects were not entirely ignorant of the great events taking place. Although there had been no official announcement, rumour was rife that the King intended putting away Queen Catherine and taking another wife. Anne's enemies lost no time in spreading her name around as the likely supplanter.

Catherine was informed of the peoples' support and took to appearing amongst them whenever she could, graciously acknowledging their cheers. Whenever Anne appeared, the mood would grow ugly; there would be jeers and shouts of whore, night crow or concubine. Anne tried not to let such things upset her, but she longed to be loved and accepted by the people. She consoled herself by entertaining lavishly in her new house, and soon Durham became to centre of the fashionable "Boleyn set".

At last good news filtered through to England; the Pope's legate had arrived in France and was shortly to set sail for Dover. His name was Cardinal Campeggio; he was very old, very gouty, and had taken an interminable time to travel from Rome to Calais.

Finally news reached Durham House that the Cardinal was safely in England. The date was September 29th and Henry gleefully told his sweetheart that they would be married before Christmas. The following day they were happily making plans for the great event when Cardinal Wolsey was admitted to their presence. Henry rose to his feet and boomed "Ah, Wolsey. And where is

Campeggio?"

Wolsey took a great swallow, and then in a small voice said "Dover".

"Still?" interjected Anne incredulously.

Wolsey executed a small bow in her direction. "I regret" he continued, "that the Cardinal has had to take to his bed due to an attack from a particularly painful form of gout".

Henry and Anne looked at each other, speechless. Then the King, scratching his beard thoughtfully, suggested "You must travel to Dover, Thomas, and speak with him. He can no doubt instruct you in the procedures he intends to adopt, then we can have everything in readiness here for his arrival".

Wolsey backed out of the presence chamber muttering "As Your Grace pleases; I will travel at once".

After talks with Campeggio, Wolsey wrote from Dover that the Cardinal seemed more interested in attempting to reconcile Henry and Catherine, rather than presiding over any divorce proceedings. As Wolsey had feared, the news did nothing to improve the King's temper. "The Pope has tricked us!" he fumed to Anne. "He sends us some gouty old idiot to try and reconcile Catherine and me, not to instigate divorce proceedings!"

Anne was perhaps even more aggrieved than the King. She had risked everything to make this marriage. Her good name was gone, for even though she was not the King's mistress, most believed her so. Her chances of making any other marriage were all but gone and worst of all, she was wasting her best childbearing years.

Towards the end of October, Campeggio reached London and met with the King. In his slow careful English, the legate said "Cardinal Wolsey informs me that Your Grace does not wish for reconciliation with the Queen?"
Piously Henry replied "She was my brother's wife. To atone for our sin, she and I must separate if we are not to incur God's eternal wrath".
"Surely" Campeggio interrupted, "your union is only suspect assuming the Queen's first marriage was consummated. I understand that Prince Arthur was weak and sickly even on his wedding night".
"Not too sickly to call for refreshment the following morning, telling all in earshot that he had been in Spain all night and that marriage was thirsty work!" replied Henry darkly.

Campeggio paused, regarding Henry shrewdly. "If you cannot be reconciled then there is another way to avoid divorce …" he began, his eyes fixed on Henry's face.
Henry's eyes narrowed with suspicion. "Continue!" he barked.
Campeggio eased his pain racked body into a more comfortable position and continued. "If the Queen could be persuaded to publicly renounce her title and retire to a religious institution, the marriage would be automatically dissolved".
The King beamed. "Excellent. Excellent. Catherine is

at Bridewell; Wolsey will accompany you".

It turned out to be a fruitless journey. Catherine received the two Cardinals graciously and listened to their suggestions and advice. "I am afraid it would be quite impossible" she told them. "Prince Arthur was too weak to consummate our marriage and I swear I went virgin to his brother. I am a true wedded wife and my daughter Mary is the King's sole legitimate heir". She paused, regarded them contemptuously, then snapped "Good day gentlemen" before sweeping regally from the chamber.

Campeggio looked at his fellow Cardinal and shrugged his shoulders in an expressive Latin gesture.
"The King will not be pleased" murmured Wolsey as they returned to their barge. "The King will not be at all pleased!"

Indeed he was not, but for once he was powerless; Campeggio had to make the next move. The legate had written to the Pope informing him that their plans for reconciliation had fallen flat and that the Queen had refused to enter a convent. With the King rampaging like a caged lion, Campeggio reasoned that the safest course of action was to take to his bed and blame the gout whilst he awaited the Pope's reply. However, whilst Campeggio was doing his level best to avoid coming out into the open and declaring his intentions, the King had another worry on his mind.

He was greatly concerned for Anne's safety. Twice whilst supping with friends in the city she had only narrowly escaped from being overwhelmed by mobs of enraged women. These women reasoned that if the King set a precedent for discarding a wife because she no longer pleased her husband, then every married woman could be under threat. The people were also aware that Durham House was her official residence, and the estate was constantly under siege. The King realised with horror that there were more guards at Durham protecting her than there were actually guarding his own person. Something had to be done. The only solution was for Anne to give up her home and return to the comparative safety of the court.

Anne had been half hoping that he would suggest such a solution for several weeks, loath though she was to give up that small amount of independence. The mobbing had badly frightened her and she did not care for the isolation of Durham, half expecting to have to flee for her life in the middle of the night should the mob gain entry to the house.

She was re-installed at court in a magnificent suite of rooms adjoining the King's own apartments, in time for the Christmas celebrations. The court had by now realised that the King truly intended to make her his wife and flocked to her standard, leaving Catherine to spend Christmas virtually alone. Even so, since the King still had not officially separated from her, they still continued to appear together at state functions.

With divorce proceedings to engineer and state

business to attend to, Henry found himself becoming estranged from the woman he had sworn to marry. Although he was sure that he loved her more than ever, she had been cooler towards him of late, he decided. So one April morning he adjourned his privy council meeting before it was barely begun and made his way to her apartments. She was quite overjoyed to see him so unexpectedly. "Henry!" she cried, dropping to the floor the book she was reading and running towards his outstretched arms. "I had not thought to see you until this evening!"

He embraced her hungrily, saying "I felt the need for your companionship. My privy councillors are all very worthy gentlemen, but sadly I only associate their presence with state matters".

"No doubt you only associate me with tedious divorce proceedings" she replied sadly.

"I associate you with love and laughter" he whispered passionately, "but we seem to have had so little time together of late, I have lost track of how you spend your days. Come ..."

He drew her back to her window seat and they sat close together, holding hands like newlyweds. His eye fell upon her discarded book. "What are you reading?" he asked, bending to retrieve it from the floor. "More French romances?" Carefully keeping his thumb between the pages so she should not lose her place, he closed the slim volume and peered at the spine, reading aloud "The Teachings of Martin Luther". He looked at her in astonishment. "You know that I published a book denouncing this man and his wickedness several years ago?"

"Indeed Your Grace" Anne replied carefully, lapsing

into formal address lest he become angered by her choice of reading matter. "I was merely interested to read the man's views and I find he makes several valid points. He reveals a side to religion I had not known existed".

Henry, far from displeased to discover in her what could be construed as heretical tendencies, found himself listening closely as she quoted to him various pertinent passages from the book.
"You truly believe it could become a rival to Catholicism?" he asked her.
"Truly" she replied firmly, inspired by her small knowledge of Luther's principles. "You should read this book Henry; it is good for a monarch to keep up with new ideas. It may be some years since this volume was published but Luther's theories have come to be known as the New Learnings".
"You are right" he told her. "I should keep abreast of the times. If you will pass me your book when you are finished, I shall be glad to read it".

She smiled at him gratefully. She possessed other tracts frowned on by the church which Henry could now be open to reading and discussing with her. If such came to pass, should any of her enemies get hold of her forbidden books and seek to discredit her with the King, she could laugh in their faces and say, 'if you believe I am a heretic because I possess such books then you should know that your King too has heretical tendencies, for he has also read them. She was hugging the thought to herself when suddenly Henry spoke. "I have a gift for you, my Anne".

Immediately her thoughts shifted. "A gift? Would that be an early birthday or a late New Year's?"
They both laughed.
"A gift because I love you so very much" he told her softly. Putting his hand inside his doublet he drew out a small velvet drawstring purse which he handed to her.

She had a child's delight in gifts; the pleasure of receiving much enhanced by the anticipation of what lay within, so she felt the contents carefully through the material, trying to guess what it could be. "An item of jewellery!" she cried triumphantly. "I believe I can feel … pearls?"
"Possibly" he answered in a mysterious tone. "I designed it especially for you, Anne. Open the pouch".

Eagerly she did his bidding, emptying the contents into her lap. "It is pearls!" she cried delightedly, holding a necklace up to the light. It was composed of a double string of pearls; a short string to lie close to the throat and a longer string to reach the bodice. Suspended from the short string was a golden letter "B", from the bottom of which hung three large drop pearls.
"It's beautiful!" she whispered, looking up at him lovingly and then hurling herself into his arms. "And so original! I have never seen the like!"

She insisted he clasp it around her neck, and once there, she patted the "B" delightedly.
"What do you take the "B" to stand for?" Henry asked her playfully.

Surprised by the question, she answered "Why, Boleyn, of course"

"Wrong"

"Wrong? I was so sure! But what else could it stand for?" She thought hard for several moments, creasing her brow with intense concentration. Then she laughed. "Tell me Henry! I cannot guess. Tell me now or I shall tickle you mercilessly!" She lifted her hand to the back of his neck and ran her fingers lightly over his skin.

He squirmed under her touch, crying out in mock terror "Mercy, gentle lady, mercy! I will tell all!"

"Speak then" she said threateningly, her fingers poised inches above his highly ticklish neck.

"Let the world think it stands merely for Boleyn" he whispered. But to you and me, it means Betrothed!"

Chapter 21

Slow Progress

Loving Anne as he did, the King continued to shower her family with honours. Her father was created Earl of Wiltshire, whilst George took over his father's discarded Viscouncy.

Soon after, the King attended the wedding of the new Viscount Rochford and Jane Parker, daughter of Lord Morley.

There had been a lull in the divorce proceedings for some months, but at last, on 31st May 1529, Campeggio assembled a court within the priory of Blackfriars to try the King's case.

The King told Anne that he and Catherine would be summoned to appear before the court sometime in June. "I would recommend that you retire from the public eye whilst the court is in session" he advised her.
"You would be rid of me?" she questioned indignantly.

At once Henry was soothing "No, no of course not sweetheart; I merely assumed you would wish to be well out of the way. It would not do for Campeggio to catch sight of you, for he would then think that the purpose of the divorce was the King's lust rather than the King's conscience.

She raised a quizzical eyebrow. "Which of course would be quite incorrect" she replied slyly.

"Quite!" agreed the King in a solemn tone.

"All the same, I would prefer to stay here" she told him. "It takes so long for news to filter through to Hever. The waiting would drive me mad".

"As you wish, sweetheart. I will arrange for a room to be set aside adjoining the courtroom so that you will be able to hear the proceedings".

So, on all the days that the court was in session, Anne sat in the small chamber the King had reserved for her. Often, he joined her, until that momentous day in the middle of June when Henry himself was called before the court to answer a charge of living in sin with his brother's wife. Catherine too was summoned to appear and King and Queen sat at opposite ends of the great chamber, facing each other. However, before Campeggio could proceed, Catherine rose from her chair and walked slowly towards her husband. Henry watched her slow, dignified progress, his chin cupped in his right hand, his fingers drumming against his cheek. However, as she halted before him, curtseyed and then fell to her knees, he straightened in his chair, hands tensely gripping its arms. The expression on his face was close to terror; what was she going to say?

Meanwhile, Anne, seated in her hiding place, became aware of the tense atmosphere in the adjoining chamber; heard the whispers and uneasy shuffling of feet. She rose from her chair and opened a small peephole in the wall which enabled her to see the scene below.

Catherine, her eyes fixed imploringly on the King's face, began to speak. "Sir, I desire you do me right and justice. Bestow your pity on me for I am a poor woman, a stranger born out of your dominions". Gesturing with her hand towards Wolsey and Campeggio she continued. "Here are no impartial judges!"

She paused and shuffled closer to Henry, her voice soft. "Sir, how have I offended you? What behaviour of mine has caused you so much displeasure that you should seek to cast me off? As Heaven is my witness I have been your true and humble wife, ever conforming to your will and desires. All friends of yours have become mine also; even those I knew to be my enemies". Stiffly she rose to her feet and stretched out her arms towards her husband. "Remember Sir that I have been your obedient wife these twenty years and we have had many children, although it has pleased God to call them out of this world".

Henry made no acknowledgement that he was hearing her; only the angry flickering of his eyes betrayed the fact that he still breathed. Dejectedly she dropped her arms to her sides, and then summoned her courage to speak publicly of the very fact upon which Henry's case was based. "And at the first, as

God is my judge, I was a true maid without touch of man. Whether it be true or no, I put to your conscience".

Eagerly she scanned his face, but his only response was to look away. Addressing the Cardinals she said loudly "This is no court of justice for me. I do not recognise its authority!" She then curtseyed once more to the King and walked slowly towards the great double doors.

Henry started, and then growled at Wolsey "Have her called back!"
Steadfastly Catherine continued her progress, ignoring incessant cries of 'Catherine, Queen of England, come into the court' until finally she passed from sight.

All eyes turned to the King. "Proceed without her" he said testily, looking towards the uncovered peephole high in the wall, behind which he knew Anne's face regarded his.

And so the tedious case dragged on towards the day fixed for Campeggio to give his verdict and the court to adjourn. As the great moment approached, the court was packed; the public gallery creaking ominously.

Awkwardly Campeggio got to his feet. "I have listened carefully to the proceedings over the past weeks" he said, avoiding Henry's eyes. "And due to the great severity of this case, I find myself unable to pass judgement until I have consulted with His

Holiness. I therefore adjourn this court for the summer recess; we shall reassemble on October 1st". His face resumed its characteristic obstinate expression as he dropped back into his seat and a hubbub of excited, incredulous voices filled the courtroom.

With a roar of displeasure, Henry leapt to his feet and stamped out of the chamber, fixing the Cardinals with a malevolent glare as he passed them. In her upstairs chamber, Anne, who had truly believed that Campeggio would find in the King's favour, collapsed on to the rush strewn floor in hysterics. Henry strode in, scooped her up without a word and together they returned to the palace at Bridewell.

Anne had completely lost consciousness due to the tension of the proceedings followed by the shock of realising it was all for nothing and when she eventually opened her eyes she was lying on her bed, still fully clothed. Raising her head she saw Henry sitting by the fireplace, staring moodily into a wine goblet. "Henry?" she said softly. He did not hear. Louder, "Henry!" He started, got to his feet and approached her bed; only then did she see the defeated expression in his eyes.

He offered her wine from his own goblet. To please him, she took a few sips, her head supported by his arm. "You are recovered?" he enquired.
"Yes, thank you" she murmured. "I am sorry, I do not usually swoon, but it was such a shock".

Henry drained the goblet dry, regarded it with

contempt then threw it across the room. "Foreigners!" he spat angrily.

Raising herself to a sitting position, Anne said casually "I blame Wolsey. Surely he could have influenced Campeggio to find in your favour, had he made the effort!"

"Your assumption may be correct" Henry said slowly, and with measured consideration. He felt extremely embarrassed by the outcome of the trial; he needed a scapegoat and Wolsey would serve as well as any. Evenly he paced around the room, deep in thought. Anne watched him in silence.

Eventually he spoke "Wolsey's failure to secure the required verdict is tantamount to treason. He shall be banished from court. I shall send him to one of his houses in the north; there is no place here for traitors to our cause!"

Now Henry's mind was made up, he lost no time. Seating himself at Anne's writing table he penned a brief note, then called for a page to deliver it to Cardinal Wolsey. Turning around in the chair to face her, Henry said "The deed is done; he will be gone by morning. Now sweetheart, we must prepare to leave on our summer progress!"

"I have been looking forward to it" she told him, smiling. "What of Catherine?"

He heaved a deep sigh, rose from the chair and crossed the chamber to sit on the edge of her bed. Patting her hand awkwardly he said "She must accompany us, I fear. She is still the Queen and the people will expect to see her. In order to keep my subjects from revolt, we must keep up appearances". Hesitantly he looked at her, but to his relief she was smiling. "I understand Henry, but you must promise me that you will not forget your loving Lady Rochford for I should be desolate without your very frequent company".

"You shall be beside me whenever possible" he told her. "Indeed during the hunting we shall always be able to ride together. Catherine has not hunted these past four years".

In early August, they set out. The Queen rode in her litter behind the King whilst Anne was relegated to the ranks of those ladies of similar status to herself.

After several weeks of travelling from place to place, they were lodged in the King's manor at Grafton in Northamptonshire when it came to Anne's ears that Cardinal Wolsey had arrived. However by the time the news was brought to her, there was nothing she could do to prevent him making his way towards the King's apartments. Worse, because the weather was so bad, Henry was forced to spend a great deal of time with Catherine since there was an endless procession of local dignitaries to meet the royal pair.

Inwardly fuming, Anne made her way to the King's outer presence chamber and mingled amongst those hoping for an interview with their sovereign. She perceived Wolsey standing alone beside a window, his eyes fixed upon the archway where Henry would shortly appear should he feel inclined to grant the interview Wolsey so fervently desired.

Anne shrank back into the shadows as the King appeared, his eyes raking the assembly. Then he saw Wolsey. From her place in the crowd Anne heard him say "Ah, Thomas. I was brought word of your arrival. Come, we shall talk privately for I have much to discuss with you". Henry then flung his arm around the flustered Wolsey's shoulders, drew him into the presence chamber and kicked the door shut behind them.

Anne was furious. She hurried back to her chambers and gave her maid orders that should the King ask for her; he was to be told that she was ill and not to be disturbed. She felt totally betrayed, for although the King had sent the Cardinal away at her instigation, he seemed only too glad to welcome him back when he thought she was not there to see.

She managed to avoid the King for the rest of their sojourn at Grafton, from whence they were to return to London. Only when the royal entourage was assembled, awaiting the signal to begin the journey southwards, did the King's searching eyes finally locate his sweetheart.

Her head held high, she stared stonily back. His face betraying his puzzlement, he nodded briefly to her before taking his place at the head of the procession.

As soon as they arrived at the place where they would spend the first night on the journey homewards, Henry sought her out. She could do nothing but receive him, her pretensions of illness played out. Stiffly she held back as he attempted to embrace her. Puzzled, he asked "What is wrong my love? You are not still unwell?"

"Yes" she snapped. "Extremely unwell with a sickness of the heart since with my own eyes I witnessed you receiving that buffoon Wolsey like a long lost friend!"

Defensively he replied "I did not see you".

"I made sure that you did not!" she flashed.

Henry slipped his arms around her unyielding frame. "But sweetheart" he protested. "He had only come to ask my permission for Campeggio to return to Rome. I would have had to receive him sooner or later to give my consent"

"But there was no need for you to greet him so lovingly, was there?" she stormed. "A nod in his direction would have served as answer to his question!"

She refused to listen to any of his explanations and in an attempt to mollify her, he promised that she would ride by his side when they entered London.

"What of the Queen?" she asked in astonishment.

"The Queen knows better than to question my actions" he growled, his mood by now as sour as Anne's.

So as the procession neared the city walls, Anne spurred her horse to the head of the procession and reined in beside the king. He was desperately eager to regain her goodwill and as they rode past one of Wolsey's houses, York Place, and Anne commented on its beauty and situation, he saw his chance.

"If you want it, then you shall have it sweetheart" he told her boastfully.

Anne looked at him with raised eyebrows "You would steal it from Wolsey no doubt on condition that I restore you to my affections?"

The King beamed. "You are very perceptive, Lady Rochford. So, is it a bargain?" He stretched out his hand towards her.

Anne turned in her saddle to look behind them at the great house, one of the finest in London. Straight faced, she resumed her forward facing seat and put her hand into the King's outstretched paw. "A bargain!" she affirmed, then laughed exultantly.

From then on, York Place became the Lady Anne Rochford's official London residence. Although Durham House still remained in her possession, she avoided going there, still fearing its isolation. Instead, she passed it to her family for their use.

Wolsey was again exiled, this time to Esher in Surrey. There he lived quietly, always in fear for his life for he had seen the malicious triumph on the face of the Lady Anne as she had watched him leave the house she coveted. She was about to extract her revenge for all the wrongs, real and imagined, that he had inflicted upon her during her brief life; he could sense that.

He knew himself to be a hunted man and it was not long before he received word that an indictment was bring prepared against him. He was to be accused under "praemunire"; his offence being that in introducing Campeggio into England, he had inhibited the power of the King. His office, the Chancellorship of England, was stripped from him and the Great Seal removed from his keeping.

Soon after Wolsey's disgrace was made public, his ambitious under secretary Thomas Cromwell left his service and travelled to London, seeking a new position. Cromwell was a shrewd and clever man; Wolsey had served as an excellent tutor but his star was on the wane and Thomas knew that if he wanted to get on in the world, the only place for him was at court, near Anne Boleyn.

He quickly gained an audience with her and told her that he had a suggestion to make to the King which could lead to the matter of the divorce being speedily concluded. Without delay she ushered him into Henry's presence where he humbly recommended that Henry lead England away from the Pope's influence and install himself as head of the English church.

Within days of Cromwell's arrival at court, the Boleyn family chaplain also gained an audience with the King. He was Thomas Cranmer, a religious scholar for whose knowledge the King had a healthy respect. "Your Grace" Cranmer began. "I have prayed incessantly to our Heavenly Father these past few days and am now convinced that Your Grace is correct in fearing that your marriage to the Queen is invalid". Cranmer paused and shot a sly glance at the King; Henry looked smug and extremely pleased. Cranmer continued "In my humble view, Your Grace should ask the opinions of the learned men of this country for I am sure that they would support Your Grace's cause".

Henry leaned forward. "You mean, consult the universities?"

"Exactly, Sire".

With the King's blessing, Cranmer was speedily dispatched to canvass the universities of England. In due course he was able to inform the King that they had all voted in favour of a divorce and remarriage. Henry was delighted and suggested they take the cause further afield, to the foreign seats of learning. Cranmer felt it would be an excellent idea and immediately undertook the task.

However, the continental canvassing was expected to take some time, leaving the King and Anne kicking their heels. The great ponderous machine that was the divorce was slowly gaining impetus, but it seemed that nothing would hurry it. Then Anne remembered her old enemy Wolsey, living quietly in retirement; the King having suspended the proposed indictment. The time had come to strike the final, fatal blow

Chapter 22

Downfalls

It was late September in the year 1530; the court had recently moved to Windsor in order to escape the stuffiness of a London which had endured yet another overpoweringly hot summer.

The King had gone hunting, an all-male affair, which left Anne to her own devices that day. She and Margaret Wyatt were spending their time ambling slowly through the great park, the vast green expanse reminding them nostalgically of their respective childhood homes, Hever and Allington.

As they wandered along, Margaret reflected to herself upon how much Anne had changed since those carefree days. The soft, loving child had turned into a hard, brittle woman whose frequent laughter held a fragile, fractured gaiety. Of late, she had made more enemies than friends and she still seemed convinced that her ill-wishers were led by the exiled Cardinal Wolsey.

Glancing sideway at her friend, Margaret asked "Nan, why do you still hate Wolsey so much?"

Immediately she replied flippantly "Because he wrecked my life"

"How so?"

"Ever since Harry Percy and I fell in love. Even then Wolsey was aware that the King had noticed me, which was why I was banished to the country for those three long years. Then, years later , when the King began to advance my father, Wolsey interfered whenever he could; always making it his business to suggest plenty of alternative candidates for any post my father was likely to get. More recently, in the matter of the divorce; when it was in his hands he made no attempt to bring things to a head. I tell you he has always hated me Meg, likely because although comparatively low-born like himself, I threaten to rise far higher than he". Exhausted by her tirade, Anne leaned weakly against the convenient trunk of an ancient oak.

"He is an old man now" stated Margaret, picking absently at the knotted bark. "Can you not let him die in peace?"

"I wish he would die" Anne replied vehemently. "Sometimes I believe that all my troubles would die with him. He is too quiet Meg. He is working against me still; I would stake my life on it!"

Margaret sensed that Anne was spoiling for a fight; needing somebody upon whom to vent her frustrations. She was about to steer the conversation towards a less controversial subject when the distant sound of a hunting horn reached their ears.

"It must be the King!" cried Anne, pushing herself

away from the tree and peering into the distance, one hand shading her eyes. "Come Meg, we must return quickly to the path. Maybe we could get a ride back to the castle!" Her ill humour quickly forgotten, Anne lifted her skirts free of the turf and ran lightly across the uneven grass towards the winding woodland path.

Margaret half turned, also shaded her eyes from the glare, and looked back at the distant castle. "Yes, Anne, I think a ride might be a good idea" she called, running to join her. "We seem to have walked a good deal further than we intended. I hope the King spots us!"

Anne laughed, looking down at her bright yellow gown and then at Margaret in her crimson. "He could hardly miss us!" she cried. "For surely we shine like beacons amongst all this green!"

Standing quietly, listening hard, they gazed at the horizon. Within minutes a party of horsemen came galloping into view, the unmistakable figure of Henry Tudor at their head. Whatever else the King lacked, he was blessed with excellent eyesight and was one of the first to recognise one of the two ladies ahead as Anne. His horse increased speed and he pulled up alongside Anne and Margaret with a flourish. "What have we here!" he exclaimed jovially.

As his gentlemen crowded round, Thomas Wyatt pushed his horse through the throng to the side of his King and said "Surely this must be the best sport we have seen all day?"

"You could be right Wyatt" beamed the King. "You could well be right!"

Noticing the pack horses carried several deer carcasses, Anne said demurely "I trust Your Grace is not intending to destroy us for trophies?"
"Indeed not!" he laughed. "Such delightful stock as yourselves would be better employed in breeding!" Both ladies laughed politely, despite his crudeness. "However" he continued "I cannot let such prizes slip from my grasp". He patted the pommel of his saddle "There is room for you here, my Anne".
"I thank Your Grace for such a kind offer" she answered. "But what of my companion?"
The King gestured towards his gentlemen. "I am sure there will be no shortage of volunteers to convey Mistress Margaret back to Windsor".
No sooner had he finished speaking, Anne's brother George piped up "I claim the honour!"

Margaret was highly delighted at this. She had harboured a childish adoration for handsome George Boleyn for many years and even now, despite the fact that he was married and she betrothed to Sir Anthony Lee, she worshipped him.

The two ladies were helped into the arms of their respective knights, and then the party galloped the remaining distance to the castle, Anne and Margaret squealing with mock terror at the precariousness of their perches.

Regrettably it was not long before Anne managed to destroy the King's good humour, for as soon as they were alone, she began talking of the Cardinal. "I am sure he is conspiring against us Henry; he is suspiciously quiet".

"Leave him be, Anne" the King pleaded. "He has given me many years of devoted service".

"Not so over the divorce!" she flashed back. "Have you so soon forgotten of the treason he committed in allowing Campeggio to humiliate you?"

Henry regarded her shrewdly, then selected an apple from a silver platter and bit noisily into it. "Wolsey is allowed no further dealings in the divorce case" he told her, his tongue in hot pursuit of the apple juice which threatened to run into his beard.

"But what if he is in contact with the Pope?" she persisted. "It could be Wolsey's hand which yet prevents the Pope from reconsidering. We are not to know what he is up to at Cawood, so far from London. He should be arrested, Henry".

"Have you proof of what you say?"

"I have no way of knowing for sure!" she burst out. "But it stands to reason that he is working against us. He hates me, you know he does. He also believes that your marriage to Catherine is valid. I tell you it is almost certain that he has advised the Pope to hold out, hoping that you become so exasperated by the delay that you cast me from you!" So violent were her protestations that she broke into hysterical sobbing, truly believing that her assumptions were correct.

Henry made haste to comfort her, unmanned as always by the sight of a woman's tears. Knowing that she was unable to cry prettily, as some ladies could,

Anne kept her face hidden as she blurted out "If this case drags on much longer I shall never be able to have your son. Wolsey's incompetence has already wasted my best childbearing years!"

With a start, Henry realised that she spoke the truth. Already she was twenty three; late by Tudor standards to begin childbearing. Holding her close he murmured softly. "You shall have your way. In trying to prevent our marriage for so long he has committed treason many times over. I will have him arrested and brought to London for questioning".

Drying her tears, she looked up into his face. "I would ask you one favour Sire".
Prepared as always to grant her anything she desired in order to cheer her, he tenderly asked "What is it?"
"Send Harry Percy to arrest him".
She felt his body stiffen slightly. It would not do for him to think she still loved the auburn haired northerner. Hastily she added "I only ask that Percy do the deed because he lives near to the Cardinal and the sooner he is in custody, the better for our cause".
It was a feeble excuse, but one that Henry was ready to accept. "It shall be as you wish, sweetheart" he told her. "A messenger shall be sent to Northumberland with the warrant as soon as I get time to put quill to parchment".

Nestled in the protective arms of her King, Anne was content. Her long lost lover would share with her the ultimate triumph of bringing down the man who had destroyed their tender young love.

However, as it turned out, Anne was to be cheated of witnessing her greatest enemy's final downfall. At the beginning of December word reached the King that Wolsey had been unable to travel very far due to illness. Eventually the prisoner had reached Leicester Abbey where he had died from dysentery on November 29th.

Henry received the news with little emotion, merely saying that perhaps it was better for Wolsey to die of natural causes and thus spare the country the expense of the trial and execution. He displayed no grief for the man he had so often called his 'dear Thomas' and ordered no court mourning.

Anne was naturally relieved that her greatest enemy was no more and her improved spirits greatly cheered the King. Christmas that year was the gayest that Greenwich had seen for some years.

The New Year, which began with such hope and optimism, was blighted by the news that Clement, still prevaricating in Rome, had issued a Brief forbidding the King of England to remarry until a decision had been reached, otherwise any resulting child would be illegitimate. The Pope also forbade anyone in England to make any decision on the affair or risk excommunication.

Henry had suspected that Clement would take such steps, so received the news with little surprise. With his agents in Rome, and Cromwell and Cranmer working industriously, there was nothing to do but wait until the deadlock was broken.

Off his own back, Henry embarked on a course of action which he hoped would bring home strongly to Clement that he was truly determined to divorce Catherine. Instead of appearing with the Queen in public as he had done throughout his marriage, he began leaving her behind, refusing even to acknowledge her existence.

If a function demanded the presence of a lady by his side, he would take Anne, sumptuously dressed in the manner of the Queen he hoped she soon would be.

When it was again time to leave London for the summer progress, Catherine was left behind; Anne riding in her place beside the King. The people would gather by the roadside to watch them pass, staring silently at Anne. The women would mutter that they could not understand what the King saw in her. The men too wondered at the King's actions until Anne turned her great black eyes to them, then in a flash they would experience her strange magnetism, they too would share the King's passionate desire to know more of her secrets.

Hunting-wise, the progress that year was a dismal failure. The wet weather which had plagued London since the beginning of the year followed them to Woodstock where the court was forced to congregate in the palace for much of the time. To Anne's horror, a combination of boredom and frustration saw Henry renew his assaults on her honour with relentless vigour.

Day after day he pleaded with her to become his mistress in fact, and when pleading had no effect on her, he launched physical onslaughts. Such insistence was hard to resist and many a time Anne was at the point of submission when a little voice inside her would say, 'surrender now and he will never marry you' and thus she would somehow find the strength of mind and body to hold him off.

Still the rain persisted, and then a message came from Windsor to say that the weather there was fine and the hunting good. Henry lost no time in travelling southwards, but not before he had made yet another significant move. Catherine was in residence at Windsor and he sent a message to her demanding that she leave the castle before the court arrived. She was told to go to The More, another house which had formerly belonged to Cardinal Wolsey. Catherine realised with a sinking heart that she had to obey, understanding that this was Henry's public declaration of their official separation. Her banishment from Windsor was only the start of the pattern; whenever she happened to be staying at a palace the King wished to visit, she would be moved away before his arrival.

By August Anne had taken over the Queen's apartments in every royal residence, having alterations made to her own specifications. Meanwhile the King wrote a curt note to Catherine instructing her to choose a house in which to live out her retirement.
So for the first time in many a year, only one lady presided over the Christmas celebrations at

Greenwich. Anne was now wearing the Queen's jewels and furs and living in her rooms; she now longed for the moment when she would wear the Queen's crown.

Chapter 23

Marquess of Pembroke

The wrangling over the divorce continued for the first eight months of 1532 with neither side making any real progress. The long wait was beginning to seriously affect the relationship between the King and Anne, with her taking every opportunity to remind him just how much she was risking for his sake. However on one occasion she went so far as to exhaust even Henry's endless patience with her, and he burst out that for her sake he was turning his country upside down and risking civil war.

She was quiet at that and clung to him, sweetly apologetic. "I am sorry Henry, but we have waited so long and it seems that we are no nearer to a happy conclusion".
"It is hard on you I know my sweet" he soothed. "But this wretched business cannot go on for much longer. I have been thinking; whilst England is under Popish domination I shall never be absolute ruler here. If a decision is not reached soon, I shall break away from Rome and put myself at the head of the

English church, like that fellow Cromwell suggested".

Anne was overjoyed. "You would really do such a thing for me?" she asked in wonder. Her eyes filled with tears for she could comprehend the enormity of such a step.

Slavishly gazing at her he replied "I would tear the world apart for you".

She could not let it rest there. "When would you do this thing?"

He sighed heavily. "It is a drastic step and one I shall only take if there is no other way for us. But whatever happens, you and I will be married within a few months, I promise".

She tried to hide her disappointment; she had hoped for an immediate break with Rome so that they could be married within days rather than months. "So I must still be dependent on you to support me and pay my debts!" she cried bitterly. Henry looked at her in surprise; it seemed she would never rest until she was safely married. He told himself that her anxiety had to be due to the great love she bore him, dismissing the inner voice which reminded him that in all their years together she had never actually told him that she loved him. Had never said 'I love you'.

He shrugged his shoulders wearily. "If it is debts that you worry about my sweet, then you shall be invested with a title on your own right which will command a modest income".

"A title of my own?" she echoed in amazement, then she sobered, realising that so great a step would be sure to have certain strings attached. It was probably better not to voice her doubts, but the words bubbled to her lips.

"I take it the title would be in exchange for my agreement to become your mistress?"

There was a pause. "Yes" he told her, shame-faced at actually having to admit it.

She thought for a moment, and then raised her eyes to his. "I agree to your terms ..".

"Anne!" His face lit up and he attempted to embrace her hungrily.

Her eyes flashing fire, she held him off imperiously. "I did not finish my sentence Henry!"

His face fell. "No doubt there are certain conditions" he said sarcastically. "I might have known that you would only give in on your own terms".

Seeing his rising anger she placated him, saying "There are only two small points upon which I would like your agreement before we strike this bargain. The first one being that you will not carry me off to bed immediately. Remember Henry, I am a chaste young lady and I would prefer to choose the time and place of such a momentous event in my life" He made as if to speak, but she held up her hand, demanding silence. She continued "The second condition is linked to the first, really. If I should conceive your child, will you give me your word that you will take the necessary steps to procure the divorce without delay so that we may marry well before the birth?"

"I certainly agree whole-heartedly with your second point" he told her, gently squeezing her cheek between finger and thumb. "After all, there must be no doubt as to the child's legitimacy. But as to the first point; you could keep me waiting right up to the day of the wedding ceremony!"

She was disappointed that he had reasoned that one out so quickly; that was exactly how she had planned to play it. There was nothing else for it. "I give you my word that I will not do that" she told him with sincerity.

He had never before had cause to doubt her promises, so he was inclined to believe her. "In that case sweetheart" he said, kissing her gently "I shall at once have the letters patent drawn up to make you a peer in your own right. You shall be the very first woman in history to hold such an honour. The investiture shall be at Windsor next Sunday and on that day you will be created Marquess of Pembroke."

True to his promise, the ceremony took place in the great chamber at Windsor Castle, before mass, on the morning of September 1st.

Anne dressed carefully for the occasion in a new gown of crimson velvet edged with ermine. She wore no headdress; her long black hair flowed freely across her shoulders and down her back.

Attended by two countesses she walked regally down the passageways and into the great chamber, and then knelt before the King, head bowed. At a nod from Henry, the Bishop of Winchester recited aloud the words on the patent creating her a Marquess, whilst the King himself slipped the crimson ermine edged mantle of estate around her shoulders and placed the coronet upon her sleek black hair. The patent having been read to the assembled noble company, she was presented with the document together with a grant allowing her to collect revenue from several estates in England and Wales which would amount to an income of at least one thousand pounds per annum. Her title and lands would pass to her male heirs, so whatever happened; even if she bore the King an illegitimate son, both the child's future and hers were secured.

Now that she had her title and a generous income, Anne realised that the time was fast approaching when Henry would expect her to fulfil her side of the bargain. She knew she was incapable of just walking up to him and informing him that she would sleep with him that night, but how else could the event be contrived?

At last a solution presented itself. The King of France had agreed to support Henry over the matter of the divorce and had invited his English counterpart to travel to France so that they could hold talks.

Coquettishly, Anne intimated to Henry that she would very much like to accompany him, and from the look in her eyes, Henry knew that if he agreed, that which he had longed for over seven interminable years may well at last take place. He could not agree quickly enough, telling Anne to choose her trousseau for he was sure that the French excursion would turn out to be their long overdue honeymoon.

They sailed from Dover on October 9th and when

Anne finally sighted the coastline of the country she had once regarded as her true homeland, she found she had mixed feelings. On one hand she was overjoyed at the prospect of returning to France; on the other, fast approaching was the land in which she would finally have to give herself to her ardent King. It was not the actual bedding which worried her, but that he may realise that she was not as pure as he believed her to be. However, being Anne, she put the matter to the back of her mind until such time as she would have to recall it, and determined to enjoy her visit.

She had barely stepped on to French soil after so long away when she heard that she would have to stay in the English stronghold of Calais. Aggrieved, she asked why, and was told that no French lady of suitable rank would deign to receive the King of England's concubine.

Whilst Anne was horrified at the slight, anger mingled with relief. Henry would travel on to Boulogne to meet Francis, so although he would need to leave her behind, at least she would be able to keep her body to herself for a little longer. She spent her time in the castle devising an entertainment to hold for Francis when he returned to Calais with Henry.

Two days later the scene was set. In the great hall in the castle of Calais, the two Kings were seated side by side enjoying a grand banquet. They had barely finished when the doors were flung open to admit what seemed to be a troupe of masked dancing girls.

They were dressed in exotic, scanty costumes of gold and crimson which floated and fluttered seductively as they performed their complicated routine.

Francis and Henry exchanged amused glances; both were well aware of the identity of the black haired beauty who appeared to be the leader of the troupe.

The set dance completed, each lady chose a Frenchman as her partner. Anne naturally chose Francis and gallantly he pretended not to know who she was, entering into the spirit of things with gusto.

He talked to her as they danced. "How well you move" he told her. "One would almost expect you to be a French lady, so elegant are your steps".
"You are most kind Sire" she replied in careful French, purposely speaking in the manner of one not conversant with the language; concealing the fluency which was as natural to her as breathing.

When the dance ended, Francis led his partner to King Henry. As she curtseyed demurely before him, he leaned forward and snatched away her mask, revealing her identity to the assembly. Francis pretended to be greatly surprised. "My Lady Anne!" he exclaimed. "I had no idea that it was you with whom I danced!"
Not fooled for a moment, she replied lightly "Then you surprise me Sire for I have been in your arms often enough in the past!"
Henry, who had been watching their exchange with some amusement, visibly stiffened at her flippant remark. Laughing, she leaned towards him and

pulled his nose gently. "But such a long, long time ago" she whispered. Immediately he brightened and was happy for Francis to partner her whenever he wished for the remainder of the revels.

The entertainment lasted well into the early hours, and although Henry had been hopeful that she would capitulate that night, he was not surprised when he tried her chamber door to find it locked against him.

The following day, the entertainments continued where they had left off only hours earlier, with much feasting and dancing, Francis had also procured for Henry's amusement, two skilful wrestlers who mixed clever holds with comic acting.

Their act was heavily applauded, Henry promising to take them on when he next visited Calais; he was very proud of his skill and strength as a wrestler.

Later, seeing Francis and Henry deep in conversation about the divorce, Anne rose from her seat and executed a pretty yawn behind her fingers. Leaning between the two royal heads, she whispered "If Your Majesties will excuse me, I shall retire". They readily gave their leave and Anne tried not to see the speculative look on Henry's face as he courteously bade her good night.

Dismissing her maids, Anne went alone to her bedchamber; a great vaulted room overlooking the stormy sea, locking the door behind her. Her heart pounded as loudly as the waves as she slowly undressed herself and surveyed her naked body in the costly full length mirror. It did not look like a body that had known a man and she prayed that Henry would be a little too drunk – both on wine and high spirits – to realise that she was no virgin.

Crossing the room to one of her coffers, she unpacked the fabulous black nightgown and matching sheer loose robe which had cost her devoted King a fortune. She lay them both on the bed and looked at them consideringly, her head on one side. Then calculatingly she donned just the overgown, clasping it carefully at her waist before returning the nightgown to the coffer. Then, seated before her mirror, gazing at her reflection in the dim light, she began to rhythmically brush her hair.

Her toilette completed, nothing remained but for her to wait. She slowly unlocked the door, then opened and shut it a few times, making sure that it freed easily and would leave Henry in no doubt when he tried the handle.

Quite soon afterwards, she heard his step on the stair; he must have excused himself from Francis with almost indecent haste, she thought to herself, suppressing a nervous desire to laugh. Swiftly she climbed out of bed and doused the one remaining torch, then stood at the foot of the bed, her eyes on the door handle, heart skipping frantically from a mixture of horror and fascination. His footsteps came closer, stopping outside her door. There was a pause and she felt almost dizzy with anticipation as the handle turned slowly and the door gradually opened.

He stood in the doorway, his huge form almost blocking out the feeble light from the torches beyond in the passageway. For a moment he struggled to locate her in the dim chamber, but then he saw her and allowed himself a moment of pure satisfaction and anticipation. He was the King of England and here was his dearly loved Marquess of Pembroke about to award him the ultimate prize for his years of devotion and endeavours on her behalf. He did not speak, merely shut the door behind him and leaned against it, breathing quickly as he waited for his eyes to become accustomed to the gloom, his gaze fixed on the dim figure before him, her oval face bathed by the weak moonlight, her flimsily robed body backlit by the low fire in the hearth beyond her. Unable to bear the tension any longer, she stretched out her arms to him and in a split second he crossed the room and gathered her to him. "You are trembling" he observed, tenderly stroking her hair. "Do not be afraid Nan, I shall not hurt you". He placed his hands on her shoulders and kissed her gently before fumbling with the clasp at her waist. Once undone, he slipped his hands inside, surprised to feel naked flesh where he had expected to find a bed gown.

Wasting no time, he pushed the gown gently over her shoulders and let it fall to the ground. She blessed the gloom which spared her blushes as she stood before him, her great dark eyes locked on his, wearing nothing but the cloak of her beautiful hair.

Gently he scooped her into his arms and laid her

almost reverently on the luxurious fur which covered the bed. As he stood looking down at her, almost unable to comprehend that the great moment had actually arrived, she suddenly felt herself seized with an unexpected passion. Carefully raising herself into a sitting position she tossed back her long hair, then with a seductive smile on her lips, stretched smooth slender arms towards him. Unable to speak the words to express how he felt, he leaned mutely towards her, allowing those ghostly pale arms to lock around his neck and draw him down onto the bed.

In the ancient castle of Calais that night, locked together in an ecstasy born of long frustration, the two lovers lay. Henry was far too bewitched by her to realise that technically she was no maid, and Anne was allowed at last to release the pent up desires that had abounded deep inside her ever since she had been awakened to the delights of love by the boyish caresses of Harry Percy.

Chapter 24

Secret Ceremony

The lovers' return to England was delayed due to stormy weather in the channel, thus another three long ecstatic nights passed before they were able to sail for Dover. Anne found herself both stimulated and humbled by the King's great passion; she had not expected their union to move her so, believing that the brief experience with Percy followed by the long years of abstinence had rendered her immune to such overwhelming desires.

If Henry and Anne had hoped to keep their new intimacy secret, then they were to be disappointed. Once they were back at court it became blindingly obvious to onlookers that there had been a significant change in their relationship.

Whereas their closeness had always been noted, now it seemed that the King could not bear her out of his sight for a moment, and she for her part was quite content to spend every available hour with him.

News that the King's relationship with the Marquess of Pembroke had at last been consummated eventually reached the Pope in Rome. He declared himself shocked and immediately issued a Brief which threatened excommunication for them both unless they separated within the month.

The Brief reached England in early December; Henry ran his eyes over the document and then burned it, saying that if the Pope thought he was going to dictate the life and behaviour of the King of England, then he had another think coming. Despite all the ominous rumblings from Rome, Henry gave orders that the Christmas celebrations were to be as joyous and lavish as his Master of Revels could devise. It had been many years since he had known such a level of happiness and contentment and he wished it to be known that nothing would be allowed to spoil it.

Anne believed it had finally happened; she had a suspicion that she may be with child. For some weeks she had felt strangely unwell and lately had felt it necessary to visit the privy almost hourly. When she could bear the suspense no longer, she sent for her sister Mary.

As her sister entered, Anne dismissed her maids and invited Mary to sit beside her on her favourite window seat. With a questioning look upon her face, Mary did as she was told. Looking anxiously into her sister's face, Anne blurted out "What does it feel like to be pregnant?"

Mary's eyebrows shot up in surprise and her gaze immediately dropped to Anne's trim waistline. "You think you carry the King's child?"

"Maybe" Anne whispered. "But before I start calling in physicians I want to be sure in my own mind that I am not just suffering from a trifling indisposition".

"I see". With a thoughtful look on her face, Mary settled herself more comfortably into the cushioned seat. "It would perhaps be easier Nan if you told me of your symptoms; there are many, and not all women are affected in the same manner".

Concentrating hard, Anne related to her sister exactly what had been happening to her over the previous weeks. Where she did not make herself sufficiently clear, Mary questioned her gently.

"Well?" Anne asked anxiously at last. "What do you think?"

Mary took her hands in her own, genuinely delighted. "I would say that you are most definitely carrying a babe, Nan dear. Congratulations!"

Dumfounded, Anne covered her flushed cheeks with cool hands. "I cannot believe that it has actually happened! My prayers have surely been answered!"

"You must not get yourself excited" reproved her sister gently. "The next thing to do is get a professional opinion from your physician, and then you can tell the King!"

Anne rose and walked slowly across the chamber, pausing in front of her mirror. Spanning her tiny waist with her hands, she turned first to one side, then the other, scrutinising herself carefully.

"There's no point in looking for any bulges!" laughed Mary, joining her. "It will be at least another two months before there are any visible signs".

"That's not what I was looking at" Anne replied, still staring into the mirror. "I was just thinking how incredible it is that I am now as slim as a reed but soon I shall be huge and rounded!" She turned to her sister. "Do you think I shall get as big as you did?"

"That depends on the size of the baby" Mary told her. "My Henry was a large child".

Anne was looking at Mary's body appraisingly. "You are much bigger boned than I" she said slowly. "What if my child grows as big as your Hal? I would never be able to give it birth, I am so narrow". She ran her hands over her hips as she spoke, raising troubled eyes to Mary's.

"You worry unnecessarily" soothed her sister. "For nature will see that the child is in proportion to your own body. There is no reason for you to be afraid".

Anne fell silent, her fears temporarily alleviated. Mary steered her towards the bed. "Now sister, you lie down whilst I fetch Doctor Butts. Let us get this pregnancy safely confirmed so that you can begin taking the proper precautions, as I did".

Anne allowed herself to be helped on to the bed where she lay down as instructed and stared unseeingly at the embroidered canopy above her. Her heart felt as though it were a bird fluttering to be free from her chest and her whole body tingled with excitement.

Soon Mary came bustling back, followed by a Doctor Butts looking even more flustered than was usual for him. He stood by her beside and regarded her carefully. "Your sister tells me that you suspect yourself to be with child, Lady Rochford" he began. "If Your Ladyship will allow, I will perform an examination to ascertain if this may be fact".

"Please proceed, Doctor Butts" replied Anne joyfully, then half raising herself she called to Mary. "Make sure no-one enters, sister". Her sister nodded in a conspiratorial fashion and placed herself firmly against the door.

Doctor Butts examined her slowly and gently, asking questions similar to those asked by Mary earlier. At last he straightened his aching back and looked down at her anxious face. "Although there are not any outward signs as yet, your symptoms confirm my diagnosis. Saying that, it is hard to say exactly how far advanced you are, Lady Rochford, but I would estimate that you should be delivered in either late August or early September". He leaned towards her and patted her shoulder. "Congratulations, my Lady. I hope I shall have the privilege of delivering the King's heir?"

Smiling roguishly up at him, Anne said softly "You saved me from the sweating sickness Doctor Butts, when my life was despaired of. I would trust no other but you to help me through my labours".

Significantly, the physician bowed his way from her presence, as though she already wore a crown. Anne eased herself off the bed and decided to at once break the news to the royal father-to-be. The time has come for him to keep his side of the bargain, she thought to herself.

Mary stood aside as she approached the door, a look of understanding flashing between then as Anne opened the door and turned in the direction of Henry's adjoining apartments. "Not a word to any" she called softly over her shoulder to Mary, who nodded fervently.

Anne calculated that the King should just have finished playing his daily quota of tennis and would therefore be either on his way up from the courts or changing in his chamber. It was the latter; Henry was standing alone in his ante-chamber, rubbing his face briskly with a soft cloth. He was still dressed in his tennis garb so evidently had only just returned.

"Anne!" he exclaimed as she appeared in the doorway. "I looked for you in the spectator's gallery but could not see you".
"Sadly I was unable to attend" she replied gravely, fighting to hold back her smiles. "I was assailed by a slight indisposition, but happily I am now quite recovered".

At once he ceased his towelling. "What kind of indisposition?"

Ignoring his question, she moved closer, tapping with her finger the golden "B" which hung from her pearl collar. "It is time this "B" was replaced by an "M" Henry" she said softly. As realisation began to dawn on his face, she announced happily "Your son will be arriving in late August or early September, according to our worthy Doctor Butts".

Wordlessly he embraced her tenderly. As they drew apart she was touched to see that his eyes were full of tears. "We shall be married tomorrow" he told her. "It will need to be a secret ceremony; one of the turret rooms will suffice. I will arrange everything and let you know the time once it is set". He clasped her to him again, murmuring her name over and over; such was the joy of the moment, she too was moved to tears.

In the early hours of the following day, January 25th 1533, an uncharacteristically white and shaking Anne was helped slowly up the winding stone steps to a small attic room in one of the turrets of Whitehall palace.

As she came slowly into the room, the King, who was already waiting, hurried forward to assist Margaret Wyatt in lowering her to a hastily provided chair. Once she was safely seated, Margaret discreetly withdrew a few paces as the King squatted on his heels beside Anne. Looking anxiously into her face he asked in a low voice "Is all as it should be sweetheart?"
Anne gave him a small apologetic smile as she replied "Rest assured that everything is very well. I apologise for my extreme pallor and apparent weakness Henry, but you know how things are with me and this hour of the day but compounds it".
He smiled adoringly at her, then got to his feet and crossed the room to speak to his chaplain.

Margaret Wyatt immediately returned to her side. "Are you all right Anne? Do you need anything?"

"No, thank you Meg. This business should not take long". Anne swallowed hard in an effort to suppress a rising nausea and looked about the tiny room with interest. It was about twelve feet square with a sloping roof, any daylight admitted through the tiny latticed window under which she sat. Her thoughts suddenly catapulted back to her clandestine meetings with Harry Percy; had they indeed spent time together in this very chamber? She swallowed hard again, this time with a nostalgic regret for those innocent days now long gone. Pulling herself out of her reverie, she saw that a makeshift altar had been erected in the far corner of the room, draped with a crimson and gold cloth. Dawn was only just breaking and the room was lit by flickering torchlight which projected grotesque patterns onto the whitewashed walls.

Henry appeared by her side and assisted her to her feet. "We are ready to begin now" he told her. Unsteadily, with Henry holding her firmly, she approached the altar and stood before the chaplain. Margaret Wyatt stood a little behind Anne; George Boleyn and Henry Norris stood behind their King.

The ceremony was brief, being merely the exchange of vows between two consenting parties. Her wedding over, the King's new wife returned gratefully to her chair and sat down abruptly; wondering vaguely why the King and Norris were in such close discussion with their backs to her. Soon she found out.

The two men approached her, and then the King motioned to Norris who produced a small package from the folds of his cloak. Henry placed the package on Anne's lap and kissed her fondly on the forehead, saying "Here is a small gift to mark this most happy occasion".

Her sickness temporarily forgotten, Anne eagerly untied the strings and opened the small wooden box. Inside was a small, beautifully wrought mantel clock, its solid silver case engraved with the royal coat of arms. Anne smiled gratefully up at her husband, and then clasping the clock in her arms said simply "Thank you Henry. I shall treasure it always".

Formalities over, the small gathering began to break up. The altar was carefully dismantled and Norris assisted the King to his apartments whilst Margaret assisted Anne back to her bed. George Boleyn prepared to leave for Hever to inform his parents that the marriage had taken place.

"What a very secret wedding that was!" Anne commented lightly as she sank back into her pillows. "Even yours and Anthony's was a more public affair than mine!" Margaret had been married to Sir Anthony Lee for just four weeks, and although she did not yet know it, was already expecting a child.

Henry did not return to his bed, but sat alone in his chamber formulating the final steps of his divorce. His first act was to pen a short note to the Pope nominating Thomas Cranmer for the vacant post of Archbishop of Canterbury. Naturally he did not mention that he had already married Anne, for Clement still believed that Henry was awaiting his final judgement on the case. Henry wanted Cranmer safely installed as Archbishop so that he could pronounce Catherine divorced, according to the rules of the newly formed breakaway English church.

Chapter 25

Coronation

By the middle of February most of Anne's sickness had subsided and she was beginning to feel extraordinarily well. Other than close friends and family, her wedding and pregnancy were still unknown to the court, although Anne was so full of herself that she could not resist dropping heavy hints.

She was with a number of friends in her presence chamber when she called to a page to bring her a bowl of apples. Wyatt, who was sitting near her, immediately commented "But you do not eat apples; you have never liked them overmuch"
Her eyes sparkling, she turned to him, her finger at her lips in a conspiratorial gesture. "I must confess that you are right Tom" she told him. "But of late I have had an insatiable desire for hard, juicy apples. The King tells me I must be with child!" Her voice rose. "Do you hear me, all? The Kings says I must be with child, but I have told him that I cannot be. Oh no, I cannot!" Then she dissolved into helpless

laughter whilst her companions looked on in amazement.

Throwing a concerned glance in her brother's direction and noting his puzzled expression, Margaret wordlessly ushered Anne towards her bedchamber. But even with the stout wooden door firmly closed, Anne's laughter could still be heard from within, interspersed with Margaret's voice begging her to calm herself.

Eventually, Anne did calm. "What makes me behave so?" she asked her friend.
"It is natural in your condition" soothed Margaret. "You are the King's wife and you carry his child. It is an exciting time for you but circumstances force you to be discreet at a time when you want to shout it to the world. For pity's sake Anne, you must keep your secret a little longer. If the Pope's spies should hear of it, Cranmer may well be prevented from becoming Archbishop and then it would be difficult for the English church to break away from Rome as planned".
"Of course you are right" Anne reasoned, sighing heavily. "I just want everyone to know because I want to talk about it! I remember Mary was the same when she was carrying her Hal. Every waking moment she wanted to discuss her symptoms, her layette… ".
"Why not talk of such things to me?" suggested Margaret coyly. "I too like to talk of babies".
Anne frowned, then realisation dawned. "Meg! You too?"
"It must be catching!" laughed Margaret happily.

"Yes, I too am with child and should be welcoming my little one around the end of September".

"That is wonderful!" Anne got to her feet and embraced her friend. "No doubt Anthony is delighted?"

"Absolutely" Margaret confirmed. "He says he thinks that I shall be embarrassingly fruitful".

"Does he, by goodness! Perhaps you should have married the King instead of me!"

Margaret pulled a wry face. "I do not think I would have been able to hold his interest for as long as you have. Anyway, I do not think I would be a very suitable queen!"

"I was not exactly born to such an exulted position" Anne reminded her.

"Maybe not" Margaret replied. "But remember, you always had to be the queen in our childhood games. No-one else could get a look in!"

Anne nodded happily, recalling those carefree days. "I hope such apprenticeship will stand me in good stead for the future!"

Despite Anne's indiscreet behaviour, somehow the news of her condition was contained within her intimate circle. At the end of February, the Pope confirmed the appointment of Thomas Cranmer as Archbishop of Canterbury; everything seemed to be going as planned.

After a suitable interval, Anne's brother George was despatched to France to personally inform Francis of King Henry's marriage and expected heir. In April a formal announcement was made to both Houses of Parliament that the King's marriage to Catherine was invalid and that the King had taken a new wife. With much bullying, Henry managed to get Parliament to pass what he termed as an Act in Restraint of Appeals, which denied the Pope any right to interfere with matrimonial cases in England.

Finally, a deputation was sent to Catherine from the King, informing her that from that day forward she was to be known as the Princess Dowager of Wales. She was offered tempting bait if she would acknowledge the King's new marriage; the company of her daughter Mary coupled with a large palace and a generous income. However her pride would not allow her to accept any of the terms and she sent word to Henry that she would never acknowledge Anne as Queen.

Despite Catherine, preparations forged ahead for Anne's coronation. Henry was planning the most lavish ceremony and celebrations ever seen for a Queen Consort. He deeply regretted that she had been denied a public wedding and the coronation was to make up for all the secrecy hitherto.

The final stages of the divorce and establishment of the church in England were implemented on 23rd May 1533 when at a special court in Dunstable, Cranmer gave his official judgement that the marriage between Catherine and Henry was unlawful. He forbade them to cohabit and pronounced them both free to remarry. Five days later at Lambeth, he judged that the marriage of Henry and Anne was lawful.

On the following day, the 29th, Anne's coronation celebrations began. Riding in the barge that had once been Queen Catherine's, she left Greenwich palace for the Tower. The Thames was alive with other craft, most decked in gorgeous apparel; some containing musicians, others containing actors performing various pageants for her amusement. Anne waved and smiled to the people on the boats and barges and to those lining the river banks, inclining her head graciously at the cheers. She also heard plenty of catcalls and hissing, but kept her bright smile firmly fixed in place throughout. As her barge approached the water gate of the Tower, just before 5 o'clock, a booming of guns from the ramparts announced her arrival. She alighted carefully, her flowing robes cleverly concealing her five and a half month pregnancy, and was lovingly received by the King who had arrived unannounced on an earlier barge.

He led her to the Queen's apartments within the Tower, newly refurbished in her honour, and then left her to the ministrations of her ladies. Despite the grandeur of her surroundings, Anne shivered as she looked about her. "I do not like this place" she confided to her ladies. "There is anguish and evil here for I feel it reaching out to engulf me!"
"Your Grace must not fret" soothed her sister in law, Jane Rochford. "Your condition makes you fanciful; you can have nothing to fear from this place".

Jane's envious eyes fastened upon Anne's swelling abdomen, then she looked down at herself regretfully. She stood no chance of ever being in a like condition for her shrewish ways had driven

George from her. Even before their marriage had broken down, George had preferred to spend his time with his sister rather than her. Jane had always been jealous of Anne's allure and in her own mind felt that George had deserted her for his sister. This fact had turned Jane's love for her husband into hatred; she never missed a chance to spy on them and hoped for a chance to one day pay them both back for what she saw as their rejection of her.

The following day, a Friday, was spent quietly within the Tower precincts. Anne needed to rest ahead of the upcoming ceremony and celebrations, meanwhile the King created and invested eighteen Knights of The Bath who would accompany Anne as she rode to Westminster the following day.

Saturday dawned fine and bright; Anne was woken early and after breaking her fast privately in her chamber, was dressed in a sumptuous white damask and velvet gown embellished with pearls and diamonds which was cunningly cut to draw the eye away from her swelling body. Around her neck she wore a necklace composed of large pearls which she had chosen from the bulging royal jewel coffers and had previously been worn by Catherine on state occasions. Her hair was left to flow free and uncovered, with just a simple gold coronet to keep it in place.

Assisted by her chosen ladies, she walked carefully down the stone stairs from her apartments and out into the sunshine where a luxurious horse drawn litter awaited her. With effort, for the dress was heavy and she encumbered and unbalanced by her growing bulk, she climbed awkwardly into the padded seat made for her, then allowed her ladies to drape her skirts becomingly, and to arrange her hair neatly. She was silent throughout this, thinking with some trepidation of the reception she was likely to receive once on the streets and close to the people. Despite her triumph, she felt less than safe in such close proximity to those who not so many months ago were pursuing her mob handed.

She was startled from her musings by the trumpets announcing the start of the procession and the protesting creak from the heavy wooden gates as they swung wide to admit her procession on to the London streets. Ahead of her went her new Knights of the Bath, followed by a selection of peers and nobles of the realm, then her litter jolted forward, dislodging her a little from her seat and requiring her to take a firm hold of the gilded railing beside her. The ceremonial canopy was hoisted above her and then she was amongst the people in the narrow streets, heading slowly for Westminster. Behind her came many other carriages and marching notables; the entire procession close to half a mile long.

Anne swallowed hard and made an effort to look down at her new subjects with an expression of kindness and humility. It certainly wouldn't do to appear arrogant or aloof. Looking about her she saw the colourful banners hanging from the specially erected poles and from the jutting upper storeys of many of the buildings. Wine flowed freely from conduits and she noticed that this had made a lot of the people very merry and more inclined to celebrate than mock her. Not that there weren't plenty of jeers; she was prepared for that, but battled hard to show no annoyance or distress, bestowing benevolent smiles upon all.

There were men-at-arms all along the route as well as a complete escort marching either side of her; Henry was taking no chances with the safety of his bride or his heir. Anne was grateful for their presence for although the streets seemed calm, she knew a single incident could change the mood in a heartbeat. It would only take one rallying call or a single menacing move towards her to spark off a stampede.

At each crossroads along the way, her litter would halt so that she could enjoy the various pageants which were performed in her honour. This was also a good way for the rest of the procession to catch up with her, for the further they progressed, the more those on foot further back were tailed off.

She smiled graciously and applauded enthusiastically at every entertainment she paused for and had her gentleman ushers distribute coins amongst the children who sang her praises in song and spoken verse.

Much as she enjoyed her progression, Anne felt that it took an interminable time to reach Westminster; holding herself erect and alert for such a long time over the bumpy roads was causing her back to ache, and keeping a benevolent smile on her face whatever the provocation was far more tiring that she ever could have guessed.

Finally the turrets of Westminster appeared ahead, the massive double doors of Westminster Hall almost dwarfed by the huge figure of the King himself, waiting impatiently and anxious to greet her.

In an impressive manoeuvre, her litter was half turned and moved almost sideways through the narrow approach to the Hall, the cobbled street made even more difficult to navigate by the press of people on all sides, until finally she drew up beside him. She felt the child stir within her as she scrambled from her cushioned seat and half fell and half jumped into his waiting arms.

Henry pressed his face into her hair, whispering "How do you like your capital city, my Queen?"
Anne, well aware that his unspoken words were more likely 'see how much I have done for you', smiled sweetly at him as his eyes met hers and told him "I like it very well, Sire. I believe a good time was had by all".

Henry placed her carefully on her feet, and then led her solemnly to her marble throne set atop the dais under the great window. The celebration banquet then began, although the King did not remain very long to enjoy it; it was Anne's day and he felt that his presence would take the attention away from her. After kissing her hand and wishing her well, he slipped quietly through a side door and boarded a barge to York Place, where he would later welcome her.

Anne found herself ravenous after her long ride through the city; although the bulk of her child limited the amount she could eat. She contented herself with eating just a little at each of the courses, and amused herself by watching the scramble at the tables below her, as the hind most members of her procession arrived in numbers, desperate for refreshment after so much unaccustomed exercise.

The banquet done, Anne was ushered away through the same side door that the King had used earlier, and settled in to a barge for the short ride up river to York Place. There, as before, she was greeted lovingly by the King, who dutifully escorted her to her apartments, advising her to retire early in order to get the rest she would need to sustain her through the morrow.

Shortly before eight o'clock the next morning, Anne again stood in Westminster Hall; this time robed in purple velvet, to greet a procession of Bishops and Abbots, headed by the Archbishop of Canterbury, Thomas Cranmer. They approached her slowly, dressed in their finest vestments complete with their crosses and croziers. Anne took her place in the middle of the clerics, and with her scarlet robed ladies walking behind, processed regally towards the Abbey. The Duke of Suffolk walked at the head of the procession bearing the crown on a velvet cushion whilst either side and slightly behind him came two more peers, one carrying the sceptre and the other the white rod.

At the Abbey doors, Anne paused under the brightly

striped awning which hung from the porch and waved to the watching crowds before disappearing into the vast chill interior and moving slowly up the central aisle towards the high altar.

After ceremonies and rites which lasted many hours, and would have taxed the strength of the most robust person, never mind a woman almost six months with child, she was crowned by Archbishop Cranmer using the same regalia used for Henry himself nearly twenty four years earlier. As expected, the great coronation crown proved too heavy for her slender neck, although she managed to bear the weight for the time it took to receive the symbolic sceptre and rod. Before the mass, it was substituted by a smaller, lighter replica made especially for her and it was thus crowned that she walked triumphantly from the Abbey and into the light of day, escorted by a huge assembly of noblemen.

As she walked regally towards Westminster Hall she felt the eyes of the Londoners boring into her and thought irreverently that the wine conduits could not have been flowing as freely as they had the previous day. Only a few cheers were raised on her behalf which did little to mask the insistent hissing of 'concubine' and 'whore' from certain sections of the crowd.

Once again inside lofty, cool Westminster Hall, she snatched a brief rest in a withdrawing room before re-emerging to preside over the coronation feast. However, her exhaustion had been little alleviated despite her quarter hour of peace; it would take a lot longer than that to recover from eight hours of solemn ceremony and ancient rite. To add to her discomfort, she found that the endless procession of elaborate dishes with their waft of spicy odours thoroughly upset her still delicate stomach. Several times she had to direct her ladies to hold a cloth in front of her face so that she could vomit unobserved into a small bowl.

It was late in the evening before the banquet came to an end. Beneath her cloth of estate, Anne rose to her feet, washed her fingers in a bowl held by her adored and adoring Thomas Wyatt, then retired thankfully from public gaze.

The following day, court celebrations began at Whitehall palace. Her pregnancy prevented Anne from taking an active part in the revels, but she and the King presided over them all and declared them excellent entertainment. It was another ten days before the celebrations petered out, after which the King ordered that there should be a little peace in the palace so that his Queen could obtain the rest she so badly needed.

The court remained at Whitehall until early August when it removed to Windsor so that Anne might benefit from the change of air and escape the stuffiness of the city. She had chosen Greenwich for her lying-in, so great preparations abounded within its walls. Anne, now nearly eight months pregnant was at the stage where she just wished to sit and dream of her coming child. Throughout her expectant months she had kept her sister close, often preferring to consult Mary rather than one of the King's numerous physicians.

Shortly before they were due to return to London, Anne expressed a desire to walk in the great park. Mary agreed to accompany her and so did Margaret Lee, herself well into her seventh month. Her other fluttering ladies were waved away and told to stay in the castle; Anne wanted only those she could totally trust about her.

Once away from the castle, Anne placed her hand over the mound which she hoped was the King's son and said to Margaret "We had better not stray as far as we usually do!" Then she burst out laughing at Margaret's shocked expression.

"Certainly no horse in the stables would be overjoyed at the prospect of carrying us on their necks" replied Meg, looking wistfully into the depths of the green park, remembering the happy day when she and Anne had galloped joyfully back to the castle with the King's hunting party.

Anne sat down heavily on a fallen tree trunk and lifted her face to the bright blue sky. "Please let it be a boy" she addressed the heavens.

"They do say it is possible to tell the sex of an unborn child by its position in the womb" Mary confided to the two expectant mothers.

"Truly? In that case, what will mine be?" asked Margaret, smoothing her gown tightly across her expanding stomach, and looking expectantly at Mary.

Mary considered for a few moments, her head on one

side. "Well, it is only an old wives tale, but yours looks like a boy to me".

"It should be" replied Meg ruefully. "For already he runs most athletically within the confines of my poor body!"

All three laughed, and then Anne straightened her back and pulled her gown back so that it lay snugly over her stomach. "What of my child?" she asked Mary.

Mary looked hard at Anne's body for a long time. "Yours appears to be between the two positions" she said at last. "It could simply be because you are further advanced that Margaret and already your child is preparing to be born".

Anne looked crossly down at her heavy body, saying "maybe it is twins – one of each! That would please the King!"

"The shock would probably kill him" broke in Mary mischievously. They all laughed again, but looked around themselves to see that they were not overheard, for it was treason to speak of the King's death, even in jest.

Momentarily Anne's face hardened as she looked at her sister. Mary has already borne the King a son, she remembered. However, maybe that was a good omen; if Henry could sire a son on the elder Boleyn, why not the younger?

Shaking the thoughts away, Anne rose to her feet, grimacing. "I feel tired now" she announced. "I should like to rest awhile before supper; and so

should you Meg."
With contented sighs, her companions got to their feet and slowly the trio made their way towards the castle.

Chapter 26

New Life

In mid-August, the court returned to Greenwich; in Anne's view a little too early, for the carpenters and other tradesmen were working up a fearful racket in their work to prepare the birthing chamber for the great event.

Anne, overheated and overtired grumbled incessantly both about the noise and the heat and became increasingly snappy to those around her. The King, feeling awkward now that this most mysterious of female rituals approached, tended to pat her arm in a conciliatory manner and then make good his escape with as much speed as possible. But no matter how much she criticised, complained or ranted, his patience never faltered.

Doctor Butts had revised his expected time of birth to the last third of September, so August 26th was fixed as the date on which Anne would officially withdraw from the court to await the birth of her child.

On the morning of that day, Anne was escorted to the Chapel Royal within the palace to hear a special mass, and then returned to her withdrawing chamber to socialise and take refreshment with the members of her inner circle for the last time before the birth.

Despite the atmosphere of jollity and the suppressed excitement of those around her, she found herself battling to shake off a feeling of impending doom as her eyes strayed to the closed door of the birthing chamber. It was called the chamber of virgins, its name taken from the tapestries which lined its walls depicting the parable of the ten wise and the ten foolish virgins. Anne was already familiar with the room, although she had not seen it since it had been prepared for the great event.

She delayed the moment of incarceration for as long as was decently possible, but finally there was no option but to focus her thoughts, thank her companions for their good wishes and move towards the door, which was thrown open at her approach. Regally she stepped across the threshold into a heated gloom, followed by her waiting women, and as the door closed, looked about her with both interest and trepidation.

The huge chamber seemed half the size she remembered; the lowered ceiling draped and tented so that it almost touched the canopy above the state bed. All the windows were covered with matching heavy material, shutting out all light so that telling day from night was impossible. The floor was also thickly carpeted, so she was even denied the sweet scented herbs which she so much preferred underfoot in less exalted surroundings.

With a sigh, she plumped herself down on an available day bed and wondered how she was going to keep herself alert and amused. She remembered Mary's confinement at Hever and suddenly wished herself there, facing her labours in the peace and quiet of her familiar childhood bedchamber. But she was no longer plain Anne Boleyn, she was the Queen, and therefore must bring the heir to the throne into the world in the expected fashion.

Gratefully she took the goblet of wine which appeared in front of her, smiled at those ladies who were regarding her anxiously and turned her thoughts inwards towards the child waiting to be born.

In the early hours of September 7th, Anne turned over awkwardly in the great bed, then suddenly awoke and struggled into a sitting position. The chamber was in darkness apart from a spluttering wall sconce and all about her was silent. She deduced from the lack of activity that it was probably night time, although was unable to see the face of her little mantel clock, the King's wedding gift to her, to confirm that it was so. Yawning heartily, she sank back into her feather pillows rubbing her eyes with her fingertips. Something had woken her, but what?

Her eyes were now becoming accustomed to the gloom and as she stared above her at the embroidered canopy, she found her eyes could just distinguish the tiny fleur-de-lys pattern. Then for a moment she was confused, her mind searching for an anchor. Was she in France? No, of course not; she was in England, at Greenwich, lying in the magnificent French bed that Henry had presented to her for her confinement.

Satisfied that her thoughts were in order, she closed her eyes in an attempt to drift back into slumber. She had been dreaming that she was in labour she remembered, labouring in great agony to bring forth the long awaited heir. Suddenly the muscles in her abdomen contracted painfully, leaving her breathless and realising that her 'dream' had been the commencement of her pains and it was because of them that she had woken.

For a moment she laid still, one hand on her frantically beating heart, the other on the mound of her child. Then as the memory of the pain receded she thought perhaps she had imagined it. When minutes later her body was gripped by another spasm she knew beyond all doubt that her time had come. Raising her head from the pillows she called hoarsely "Margaret…. Margaret!" There was no response. Clearing her throat she called again, louder this time "Margaret. MARGARET!"

Cumbersome through her own pregnancy though she was, moments later Anne's bed curtains were parted to reveal Margaret Wyatt-Lee, clad in a voluminous nightgown, a candle in one hand with its flame shielded by the other.

"Anne" she whispered. "Is it the babe?"
Mutely Anne nodded, her bottom lip crushed between her clenched teeth as another contraction tore at her body.

Suddenly the chamber was ablaze with light and movement. Doctor Butts appeared by her bedside, gazing owlishly at her. "How long have you had the pains Your Grace?" he asked her.
"I have been vaguely aware of them for some hours, I think" she told him. "You see, I was dreaming that I was in labour then I suddenly awoke to find I truly was".
"Hmmm" Doctor Butts gently palpated her swollen body. "That is often the way of it; women at their time often dream of their coming labours when the child is on its way. Think of it as nature trying to bring you as much rest as possible to see you through your ordeal".
Anne said nothing; she was beginning to feel a little light headed due to the combination of the pain and lack of sleep. Dr Butts continued "At what time did Your Grace retire last evening?"
"Between nine and ten" she replied. "I was very tired and fell asleep almost immediately. What is the time now?"
"It was but a few minutes past two when I left my chamber to attend Your Grace" he told her. "Try to rest between your pains Madam, for they are but the prelude to the rhythmic spasms which will eventually expel the child".

Anne gripped his wrist as he made to leave her bedside. "Then how much longer before the child is born?" she asked urgently. "I felt sure that the birth was imminent!"

"Your Grace is mistaken" he soothed. "When the child is truly on its way your pains will come much closer together. I would estimate that you still have at least twelve hours to go".

Her grip on his wrist slackened, her hand falling back down on to the coverlet. "Another twelve hours?" she repeated blankly. "God give me strength".

Bowing courteously, Butts left her bedside. Through her half drawn curtains she saw him consult briefly with one of the midwives before sinking his tired body into a chair to prepare for the long wait.

She closed her eyes as another spasm caught her and when she opened them again she found her sister Mary beside her. "How is it Nan?"

"Doctor Butts said that it could be another twelve hours before the baby is born, Mary. So long!"

"Surely not!" Mary looked across at the physician who was dozing, slumped in his chair. "That cannot be Nan, for already you are almost eight hours into your labours".

"Eight hours!" Anne mouthed silently. "Then I have slept?"

"It is now almost ten o'clock my dear. Evidently your weariness overcame the intensity of your pain allowing you several hours of precious rest. I am sure it will not be too long now".

Anne sighed, shifting her cumbersome body with difficulty. She screwed up her face as another contraction set in, then when it was over, said "It seems strange, but the stronger and more frequent the pains, the easier it seems to bear".

Mary smiled down at her lovingly. "That is because every pain brings you nearer the birth, Nan. Do you not remember that I told you an expectant mother welcomes every agony which brings the moment of birth closer?"

"I believe you did say that" Anne smiled weakly at her sister. "It is such a comfort to have you here Mary. You will not leave me?"

"I promise I will not leave you".

Suddenly Anne remembered her husband, the direct cause of her present suffering. "Henry! Has he been told?"

"Immediately he woke" Mary replied. "At present he is no doubt pacing anxiously about his chamber waiting for news of you".

"Waiting for news of his son, you mean" retorted Anne tartly, a bitter edge to her voice. "Tell him to go and hunt, or play tennis or something. He will be better if active; his part of this business is long done. It is up to me to see it through."

As her sister was gripped by another vice-like pain, Mary rose hurriedly. "I will send word to him that you are doing well and that you desire him to do as he would".

Henry was indeed restless and much relieved by his wife's message that all was going well. He would go hunting in the deer forest, he told the messenger. As soon as the child was born he wished to be recalled to the palace.

Anne's labours dragged on and on. Seated either side of her bed, her mother and sister talked soothingly to her and encouraged her to grip their hands as the pains became stronger and more insistent.

It was approaching three in the afternoon before Anne's spasms became so frequent that she had only seconds to recover from one contraction before the next gripped her. Her eyes closed, her face contorted, she cried out in her agonies as the birth approached. Her body was slippery with sweat and she writhed so strongly it was difficult for the midwife to assist her. Finally with an ear-splittingly loud shriek, she expelled her child onto the priceless French bed.

Delivered at last, Anne lay quiet and exhausted. Her eyes were closed but a faint smile curved her lips as she heard the lusty cry of an infant break the silence of the birth chamber. She opened her eyes. Why did no-one seek to congratulate her on the birth of an heir? Why did her sister and mother look down on her with troubled eyes?

Clearing her parched throat, she croaked "The child is healthy and well formed?"
Doctor Butts appeared beside her with the baby in his arms, wrapped securely in linen. "Perfectly healthy Your Grace" he replied, non-committally. With the help of her mother, Anne eased herself into a sitting position and held out her arms for the child.

Hesitantly the bundle was held out to her. The new

mother snatched it to her then parted the bindings and looked lovingly upon the red crinkled face of her child. Tenderly Anne laid the infant upon her knees and uncovered the tiny body; then she saw the reason for the silence. She had borne a daughter; healthy, yes, but not the son for which Henry had married her in such haste.

Licking her dry lips, she wrapped the child warmly then lay back amongst the pillows with her daughter in her arms before asking "Is the King told?"
"He is told that the child is born, Nan" replied her mother. "The messenger did not wait to learn whether it was a boy or girl; he rode for the King when the pre-arranged signal was given from the window above the courtyard."

Proud Anne refused to show her disappointment to those around her. "Leave me, all of you" she commanded. "I would be alone when my husband arrives".

The midwife was visibly concerned. "But Your Grace" she protested. "Your ladies and I must see you cleaned and comfortable before we leave your presence".
Anne rounded on her furiously. "There will be time enough for all of that after I have seen the King" she snapped. "Now be gone. All of you".
Slowly all trooped out shutting the door behind them and leaving her alone with her new daughter.

The child opened her fair lashed blue eyes and regarded her mother solemnly. Anne caught hold of a tiny waving fist and said softly "Oh my little one; what trouble have you brought upon your poor mother by not being the hoped-for boy?"

Anne had planned to face her husband with defiance, intending to play upon the fact that although the child was female, it had at least proved her ability to bear healthy children. But as she gazed at the fruit of her labours, her defiance melted away and her eyes misted with tears.

With the child still cradled in her arms, Anne bowed her head and wept. As she felt her mother's tears fall upon her face, Anne's daughter roared her disapproval of the miserable world she found herself in.

So immersed in her grief was she that she did not hear her chamber door quietly open and shut. Henry Tudor, his heart touched by the pathetic scene before him, trod softly across the floor and gently touched his wife's wet cheek. She did not start or look up; she knew who it was and she could not bear to look into his eyes and see his disappointment.

"I have borne you a daughter" she sobbed, releasing her hold on the child as he bent to take the infant. Humbled by this miracle of life, the King could not bring himself to reproach the child for her sex.
"But what a daughter!" he breathed in amazement. "She is so large and well-formed; and so strong!" Look Nan, is she not the most beautiful creature you have ever seen?"
Anne raised her reddened eyes to her husband's face.

"You truly love her then? You forgive me for not birthing the son you craved?"

"My sweet Nan, this girl is worth ten of the half Spanish female I had by my brother's wife. Mary was never as healthy as this one; she never wriggled so strongly nor cried so lustily. You have given me a beautiful, perfect daughter. We are young, sweetheart, and no doubt this little one will soon have a brother to share her nursery".

Anne felt fresh tears welling into her eyes. He was being so kind and taking such pains to hide his disappointment. "Then you will not put me from you?" she pleaded. "You will give me another chance?"

Henry carefully deposited his daughter into the waiting cradle then sat himself on the edge of Anne's bed and took her hands in his. "You will have many more children" he told her tenderly. "And as for putting you from me, what sort of talk is that? I tell you I would rather lose my throne and beg my bread from door to door than desert you".

Gratefully she gave herself into his embrace. "A son next time" she whispered. "I promise you a son".

"You must be fully recovered before we try again" he told her firmly. "We have many years ahead of us; there is no hurry".

Anne's adoring eyes strayed to her daughter's cradle. "What name shall we give our child Henry? I should like to call her Elizabeth".

"Then Elizabeth she shall be my sweet" he told her.

"Elizabeth; named for my mother and yours".

Chapter 27

Hope & Despair

Three days later the state christening of the infant Princess Elizabeth took place in Greyfriars church, which was contained within the sprawling complex of Greenwich palace.

Anne was unable to attend, barred by both tradition and the state of her health. However she was well represented by her family for both her brother George and her father played prominent parts in the proceedings

After the christening, the child was carried in state to its mother's chamber in order to receive her blessing; then borne away to the royal nursery. This ceremony heralded a steady stream of people bearing elaborate and expensive gifts, each hoping that their offering would procure the favour of the King's new Queen.

With a heavy sigh, Anne leaned forward in her bed so that Margaret Lee could slip the purple mantle of estate around her shoulders before the gift bearers arrived. Margaret took the opportunity of being close to Anne to whisper "All is not well?"

Anne looked up quickly into the face of her friend, then forcing a smile to her lips replied "Bodily I am well; I thank God for the youth and strength which so aided my recovery after the birth. But mentally … come closer Meg; I suppose this could be counted as treason and I want no word of it to get to the King. To put it bluntly, I am dreading Henry's renewed nightly visits in order to get his son"

Margaret made pretence of adjusting the bed coverlet, waving away those who made to assist. Looking into Anne's troubled face; Margaret could well guess her thoughts. "You think he loves you less for birthing a daughter?"

Anne closed her eyes momentarily, before forcing herself to admit that she feared that was so. "His love for me seems to have undergone a transformation" she confided. "Only days ago I was the love of his life; he said he wished for nothing more when I was with him. But now, when he comes to see me and talk with me, his eyes run over the shape of my body under the coverlet, almost as though he is gauging when next he will be able to share my bed. He thinks of me as a brood mare, Meg. A brood mare for his colts!"

As always, in moments of deep emotion, Anne was perilously close to hysteria; her voice had risen dangerously in both pitch and volume as she finished her piece.

"Compose yourself Anne" Margaret whispered urgently. "Already you have attracted the attention of others. I beg of you, be calm and make ready to receive the Princess's gifts".

Margaret's sound advice happily had its usual effect upon Anne. Suddenly she remembered that she was a Queen and must behave as one. Shrugging off her melancholy thoughts, she composed her features and ordered that the guests were to be admitted.

Whilst the doors were swung open and her Grand Almoner prepared to announce the names of the first to enter, Anne glanced quickly at Margaret, standing to attention beside the bed. With a shock she remembered that Margaret was very near the end of her own pregnancy and that the strain of almost constant attendance upon her Queen was telling on Lady Lee.

Looking into the ante-chamber beyond the open doors, Anne could see a long line of gift bearers making their way slowly towards her. "Margaret!" she hissed. Immediately Margaret bent towards her mistress. Anne caught hold of her arm and continued "Forgive me, I have been very selfish. I have been so immersed in my own problems that it completely slipped my mind that you too will be in childbed within the next few weeks. You must retire from my service until after the child is born, Meg. Get as much rest as you can and conserve your strength".

The first guests were approaching and within hearing distance, so Margaret and Anne dropped their first name terms. Performing an awkward curtsey, Meg replied gratefully "I thank Your Grace for such concern. I shall be glad to take up your most generous offer and will look forward to returning to your service once my child is born".

"You are dismissed, Lady Lee" Anne said kindly. "Kindly have me informed when the child is born and I will endeavour to visit you once I am churched. Take care".

Anne's eyes followed Margaret sadly as she walked from the chamber. She knew that Meg was her most faithful friend and in such a public position where envious eyes watched her every move, Anne felt more deeply than ever that Margaret Wyatt-Lee was the only woman of her household whom she could trust.

However, it was time to turn her attention to her guests and receive both their congratulations and their gifts. Summoning a bright smile to her face, although inside she felt more like weeping, Anne turned to the first of the long procession.

When Elizabeth was three months old, Henry told Anne that it was time the child had her own household away from the court. "You mean you want to send her away from us?" she asked incredulously.

Although Henry was exasperated, he tried not to show it. "It is tradition sweetheart" he explained. "Elizabeth is my heir and as such she must have a separate household".

Anne could see his reasoning, but she wanted to

keep her daughter near her. "She is still a tiny baby!" she burst out. "She needs her mother's love. Send her away now and she will grow up barely knowing who her father and mother are!"

She had pushed her argument too far. Henry was less tolerant of her outbursts than he had been prior to their marriage. His fists clenched by his sides and his face rapidly colouring, he walked menacingly across the room and stood close in front of her, his breath fanning her face as he spoke. "If the maternal instinct in you is so strong Madam, why have you not yet conceived my son?"

Anne stood her ground, fighting to subdue the temper which threatened to rise and match his. "Because you returned to my bed too soon!" she screamed. "As soon as I was churched you resumed your nightly visits. Evidently you managed to forget how lovingly you told me that we would wait a little, so as not to risk my health or a future babe's".

"My first wife required only a few weeks to recover from her labours"

Deadly as a viper, Anne turned on him. "Then maybe that is the reason she lost all those babes" she hissed. "And kindly refrain from calling the Princess Dowager your first wife. She was your brother's wife according to you, unless of course now I have committed the ultimate crime of bearing you first a daughter then failing to conceive again immediately, you are thinking of changing your mind and taking Catherine back?"

Henry knew when to withdraw graciously. Clearly he was not going to win the argument, for she had

far more ammunition to sling at him than he had to fire at her. Characteristically completely changing his mood, he said "Your temper is high today, sweetheart; you are sure that you are not …?"
"With child?" she interrupted aggressively. "No, I am not!" She turned her back on him, knowing that she had angered him dangerously but that he was at least making moves towards reconciliation. Desperately she racked her brain for the appropriate words to respond, without him thinking that he had won the day. Finally, in a sad little voice, she asked "Will you promise to take me to see our daughter often?"

Both grateful and relieved that she was making the effort to be amenable, Henry almost fell over himself to grant her wish. "Whenever you like, sweetheart" he told her tenderly. "And as Elizabeth is now my heir, I shall take immediate steps to have Catherine's daughter officially declared illegitimate."

Anne's eyes sparkled as she looked up at him; it was all turning out better than she had hoped. That request had been hovering on her lips since Elizabeth's birth; she had been trying to think of a diplomatic way to phrase it but now he himself had suggested it. "That will be most acceptable" she replied. "Such a declaration will make our daughter's position secure".
"Until we have a son" the King broke in, his eyes twinkling as he ran them lasciviously up and down her slender body.

Remembering that although he had married her, her

own position was precarious until she bore his son, she pressed her body invitingly against his and then taking his hands, drew him towards her bedchamber.

By the time Elizabeth had been at Hatfield for two months, Anne knew that she was again pregnant. Characteristically she could not keep the news to herself and immediately ran to the King. He declared himself overjoyed and his hitherto growing indifference towards her turned once again to slavish devotion.

However their joy was tragically short lived. Only weeks after she had broken the news, she was seized with severe cramping pains whilst supping quietly with the King in her rooms. Without delay she took to her bed, summoning physicians and midwives who did all they could, but within twelve hours it was all over. She had miscarried her child.

Anne took far longer to recover from her miscarriage than she had Elizabeth's birth. She stayed in her bed for a full week, lying motionless and frequently breaking into bouts of pitiful weeping. But being Anne, she could not long wallow in self-pity and she left her bed for the very first time on the same day that her dear friend Margaret returned to her service. Margaret had borne her child three weeks to the day after Elizabeth's birth; a fine boy.

The King was understandably upset that Anne's second pregnancy had come to nothing, although he kept telling her that there was plenty of time whilst they were both still young. In private however he was only too sure that this was not so. Already he was forty three years old and Anne herself was in her twenty seventh year. He made up his mind that unless she showed him very soon that she was able to bear his son, he would look elsewhere for a fertile Queen.

Less than one week later, news reached England that Pope Clement had finally reached a decision on the union of Henry and Catherine; he pronounced the marriage valid. Henry had been expecting such a declaration for some time and had already drawn up what he termed as the Act of Succession. Parliament was promptly presented with the draft and obligingly passed it with very little trouble. The Act totally abolished the power of the Pope in England and settled the succession on Anne's children.

Still deeply affected by the trauma of miscarrying, Anne spent a great deal of time at Hatfield with her daughter. Elizabeth was now six months old and very advanced for her age. Although she saw her mother infrequently, the child was well aware that Anne was the important person in her life; as soon as she appeared in the nursery the little girl would hold out her arms and gurgle delightedly. It was such sweet music to Anne's ears after her disappointment.

Catherine's daughter Mary was also at Hatfield. At her father's insistence she occasionally waited upon the baby Princess, but made sure she was hidden away whenever Anne visited. Every time she went to

Hatfield, Anne sent messages to Mary's apartments beseeching her to let bygones be bygones and acknowledge her as Queen. Sometimes Mary would not even read Anne's messages and at other times she would send the curt reply that she knew of no other Queen in England except Queen Catherine.

Anne tried every possible way to force an acknowledgement from stubborn Mary. When bribery did not work, she tried threats. They too were ignored until finally Anne's patience was exhausted. Many times she returned to London exasperated and despondent in equal measure; exasperated because her friendly overtures were repulsed and despondent because she knew that to have Mary on her side would be to possess a valuable ally.

Then happily something happened which pushed all the irritations into the background; in April 1534 her third pregnancy was confirmed.

Chapter 28

Seymour's Move

When Anne broke her glad news to Henry, he displayed little emotion. "But I thought you would be pleased" she said in a small voice. "This will be your son".

Staring out of the window, his back to her, he moodily replied "My son? According to you Madam, so was the last pregnancy and that came to nothing. Before that you bore me a live child you swore would be a prince and what was it? Another useless girl!" He swung round to face her, waggling his finger menacingly. "I am warning you; you must try harder to keep your promises if you wish to keep your place!"

Overwhelmed by his cruel reaction to her news, she stared at him uncomprehendingly for a moment. Then her old spirit awoke. Sarcastically she said "So you obviously expect nothing this time either, then. After all those years of love and devotion, I make two mistakes and you turn from me!"

Henry looked at her, his gaze both searching and assessing. She had changed since they married; she had grown thin and bitter and all her gaiety had left her.

"I know the source of all our troubles" she said suddenly. "Now that you know the secrets of my body, all the thrill of the chase has gone. I am no longer a mystery to you, only an encumbrance because I have not birthed a son!" She paused and threw a crafty glance in her husband's direction. With a rising horror she saw by the look on his face that she had hit the nail on the head. Her pride badly bruised, she made for the door at the same time shouting "No doubt you already look to one of my maids of honour to replace me as I replaced Catherine!" Without waiting for his reply, she slammed out of the chamber.

He pondered on her parting statement, and then with a cruel smile murmured "Maybe I do Madam. Maybe I do!"

The longer Anne's pregnancy continued, the more reconciled the married pair became. Henry knew he had to look philosophically on the matter; he no longer loved her but she was the mother of his daughter and presently carried his unborn son. Every morning he dutifully went to her chamber and solicitously enquired after her health, often staying to talk to her if she craved his company.

One particular morning she had been extremely sick and it was with great distaste that he stood at her bedside looking down on her gaunt, white face. He did not like to think of himself as a heartless man, but he realised in that moment that he no longer really cared about her health or welfare. All that mattered was that she should carry the child to full term and that it should be born alive, healthy and male.

After his usual enquiries and good wishes for the day, he made a paltry excuse and left her, deciding as he did so that he was in need of a small diversion to cheer him.

One of the Queen's maids of honour, Jane Seymour, waited until the King had left Anne's chamber, then slipped out behind him, unnoticed by any. Silently she followed him; he appeared to be making for his privy garden.

His hand was on the latch of the door to his walled garden when he heard a sharp cry behind him. Jane, obedient to the whisperings of her Catholic friends was carrying out her first attempt to prise the attentions of the King away from the Queen who had split their church and headed the much feared reformation. Jane's deception was a simple one; she and the King were out of sight of the private apartment windows and quite alone, so to attract his attention she pretended to twist her ankle and fell down on to the gravelled path.

At the sound of her cry, the King looked over his shoulder and on seeing a lady in distress, strode gallantly to her rescue. Jane, moaning effectively, pretended not to notice his arrival, then looked up into his face and blushed right on cue. "Your Grace" she breathed. "Forgive me for not curtseying but I appear to have damaged my ankle".

Henry found her quite charming in her distress. She was delicately made, like Anne, but did not appear to be as tall. Her hood had slipped back a little to reveal a small amount of honey coloured hair which perfectly complimented her clear and becomingly flushed skin. She fixed her china blue eyes on his and smiled apologetically. Henry was struck temporarily dumb; she was the complete antithesis of his black haired wife, both in looks and apparently in character, judging by her demure glances and soft words. He liked the way she looked at him; there was admiration in her eyes and he felt himself sorely in need of a little admiration. Moreover, in her distress she clearly needed him and it had been a long time since Anne had been anything but fiercely independent.

Squatting down beside her, he looked searchingly into her face and found he recognised her. "Mistress Seymour, is it not?"
"Yes, Your Grace" she murmured, her eyes downcast as though she feared to meet his gaze.
"How painful is your ankle?" he asked kindly. "Are you able to walk back to the palace?"
"I do not know" she replied, in apparent confusion. "I will try my weight upon it and see".

He helped her to her feet, and then with his arm supporting her, Jane gingerly placed her tiny satin shod foot on the ground. After an effective pause she applied her weight, then with an agonised little cry, crumpled into his arms.

"I will carry you back to the palace" he decided, sweeping her into the air.

"But Your Grace" she protested prettily. "What of the Queen?"

"The Queen is abed" he replied shortly. "And even if this should reach her ears, she knows better than to question my actions".

So an exultant Jane was carried gently back to the palace by her gallant King. "Your Grace is so strong yet so tender" she murmured. He smiled approvingly at her but said nothing, merely flexing his shoulders a little and puffing out his chest still further.

At the outer door of the palace, he lowered her carefully to the ground. "I thank Your Grace for such kindness" Jane whispered. "I must go now to wait upon the Queen". She curtseyed elegantly before walking away from him down the narrow passageway.

He watched her out of sight, standing in characteristic pose of legs apart and hands on hips. When she had disappeared, he made for his chambers, his desire for garden solitude forgotten. Mistress Seymour with her simple elegance and demure ways had captured his thoughts. However, had he used those thoughts a little more carefully, he would have realised that as she walked away from him, she displayed not a trace of a limp.

His Queen and her ladies joined him a little later. Caring not for the presence of others, Anne launched straight into her attack, for friends and enemies alike had wasted no time in running to her with news of the garden incident. His smile of greeting died on his lips as she railed at him. "And what, pray, were you doing with that cow-eyed bitch in your arms this morning?" She swung round, pointing an accusing finger at the cowering Jane. "I mean her, the Seymour!"

"Calm yourself" Henry blustered. "Remember the child".

"The child, the child" she taunted. "It is always 'remember the child' ". The words she had voiced secretly to Margaret after Elizabeth's birth at last rose to her lips. "All I am to you is a brood mare!" She stamped her foot. "I won't stand for it, I tell you. I am Queen here and I wish to be treated as such!"

Henry dismissed all onlookers with a wave of his hand. When he and Anne were alone, he took her by the shoulders and shook her gently. "You know that is not true" he told her reprovingly. "You are my dearly loved wife and Queen and with God's grace will be the mother of my son by Christmastide. Yes, I beg you to take care of yourself, but not only for the child's sake Nan, for your own also!"

Angrily she shrugged his hands from her shoulders. "So I may live to try again, no doubt! I still await your explanation for your conduct this morning!"

"I am not answerable to you for my actions" he growled. "Mistress Seymour simply twisted her ankle and I did what any man would have done and helped her back to the palace".

"You did not have to appear to enjoy doing so quite

so much!" she snapped, her black eyes locked on to his, trying to see into the recesses of his mind.

Uncomfortably he turned away, saying quietly, "it was a pleasant change for someone to treat me as though I am King here, with the appropriate deference".

"Deference?" Anne screeched. "I'll give the little cat deference when I next lay eyes on her. She is too quiet and demure, that one. She seeks to replace me; to oust me from your side. You might well look at her and lust Henry, but see how fragile she is. Even if she could conceive your boy, birthing him would surely tear her apart!"

Henry was shocked. "How can you say such things? I do not seek to replace you. I love you; none other"

She grimaced. "None other? For the present maybe". She drew in a deep breath and winced, her hands rubbing the ache in her back. "I am weary; I shall return to my chamber and rest before supper".

"You will dine privately?" he asked hopefully.

She looked at him appraisingly. He would have to be watched. "No" she replied slowly. "I will eat in the great hall. With you".

Later that evening, gorgeously dressed and with her girdle loose to give room to her six month pregnancy, Anne took her place beside the King. She noted the lascivious glances Henry threw in the direction of Mistress Seymour and observed the way Jane demurely lowered her lashes whenever she caught the King's eyes upon her.

As the tables were cleared and moved aside and the dancing about to begin, Anne made the decision over which she had been mulling all night. It was the custom for the King to lead the opening dance, either with his Queen, or if she be indisposed, with the lady of his choice.

As he rose to his feet and made to leave the dais to choose his partner, Anne also got to her feet. "I will dance with Your Grace" she said quietly.

Not looking at her, he smiled over the heads of the company, saying from the side of his mouth "Do not be so foolish Anne; you cannot dance in your condition. Anyway the opening dance is always a galliard to get the blood leaping, you know that".
"That is exactly why I wish to open the proceedings with you" she told him. "I do not wish to witness your blood leaping with Jane Seymour's!"

Angry that she had read his mind and was seeking to thwart his plans, the smile immediately vanished from his face as his head whipped round and his eyes sought hers. "You are going to risk losing our son for the sake of denying Mistress Seymour the opportunity of dancing with her King?"
Anne slipped her hand into his. "If you wish to put it that way, yes!" she answered firmly, leading him slowly down the steps of the dais.

He had no alternative but to follow her. Annoyed as he was, he was not going to risk a scene in front of five hundred people, amongst whom were a large number of foreign ambassadors and spies.

As he and Anne took the middle of the floor, Henry signalled to the musicians to play a pavane. "The Queen wishes to dance" he told the company pompously, stating the obvious. "A pavane is more suited to her condition".

So a pavane it was. The court lined up around them and the dance began. Piqued though he was that she insisted on dancing, as he led her back to the dais afterwards he told her that despite her bulk she was by far the most adept and elegant dancer on the floor. She bowed her head graciously at his compliment and threw him a flirtatious glance. His eyes twinkled as he squeezed her hand in reply, and in that moment she knew that for all the differences between them, she still had the power to attract him.

Glad of the rest, she sat quietly in her chair whilst the dancing continued. Eventually as she had suspected, Henry chose Jane Seymour for his partner. Her excellent eyesight standing her in good stead, she noticed with concern that the two seemed to be in earnest conversation, which worried her greatly. By the time Henry and Jane had danced together three times in succession, Anne had been pushed to her limits.

Immediately the dance finished, she rose to her feet and indicated to Henry that she wished to step the next measure with him. Several more times during the evening she found herself forced to take similar action in order to force her maid of honour away from the King.

In all, Anne took the floor seven times that evening and insisted on staying until the merrymaking was over. Unknowingly she had played right into the hands of the Catholic party who had been hoping for such a reaction to Jane's presence. Their greatest fear was that the child she carried would be the prince whose birth would cement the breach with Rome; therefore the greater the strain on the Queen's health, the more likely a premature birth.

As her ladies helped her to bed, Anne was aware of a strange light headedness which she put down to the wine she had consumed together with the exhilaration of the exercise. However, despite her extreme weariness she seemed unable to sleep and tossed incessantly in her quest for comfortable oblivion. Her body seemed to have developed a mind of its own; her muscles clenching unbidden, leaving her fighting for breath.

Finally, the awful truth was revealed to her; her labours were prematurely begun.

Chapter 29

Diversions

By the time her physician arrived, the cramping pains were attacking her with ominous regularity. She recognised the pains as a slightly less intense version of those she had experienced whilst giving birth to Elizabeth and feared they would only intensify to an unfortunate conclusion.

Doctor Butts examined her gently, asking questions as he did so, before bowing his way from her bedside to consult with a colleague. Minutes later he was beside her again and said gravely "I greatly regret that Your Grace is in premature childbed".

"I am well aware of that!" she snapped. "Can you do nothing to prevent the child being born?"

Butts shook his head emphatically. "Sadly no, Madam. Although, should the pains cease within the next hour or two, there is a chance that the child will not be harmed and the pregnancy continue .... "

"But it is unlikely" Anne finished for him. "Then we can only wait and see, must we not?" Sighing dejectedly, she dismissed Doctor Butts with a curt nod.

As the hours passed, the birth pangs became more insistent, tumbling Anne into a sea of agony. She suffered all the more because she was only too aware that no good would come from such an early birth; this time there would be no babe to cuddle and help wipe away the memory of the pain.

The child was born soon after dawn. Anne held her breath expectantly, hoping against hope that she had been incorrect in her calculations and that the child was nearer term than had been thought. But listen hard though she did, there was no welcoming cry heralding new life. Raising her head slightly, she caught sight of a midwife wrapping a tiny body in a scrap of white linen. Anne had to know that which they seemed afraid to tell her; raising her head higher she called for Doctor Butts.

Reluctantly he came to her, wringing his hands anxiously. "A most unfortunate still birth, Your Grace" he said gently. She said nothing, merely keeping her eyes on his face. In answer to her unspoken question, he continued. "Regrettably it was a well formed male child".

Totally dismayed, she fell back on her pillows, her hands flying to her face in an effort to fight back the tears. Henry might have been forgiving had she lost him a daughter, but a son! How was she possibly going to face him? Her face still hidden, she asked in a broken voice that the King be told as soon as possible.

Once cleaned and made comfortable, she slept for a while and was only awakened by the slamming of her chamber door and the sound of heavy footsteps approaching her bed. In her heart of hearts she knew what this meant and opened her eyes to find herself confronted with the King. It took only the merest of glances at his contorted face for her to see that he was in a fearful rage. "So Madam, you have killed my son with your inane capering!" he roared.

Anne had been too tired after the birth to even consider how she would handle the inevitable confrontation, but feeling rested and stronger she decided in a flash that in this instance, attack might be the best form of defence. Struggling into a half sitting position, she leaned towards him and hissed "It is entirely your fault!"

Henry was taken aback; his mouth gaped in shock. He was not used to being blamed for anything. "How so?" he bellowed. "How dare you blame me for your own stupidity?"

Courageously she drew herself up further and faced him. "If I, your wife, had not had to compete with that Seymour bitch for your attentions, this might never have happened!"

Henry had a distinct feeling that she was about to get the better of him yet again, so turned his back on her and stamped angrily around the chamber. Anne watched him with contempt then asked in a scornful voice "Well, have you lured her to your bed yet?"

"Do not be coarse Anne!" he snapped. "I have no intention of making the lady my mistress, and even if I had, I do not expect to have to answer to you for it".

"She may look simple, but she is far too clever to

sleep with you!" Anne taunted. "Not with an example like mine in front of her every day, you will see! She will return your gifts, repel your advances and declare that she wishes to keep herself pure for her husband. Given encouragement, she will lure you into marriage!"

"Even as you did" he sneered, in a deadly calm voice.

Her scornful laughter filled the chamber. "I … lure you? I think you should look a little closer into the not too distant past before you start making such observations. Who took care to break up my friendships with other men? Who came sniffing round my skirts at Hever? Who sent me expensive jewels and passionate love letters? Who …?"

"Cease your prattle!" he roared. "In the matter of Mistress Seymour you would be wise to close your eyes as your betters did before you!"

"Betters? Catherine, no doubt".

In extreme rage, the pitch of the King's voice became almost falsetto. "Do not interrupt me!" he screamed. "But yes; Catherine was by far your better. She had dignity, breeding ..."

"And she gave you dead children!"

"You have done no better for all your promises". He advanced towards her bed, a warning hand outstretched, and forefinger jabbing aggressively. "Remember Madam that it is within my power to bring you down from your lofty position in this land. You would do well to recall all I have sacrificed for your sake for I am beginning to wonder if it was all worth it!"

"So am I!" she retorted.

He paused by the door, raking his eyes over her dishevelled appearance, an expression of intense dislike on his face. "I will give you one more chance" he told her. "Remembering all the love that there was between us, you will have one more chance to keep your promise. If you know what is good for you, you will not fail me again!" With that, he was gone. Anne, trembling from the vehemence of their verbal battle, flung herself back on her pillows with fists clenched against her teeth as she fought back her rising hysteria.

Anne was ever a fighter. Within days she was up and about, flirting as merrily with the King and his courtiers as she had in the days before her marriage. Publicly she assumed a mask of gaiety; devising plays and masques for the King's entertainment and luring him back to her side with her infectious laughter and bantering talk.

"You are looking very run down, Nan" her brother George observed one evening.
"That is no wonder" she replied bitterly. "Think of the strain I am under George. During the day I have to watch him constantly lest the Seymour gets her claws into him; the evenings I spend devising entertainments for him – and I am sure you are well aware how I spend my nights!"
"You are not yet with child?" George enquired.
"Most definitely not" she admitted sadly. "If only I could conceive again I could give up this useless course upon which I am set and retire until the birth

of my child".

Desperately wishing to cheer her up, George slipped an arm around her thin shoulders, pulled her to him and kissed her cheek affectionately. "If the King is as relentless as you say in his attempts to get an heir, surely it cannot be long before you again experience the delights of morning sickness!"

"I would welcome it" she told him frankly, trying to raise a smile at his little joke. Lifting her chin in a determined fashion, Anne noticed Jane, George's wife, standing a little aside from them, watching their exchange of affections jealously. The sight of her jogged Anne's memory. "I have been meaning to ask you something, George" she began on a low voice. "Have you noticed that whenever you and I are together, either your wife or one of her confidants are in close attendance?"

"Yes I had noted that" he admitted. "But I did not draw it to your attention for fear of worrying you".

"Why should it worry me? For God's sake George, we are brother and sister. What have we to hide? Apart from being family, you are one of the few people around me that I can trust!"

"I have a suspicion that my wife has become an active member of the Catholic party, hoping to discredit you with the King" George confided. "As you know, Jane Seymour is their bait".

"Henry does seem to have become enamoured of blonde hair, blue eyes and insipid colouring lately" Anne mused. "I am not sure if it because the Seymour is mousy or if he really has a penchant for the colour". She screwed up her face, trying to remember "Wasn't his mother yellow-haired? At any rate, it seems he is desperate for a change from black hair and eyes".

"Perhaps we should throw in our own bait" suggested her brother.

Immediately Anne was interested. "You mean find a blonde temptress from our own circle?"

"Why not? There is nothing to lose"

With her forefinger tapping her lips, Anne thought very hard. "It must be someone he hasn't seen much of before. Your wife is no good, he doesn't like her …"

"The King displays much good taste there" George interrupted with a grimace.

"We have a blonde cousin" Anne remembered. "Madge something… Shelton! Madge Shelton. But I have not seen her for years".

"Bring her to court anyway" suggested George. "If she is suitable, we can then find out if she is agreeable to our plan".

Within a few weeks Madge was at court under Anne's patronage, being surreptitiously schooled in the ways of tempting Kings. As soon as Anne saw her again, she knew the girl was eminently suitable. She had a look of Mary Boleyn, but was even fairer and more voluptuous.

Obviously before Anne could thrust her cousin under the King's nose, she had to be sure that the girl herself had no ambitions of queenship. It did not take long to discover that Madge was totally devoid of any ambition; again displaying similar traits to

Anne's sister Mary.

When Anne eventually confided to Madge the nature of her plan, the girl was shocked and protested that she did not desire the King for her lover.

"You have had a lover before?" Anne enquired sharply.

"One or two" Madge admitted cautiously. "But I have not really had a great deal of experience in such matters.

"All the better" said Anne with satisfaction. "For in many ways, at this stage of his life, the King feels unmanned by the attentions of hard, experienced women. You would be ideal for our little scheme Madge. Will you do it for me? For our family?"

She took a lot of persuading, but eventually Madge agreed with reluctance and Anne lost no time in bringing her to the King's attention. At first she was subtle, keeping the girl quietly by her side at all times so that the King could not fail to notice her.

He noticed her at once, which led Anne into the second phase of her plan. Madge was frequently sent to the King's chambers bearing private messages from the Queen. One night, Madge did not return from the King's rooms until well after midnight and was able to report triumphantly to Anne that Henry had well and truly taken the bait.

Anne was both delighted and relieved. The King thought he was indulging in a private love affair of which his wife knew nothing and would have been extremely shocked to know that she had engineered the whole scheme.

Despite spending a good deal of his private time with Madge, the King did not neglect his visits to the Queen, or stint in his efforts to get his heir. However it was a great source of worry to Anne that by the end of June 1535 she still had not conceived the King's child. Although it seemed, neither had Madge.

Preoccupied though she was with her own troubles and schemes, Anne had lately observed a distinct roundness to her sister Mary's body and suspected that she at least was proving fruitful. The question was, by whom was she pregnant? Mary had been a widow since the 1528 epidemic of sweating sickness had carried off William Carey.

Discreetly, Anne watched Mary for several weeks before she accused her to her face. When the sisters were briefly alone one afternoon, Anne asked slyly "Do you have something to tell me sister?"
Mary looked fearfully at her, confirming Anne's suspicions. "It is not the King's?" Anne continued sharply.
"Of course not!" Mary exclaimed in disgust. "You may have thought me promiscuous in sharing my bed with so many, Anne, but I am not so depraved as to wish to share the King's bed with my own sister!"
Anne was at once apologetic. "I am sorry Mary, but you must understand how I feel. I have been trying to conceive for months, and then you, without a husband, appear miraculously with child!"
"I have a husband" Mary said quietly, refusing to

meet Anne's incredulous gaze. "I married Sir William Stafford four months ago, secretly".

"Do you realise what you have done?" exclaimed Anne angrily. "You, the sister of the Queen of England to throw yourself away on a simple knight?"

"Why should I not?" Mary retorted, displaying a rare flash of temper. "For all our family's present lofty eminence, you and I were merely knight's daughters before the King noticed us. Anyway, which is the greater shame; marrying for love or bearing a fatherless child?"

Anne had to admit that Mary had perhaps done the right thing by her child in marrying its father, but her sister's fruitfulness did nothing to assuage her personal frustration at her own apparent inability to conceive.

However, apart from that, things were going reasonably well; Madge was continuing to divert the King's attention away from Jane Seymour, which gave Anne the opportunity to send her faithless maid of honour back to her family in Wiltshire. With Jane absent, the Catholic faction were quiet. Most importantly, the King continued to spend his nights in her bed and often during the day sought out her company as he declared that no other could provide such mental stimulation. It seemed that despite his other fancies, he could not do without his Anne Boleyn.

Chapter 30

Misery & Joy

However, whilst Anne was reasonably happy with her life, the King was not so pleased by his. He felt that he had lately endured more than his fair share of disappointments and was not prepared to admit to anybody that he was beginning to feel that he had been wrong in choosing Anne to be his Queen.

Henry the King was a man who always had to be right, and as a result of his turbulent life with Queen Anne, he began looking around for a scapegoat on whom to vent his spite.

Eventually his ex-Chancellor Sir Thomas More came to mind. Thomas More had been a great friend of both Catherine and himself, but had not supported the divorce. Being a quietly spoken, well-educated man, he had not railed against it like some, but had shown his disapproval by resigning his Chancellorship in May 1532.

Although the King had been angry with him at the

time, he had taken no action against his old friend and had allowed him to live quietly in retirement with his family at their riverside house in Chelsea.

Thomas More had also refused to sign the Oath of Supremacy recognising Henry as supreme head of the English church. As the King remembered More's gentle but firm refusal of his support in that matter, a fresh paroxysm of rage took hold of him. Henry had always been possessed of the childish desire that a person whom he loved and admired should also love and admire him. Thomas More had trespassed upon that unwritten rule; he had rejected his sovereign and now approached the time when he should pay for that betrayal, along with all those others who had equally thwarted their King.

Sir Thomas More, arguably the greatest Englishman of his time, was arrested, brought to trial and marched from his prison in the Tower to face the executioner on Tower Hill at 9 in the morning on 6th July 1535.

Henry and Anne, standing silently together at the great oriel window overlooking the river at Whitehall, heard the Tower guns booming the tragic news that More was dead.

As Anne stared through the window, in the direction from whence the firing came, she pressed her clasped hands to her chin as an involuntary shiver overtook her whole body. Was her fear some terrible portent of her future fate? Without turning her head, she threw a swift sidelong glance at her husband. Henry was breathing quickly through clenched teeth, his expression one of evil resentment.

Turning so suddenly that he caught her eyes upon him, he hissed "Perhaps now you are satisfied. The greatest man in my kingdom has died this day so that you may sleep peacefully in your bed of nights, safe from your enemies!" With that, he turned on his heel and stalked down the gallery. As he reached the top of the flight of stone steps, she heard him call out for his horse to be made ready.

Sighing with exasperation, Anne made slowly for her apartments, musing as she walked on how shallow the King's love had turned out to be. From the King's sweetheart to the King's encumbrance, she thought dejectedly.

On reaching her great presence chamber, she found it to be a scene of merriment. Her musicians and dearest friends appeared to be working on a new play amid much hilarity. Ever ready to throw out sadness in exchange for joy; for she did not care to ponder on her future, Anne cried "Greetings all. So my apartments are become rehearsal rooms?"

Henry Norris detached himself from a cluster of bodies and bowed low before her. "It is an extract from an old English legend" he explained. "A tale of a lovely maiden who is rescued from the very jaws of a fearsome dragon by a handsome, gallant knight. Your Grace shall have the star part!"
"And what would that be?" she laughed. "The dragon?"

"You jest, Madam" Norris replied, entering into the spirit of her banter and so far forgetting himself as to chuck her under the chin. "There is only one part fit for Your Grace".

The intimate tone of his soft voice delighted her and was balm to her wounded pride. It was in her very nature to wish to inspire love and admiration from the opposite sex; she needed to feel herself desired by many.

One of her musicians, a certain Mark Smeaton, had been avidly listening to the lively exchange of words. He was but a simple lad, low born but plucked from obscurity by Anne and the King who had heard his singing and playing whilst on a summer progress together. Mark was inordinately sensitive; his great love of music made him so. However there was also another great love in his life; Anne the Queen.

Seeing a chance to bring himself to her notice he broke in "Our good Norris forgets himself" he began, pausing as her bright eyes turned to his face. "He should have acquainted Your Grace with the fact that the maiden of the legend is the most beautiful and virtuous creature of her times, therefore she could be played by no other than yourself".

Anne was slightly taken aback by this passionate statement as she had never before realised quite how devoted the boy was to her. Looking into Mark's spaniel eyes which mutely begged that she give a sign to show that she approved of his words, Anne stretched out a tentative hand and patted him gently on the cheek. As she made to withdraw, he seized her hand and kissed it fervently. Although her impulse was to snatch her hand away, she did not wish to hurt his feelings or kill the slavish devotion which was so gratifying to her senses. Instead she said softly "Play, Mark. Let me hear the music to which I must perform".

At once Smeaton reluctantly released her hand and reached for his lute. The other musicians struck up on cue, and as the haunting melodies filled her chamber, Anne found herself transported back to the days of fire breathing dragons, giving her vivid imagination full rein.

As the last notes died away, Anne clapped her hands in delight. "Quite magical!" she declared. "Who wrote the music?"
"Myself and Master Smeaton" replied a well-known voice behind her.
Anne threw back her head and laughed joyously, then without turning around, flung her outstretched arm behind her. At once fingers grasped hers and he came into view. "Tom Wyatt" she murmured intimately. "I had no idea you had returned to court".
"I could not long stay away from Your Grace" he replied seriously.
Then there was silence; the two drank in the others every feature until Anne became uncomfortably aware that all eyes were regarding her and Wyatt with great interest. Reminding herself that she was wife to a jealous husband and that spies were everywhere, she released her hold on Wyatt's hand

and cried gaily "So, I am to be the gentle maiden, but who, pray, shall be my rescuer, and who is the dreaded dragon?"

At once a hubbub of excited voices rose about her. Raising her eyes to Wyatt's once again, she saw in his face that which she had been desperate to know still existed. Despite all that they had been through, both together and apart, he still loved her. With a start she realised that his continued affection meant more to her than anything in the world; even her desperation to bear the King a son paled into insignificance beside Wyatt's love.

Although she threw herself wholeheartedly into the preparations, she found her eyes continually searching him out so to allay any suspicions she made a concerted effort to mix with all present and not show favour to anyone in particular.

The play was rehearsed time and time again; indeed the idea was two weeks old before Anne decided that all the players were sufficiently accomplished to risk a public performance.

Finally, the evening before the court was due to leave London bound on its summer progress, the play was performed before a delighted assembly. Anne excelled as the maiden in distress and Francis Weston was totally evil as the dastardly dragon; whilst handsome William Brereton played Anne's saviour with great panache.

As the flushed and excited performers took their

bows before the appreciative audience, Anne was surprised to see that the King was applauding most enthusiastically of all. Lifting her head, Anne looked into his eyes, pouring all her mysterious sensuality into one intense expression. The King leered back at her, then holding her gaze, clapped harder than ever.

Anne was content. She felt that she had ensured his visit to her bed that night and hopefully she had inspired the sap in him to rise so strongly that at last their prince would be conceived.

Anne, sure in her own mind at least that she at last carried the heir, made a scintillating companion on the summer progress. Henry caught her abandoned mood and together they enjoyed some of the happiest times since their marriage.

It was at Wolf Hall in Wiltshire that Anne's merry mood rapidly evaporated for it was there that she found she had not in fact conceived as a result of Henry's enthusiastic attentions on the eve of the progress.

Her disappointment was so great that she found it impossible to hide and became sullen and argumentative. The King was thrown into an equally tetchy mood and felt himself rejected which prompted him to look around for some small diversion. Anne was aware that his eye might wander and remembered too late just in whose house they were lodged. Their host was Sir John Seymour and it was his daughter Jane who had been the subject of the last violent disagreement between the King and Queen.

At twenty five years of age, Jane Seymour was still unmarried, but behind her meek and mild countenance there lurked a shrewd and calculating brain. She had failed in her previous attempt to lure the King and made up her mind that she would not fail again.

Carefully she watched the Queen, quickly ascertained her moods, and then set out to be Anne's exact opposite. Anne, being mostly irritable and sour, allowed Jane the golden opportunity to be bright and sunny tempered, which she seized gratefully with both hands.

The King became so absorbed with the daughter of the house that when the time came to leave Wolf Hall, he commanded that Anne appoint Jane as a lady in waiting. 'Lady in waiting for what?' Anne asked herself, but feeling totally dejected and defeated, she could do nothing but accept the girl.

Once back at court the relentless wheels of fate rolled slowly on. History was seen to repeat itself as Jane, openly pursued by her lustful King, primly returned all of Henry's gifts of money and jewels, solemnly declaring that no man could buy her virtue.

Each day, Anne dragged herself from her bed and steeled herself to face yet another day of the Seymour's relentless competition. Was this how

Catherine had felt as she had been ousted from the King's affections by Anne herself? The only small consolation was that the King rigorously continued with his regular nightly visits to her, so not all hope was lost.

Day followed miserable day; making a supreme effort to be bright and charming towards a man she had grown to hate, and who certainly no longer loved her, was totally alien to Anne's nature, but somehow she achieved it. Nights were even worse, pretending a passion she did not feel. Then a morning dawned when she was too ill to leave her bed, her head swimming every time she tried to stand. It was late afternoon before she felt able to rise and even then she felt uncharacteristically sluggish and nauseated.

Although hardly daring to hope that her object might at last have been achieved, she was obedient to her body's promptings. She stayed in her bed for the best part of three weeks, keeping Jane Seymour especially close and occupied, only finally emerging after a successful consultation with her physician. The prince was on his way at last.

Still feeling very weak from her extended bed rest, Anne made her way unsteadily through her outer chambers, intending to find the King and inform him of the happy news. But at the door of an ante chamber she stopped dead in her tracks, blinking in disbelief.

Oblivious to any passers-by, Henry was blatantly

caressing and kissing Jane Seymour, whilst she, brazen hussy, sat unashamedly on his lap with her bodice in disarray and her arms around his neck.

"So this is how you spend your time whilst I am sick!" Anne cried.

At the sound of her voice, the guilty parties leapt apart and Henry rose to his feet. Walking past him to the cowering Jane, Anne hissed "You were always the one to make the most of your opportunities were you not? Even the last time you were here you did your best to come between the King and me. And now, the minute you escape your duties in my sickroom, here you are again, whispering and pouting in private whilst primly flaunting your chastity in public!"

Anne stepped back and surveyed them both triumphantly. "Well I am afraid your hand is played out Mistress Seymour" she crowed. "I have outwitted you yet again for in seven months' time I shall give birth to the King's son!"

Chapter 31

Failure

On 9th January 1536 a message reached the court that at last sad, obstinate Catherine of Aragon had released her hold upon life.

Henry shed a few crocodile tears, stating to all who would listen that she had been a good woman, and then ordered new yellow garments for himself and Anne. For yellow was the colour of Spanish mourning, he twinkled, carefully omitting the fact that in England yellow was the colour of gladness.

When Anne was brought the news, she cried loudly "At last I am free; the only true Queen in England no matter what my enemies may say!" Then turning to Margaret Lee, who of all her ladies was never far from her side, remarked "But although this should be one of the happiest days of my life, I cannot truly rejoice. Catherine's death only makes my private position all the more perilous!"

Margaret was close. "How so, Anne?" she

questioned. "You cannot deny that you have prayed for her death these many years".

"Yes Meg, but think! You know how relations between me and the King have been slowly worsening since the birth of Elizabeth. And then, after I lost his six months son he told me he would give me one more chance to produce a prince. If I was to fail again, he swore that it would be the worse for me!"

Margaret's face registered shocked surprise. "He said that to you? A woman who had recently suffered so cruelly in fruitless childbirth? How could he be so callous?"

"He has many facets to his character, Meg" Anne murmured. "Sometimes he is cruel and coarse; at other times the most kind, gentle and cultured man a woman could wish for. The trouble is, I never know which man I will get; he is never the same for two days in succession".

"And you yourself are so changeable" Margaret observed.

"Precisely" Anne agreed. "We are similar in that respect but sadly our good moods never seem to coincide these days as they did in times past".

"Then you are afraid he wishes to be rid of you?"

"I am sure of it" Anne replied. "And now Catherine is dead he can put me aside with a clear conscience should he so wish. Whilst Catherine lived I was safe, for if he wished to divorce me he would have been forced to take her back. I have terrible dreams and visions when I am alone at night! I am sure some terrible fate will befall me if I do not carry this son to term!"

Margaret could see by the tell-tale high colour of Anne's usually pale complexion, and by the way that her expressive black eyes protruded slightly, that she was close to another bout of hysteria. Such outbursts had occurred all too often since Anne became Queen, Margaret remembered. It was imperative to distract her from such destructive thoughts, but to tell her to calm herself and think of the child would be to topple her over the edge of her reason.

Walking briskly to the chamber window, Margaret observed brightly "The gardens are looking charming; it is inordinately warm for early January and a walk would do us all some good".

Anne mutely nodded her assent so Margaret quickly called other ladies to assist her in dressing the Queen warmly for a short stroll.

It was indeed a most pleasant walk and Anne and her ladies returned from the palace gardens with glowing cheeks and frost tinged veils. The weather was really not particularly warm; Margaret had made that comment purely to lure Anne away from her misery. It had worked though; the inconsequential chatter of her younger maids had amused Anne, who kept her eyes averted as much as possible from the figure of Jane Seymour walking quietly at her left side.

Whilst the weather remained kind, with just a nip of frost in the air, Anne insisted on a daily walk for her health. And it was walking thus in the gardens towards the end of January that Anne received the calamitous news which wrecked all her hopes.

The King had organised a joust, promising to take on all-comers whether they be courtiers or commoners. Anne, in an uncharacteristic expression of wifely concern, had warned him to be careful in the slippery conditions. He had promised to take the utmost care, kissing her heartily on the lips as he prepared to leave for the tilt yard. "You too must take care" he told her solicitously. "For you are shortly to become the mother of my prince and together you will be the jewels of my kingdom!"

Anne had nodded her head ruefully as he had left her. 'The jewels of the kingdom' she muttered, more to herself than any, laying her hand on the bulge of her four months child. 'Certainly the boy will be of far more import to the King than the mother who bears him'. Then sighing gently she had summoned her ladies and prepared for her daily stroll.

It was strolling thus some time later that she heard a great tramp of feet approaching from behind. Half expecting it to be guards come to arrest her, she spun round awkwardly, but smiled with relief to see it was merely the Dukes of Norfolk and Suffolk accompanied by her father and lesser minions.

However her smile of relief faded as she read their serious expressions. "What is it!" she cried in alarm. "What has happened? Not the King?"
"He had had a serious accident" Norfolk burst out, never the most tactful of men and careless of the shock it would cause to her in her delicate condition.

Both hands clasped to her mouth, Anne said nothing, watching his face fearfully. "We fear he may be dead" Norfolk continued lamely, "or at least even if he has survived the fall, it is possible that he will not regain consciousness. The accident came about when …"

Anne heard no more. Visions of a future without the protection of the King assailed her. She would be alone and hunted; hated as she was by her enemies within the court and the common people. Her child would never be born for surely the pair of them would be murdered before she had a chance to give birth. The grey landscape in front of Anne's eyes turned rose pink, then darkened to an inky blue. She had a vague awareness of the pathway tilting up to meet her before she hit the ground with a sickening thud.

When she regained her senses she was lying on her bed with her ladies fluttering anxiously around her. Despite her very public resentment at being merely the King's brood mare, her thoughts flew immediately to her unborn child. She searched the faces around her, moving from one to another until she found Doctor Butts, then weakly motioned him closer. "Doctor Butts" she murmured. "Is the child safe?"

It was with great relief that she heard him say "Your Grace has had a severe shock but happily it does not seem to have affected the royal infant".

"Thank God!" she sighed, relaxing into her pillows. Then suddenly she remembered the reason for her faint. "The King! What of the King?" she cried in alarm.

Her physician gritted his teeth. He had very much hoped that she would not ask about the King; he had hastened to give her a potion to make her drowsy and muddle her thoughts the moment her consciousness began to return, hopeful that she would remain docile and calm. However, she was the Queen and if she demanded to know the condition of her husband, he had no choice but to tell her. "He has not yet regained consciousness, Your Grace" he told her gravely.

With a swiftness which belied her drugged state, Anne swung her legs to the floor and attempted to stand. However in her haste she had mistaken the footstool beside the bed for the firm floor and as she applied her weight to its edge, the stool catapulted away, causing her to fall heavily to the floor. Again she lost consciousness.

When she awoke for the second time, there was no need for her to ask about her child. She knew by the ominous pains gripping her body that the shock of Henry's accident coupled with two heavy falls in consecutive hours heralded the onset of her labours and sure death for her prince.

So tiny was the infant that she barely felt it pass from her body, although she knew from the whispering voices and hands about her that the moment had come. Jane Seymour's foxy little face swam into Anne's vision. "A little boy, Your Grace" she said harshly, making no attempt to mask her triumph. As Anne's loyal ladies removed Jane forcibly from the chamber, she called back over her shoulder "Yet another dead boy!"

Anne pulled herself up the bed with difficulty. Looking towards her kind Doctor Butts she cried "No! Please tell me it was not a son! Please say it was a girl!"

Coming swiftly to her bedside Doctor Butts awkwardly begged her to calm herself. Distraught and hysterical she clutched at his robe, drawing herself close to his face. "Tell me it was a girl!" she pleaded. "That is why I have come to this. It was a girl, was it not?"

His face grimly set, Doctor Butts cleared his throat then gently prised her fingers from his clothing and eased her back on to her pillows. "It was difficult to tell" he admitted slowly. "The child was not … whole".

She stared at him, horror-struck, then whispered "You mean it was deformed?"

"No, no" he soothed. "I believe the infant may have been dead for some little while, long before you fell. It seems that your body had been in the process of breaking it up prior to expulsion".

She could well imagine it and grimaced delicately, huge tears rolling soundlessly from her eyes. "So you could not tell its sex?" she asked in a faint voice.

"It is difficult to be sure" he admitted. "But the evidence does point to the child having been male".

Anne could take no more; she closed her eyes, turned her face into her pillow and gave herself up to the bitterest grief she had ever experienced. She was in her twenty ninth year and past her prime. Even if Henry was disposed towards giving her another chance, her childbearing history looked like following a course distressingly similar to Catherine's before her.

A gentle hand was lifting her head, wiping away her tears and replacing her tear sodden pillow with fresh linen. Anne opened her eyes expecting to see a member of her family or Meg but instead fastened upon the smiling face of Jane Seymour. "I have conveyed the news of Your Grace's unfortunate occurrence to the King" she whispered, viper like. "You will be delighted to hear that he appears to be recovering, for his accident was not as serious as first thought. He was not … very amused, shall we say, to hear that you had cheated him of his son yet again".

With strength she did not know she could possible muster, Anne lifted her hand and slapped the Seymour's long nosed face as hard as she could. With some sort of savage pride she surveyed the wheals her rings had made on the soft white cheek, then raising herself on her elbow, screamed "Get that slut out of my sight! Away, I say, before I squeeze the breath from her sly little body with my own bare hands!"

Days later the King hobbled painfully across the threshold of her bedchamber, his leg heavily bandaged and the pain of his injury written across his face.

Anne, who was fast recovering, glanced fearfully up at him, waving her women away from the bedside. "I was so worried for Your Grace… " she began humbly. Henry silenced her with an irritable wave of his stick, which caused him to place his full, not inconsiderable weight upon his bad leg.

He swore horribly, then limped to within inches of her. "You have killed yet another boy, I hear!" he snarled, displaying broken yellow teeth, his stale breath fanning her face. "I told you to take care, but you insisted on rambling around slippery paths in wintry weather!"

"It was not my walking which brought me to this" she protested. "My concern for your safety prompted both my falls and the cruel way in which my uncle of Norfolk broke the news of your accident helped my condition not at all!"

He regarded her silently for some moments before speaking in a voice thick with contempt. "It becomes increasingly obvious to me that any boy I give you will be killed long before his time by your shrewish ways and violent tempers. You have squandered your last chance Madam; you will get no more boys by me!"

Before she had time to protest further, he was clumping his way towards the door. As it opened to allow him out, Anne caught sight of Jane Seymour waiting for him in the chamber beyond. With a muffled oath which would have done credit to the roughest commoner, Anne picked up a precious crystal goblet and hurled it with all her strength at the closing door. As the jamb met the door frame, the goblet hit the carved panels and smashed into a thousand tiny pieces. "Shattered! Even as my life" Anne murmured bitterly.

Chapter 32

Impending Doom

The obviously serious rift between the King and Queen had not gone unnoticed by the powers that be at court.

Master secretary Cromwell, ever seeking ways to ingratiate himself still further into Henry's royal favour, one day conceived a plan which he believed would promote his own interests beyond his wildest dreams.

Henry Tudor was seated at his work table whilst Cromwell stood beside him, slipping various papers in turn in front of the King for the royal signature. Henry trusted his master secretary implicitly, so only gave each document a cursory glance before appending his signature, handing the paper to a clerk for sanding and looking for the next.

When at last state matters were done, Cromwell took the documents from the clerk and sent the boy away. Flipping absently through the folio, Cromwell observed slyly "It seems Your Grace's mind wanders from state matters this day".

Henry swung round angrily to face him. "You are implying that your monarch becomes senile?"

"No, Your Grace" interjected Cromwell hastily. "I only feel concern that Your Grace appears to have problems which far outweigh the monotony of autographing state papers".

"Your intuition is correct" replied a glum monarch. "It is a personal problem which afflicts my heart and my conscience". He paused, momentarily reluctant to voice his thoughts to another then continued. "I feel that my marriage to the Queen has broken down and that for the sake of my realm I should marry a younger woman who can give me children".

"Divorce?" suggested Cromwell glibly.

Henry shook his head emphatically. "My people would never condone another divorce so soon after the first. No, divorce alone will not do". He rested his elbows on the table before him musing "If only the Queen's conduct were suspect…"

Cromwell suppressed the crafty expression which crept across his face before breaking in. "Supposing I could prove such?"

Henry's mouth dropped open in surprise as he met Cromwell's unreadable gaze. "You have information which could make us doubt the integrity of our Queen?" he roared.

Cromwell inclined his head slightly, searching for the words with which to construct his answer. After a pause, he said slowly "I could perhaps provide written testimonies proving that Her Grace has been somewhat indiscreet".

Henry stood up suddenly, his chair tumbling backwards. "Tittle tattle and bedchamber gossip will not do" he warned.

Cromwell waved his hand dismissively. "I am a lawyer Your Grace; you can trust me to sift the fact from the gossip".

Henry moved towards the great fireplace, hands rubbing his face thoughtfully. Suddenly he stopped and wheeled round. "Such matters must be thoroughly looked into, Master Cromwell. See to it!"

Thomas Cromwell had been about the King long enough to know that such words signified that he should leave the royal presence at once and set about gathering his information; but he could not resist one final parting shot "Mistress Seymour would make Your Grace a meek and loving Queen" he said silkily, as he bowed himself out.

Henry, by now back in front of his work table, set his jaw consideringly, then thumped his fist hard upon the table top, scattering quills and ink. "By God she would!" he roared approvingly.

Since her miscarriage Anne had been shunned openly by the King and his immediate circle. Her sense of impending doom had been in no way alleviated when information had been brought to her that at the very same time she had lain in premature childbed, Catherine of Aragon had been interred in Peterborough Abbey.

The only members of the court who visited her in her disgrace were her own family and long standing close friends. Looking about her vast chambers, peopled by only a few dozen whereas months before there had scarcely been room to stand, Anne could not help but observe that in her adversity she had at least learned the identities of her true friends and supporters.

"You must force your way back into the King's affections!" urged her brother George. "After all those years waiting in the wings, you cannot resign centre stage without protest!"

"He no longer desires me" Anne replied frankly. "My brief enchantment soon lost its significance once I had miscarried a brace of boys".

"You have indeed flown too close to the flame" muttered George, alluding to a conversation they had shared many years before.

"And scorched my wings beyond repair" Anne agreed sadly. "There is no way I can lure him back now, George. I have lost the power to bewitch him; he knows all my ways too well".

"You still have power over some of us though!" interrupted Henry Norris gallantly. "For all of us present today, you are the light of our lives! See how we dodge our duties to our sovereign lord in order to dance attendance upon Your Grace!"

Desperate to know herself to be loved and desired still, Anne was all too ready to respond. Looking about herself, she laughed lightly. "I must admit that the majority of my adherents are male" she observed, curving her mouth into that mysterious smile which had captivated Kings on both sides of the channel. "Come Norris, Wyatt … all of you. We shall dance away the tediousness of this sheltered existence". She signalled to her musicians to strike up a merry tune, and then abandoned herself to the arms of first Henry Norris, then her brother and finally Thomas Wyatt.

At last she stood, breathless and laughing, within the circle of her admirers. "Goodness!" she gasped. "You gentlemen dance with such energy and ardour that it seems that you quite forget that I am your Queen!"
Believing them to be amongst friends, William Brereton broke in "And surely if you were not our Queen, we would all be suitors for your hand!"

Anne smiled delightedly before her face assumed a serious expression. Looking towards Brereton she said softly. "If that be so, then maybe it is better for you gentlemen not to speak of that which is in your hearts. You and I know such words to be merely courtly jest; however the King's spies may twist it to something other than that".

Their faces stared back at her in amazement. "You think yourself spied on, Nan?" asked Wyatt incredulously, betraying the special feelings between them by using her pet name publicly and without rebuke.
Curling her finger, she motioned them all closer. "I am sure of it" she confirmed. "Although I feel sure that there cannot be any spies amongst today's gathering".

Mark Smeaton had left his place amongst the musicians and unnoticed by any, had crept closer to her. Suddenly, his boyish passions so aroused that he could bear no more, he forced his way through the little circle of her friends and dropped on his knees before her, "They have no evidence against you Madam!" he cried. "And even if they could concoct any, I for one would gladly die for you!" With that, he reverently kissed the hem of her gown.

Anne looked thoughtfully down at his bent head, then leaned forward and lightly caressed his crisp dark curls. "I pray to God that you will not be called upon to do any such thing" she whispered gravely.

Whilst Anne's attention was diverted, Jane Rochford slipped quietly from the chamber, a spiteful smile about her lips. She had done her job well, she decided. Master Cromwell would be most interested to learn of the conversation that afternoon in the Queen's privy chambers.

Cromwell was indeed interested; he listened solemnly to Lady Rochford's account then sent her away with a generous monetary reward. As the door closed behind her, Cromwell rose from his desk and pulled aside a curtain behind it to reveal a recess, wherein sat a clerk scribbling swiftly upon a large sheet of parchment. "You recorded the Lady's statement?" Cromwell asked shortly.
"Indeed Sir" replied the clerk, sitting back in his chair and regarding the document before him with satisfaction. "Every word the Lady Jane uttered has been recorded and suitably embellished as per your

instructions".

Cromwell's tense features dissolved into a smile. "Let me have a copy as soon as possible. Then, issue an invitation to Master Mark Smeaton to dine here with me tomorrow evening".

Without waiting for his menial's reply, Cromwell allowed the curtain to swing back and returned to his desk. At last I have found the weak link in the chain, he thought to himself with satisfaction. Humble Mark Smeaton would be easy to break, especially if he had not the wit to suspect an ulterior motive behind the magnanimous dinner invitation!

And so it was that the dinner for which Mark set out with high hopes and dressed in his finest clothes, turned into a tortuous nightmare. Once the boy was seated at his table, Cromwell signed to two ruffians who tightened a knotted rope about Mark's head until he half fainted away in agony, whilst Cromwell barked a series of unthinkable questions at the terrified youth.

Poor Mark had neither the will nor the depth of character to bear such torture with fortitude and soon Cromwell was in possession of the desired confession. Under cover of darkness, Smeaton was transferred, broken and bleeding, to the Tower of London, from whence he could only expect to finally emerge to die the traitor's death. Smeaton had confessed himself guilty of high treason; he had stated that on no less than seven occasions he had committed adultery with Anne, Queen of England; moreover, he had also been persuaded to implicate four others from her circle.

On 30th April, Cromwell placed written evidence of the Queen's indiscretions before his King. The document included the names of five men with whom Anne had apparently both slept and plotted together with times, dates and the places where the offences were committed. Also included were the results of Jane Rochford's spying and Mark Smeaton's personal confession.

"You believe all this to be true?" Henry tapped the document with his finger as he spoke.
"It is all there in black and white Your Grace" Cromwell replied smoothly. "It seems that the Queen was prepared to go to any lengths to secure an heir for England; even to foist a bastard on the throne".
Henry looked suitably aghast at such a suggestion, then his thoughts flew to the one child she had borne him, Elizabeth.
He voiced his thoughts "What of Elizabeth?"
"There is no doubt that she is Your Grace's true daughter" Cromwell soothed. "If Your Grace will quickly read through the dates of the Queen's offences, it can be seen that the first of these acts only took place after the child's birth".
Henry was still not convinced. "These dates are only based on the information that your people were able to uncover. What if she slept with another man at about the same time as she became my mistress? She may have cleverly covered her tracks".
"Possibly…" Cromwell admitted dubiously. "But I believe Your Grace need not trouble yourself over the paternity of the Princess; remember that the

majority of the testimonies come from Lady Rochford, wife of George Boleyn. She was a member of the Queen's circle long before Your Grace's marriage".

Henry pondered. "We are relieved to hear it" he said at last. "For despite the fact that the Queen's only living child is but a girl, Elizabeth is a bright and gifted child and we are proud to be her sire".

Gathering up the papers, Henry paced uneasily about the chamber, his eyes scanning the incriminating evidence. "This testimony naming Norris as one of her lovers" he indicated the place on the document. "I cannot believe that of him!"

Cromwell sighed deeply but silently; he had been expecting such a reaction. "Your Grace, Smeaton himself implicated the gentleman".

"But Norris is always in or near my bedchamber" protested the King. "As a gentleman of my privy chamber he is always in close attendance and I for one cannot remember a single occasion when a long absence was noticed". He dropped his eyes again to the document. "Brereton though, I can well believe it of him. Weston too; I have often seen him leering in the Queen's direction". Henry paused and looked piercingly at Cromwell. "Smeaton surprises me though; he is very young and untidy and the Queen has always been so fastidious".

"There is also the question of the Queen's relations with her own brother" Cromwell reminded him gently.

"Incest is an ugly word and a heinous crime" Henry conceded distastefully. He lowered the document and fixed Cromwell with a baleful gaze. "I shall expect such an allegation to be fully proved, Cromwell".

Cromwell inclined his head in a gesture of assent. "In order that these accusations can be made clear in Your Grace's own mind, may I suggest that Your Grace closely observe the behaviour of the Queen and her lovers at tomorrow's May Day joust?"

Henry considered for a moment. "A good idea, Cromwell; a most excellent suggestion. I shall watch all concerned with the utmost diligence".

Chapter 33

May Day

The brightly coloured bunting fluttered gaily in the gentle breeze; the cornflower blue sky and slight chill in the air proclaiming a typical English spring day.

Anne had dressed most carefully for this her first public appearance with the King since her miscarriage; indeed had paid such minute attention to every detail that as she approached the royal dais with her ladies, could see that she was late in arriving as the King had already taken his seat.

Once in front of the dais she performed the required obeisance to her monarch then gracefully climbed the three steps to her own chair, placed alongside his. All through this little ritual it had not gone unnoticed by Anne that the King had never once looked directly at her. It was only as she took her seat that she sensed his eyes upon her and only by looking up quickly did she meet his suspicious gaze before he averted his eyes.

So he sulks still, thought Anne to herself, as with pursed lips she arranged her skirts. Then, as a little of her natural rebelliousness surfaced, she decided that if he did not want to speak to her, she would also remain silent.

Out of the corner of his eye, Henry regarded the woman for whom he had turned his realm upside down. Anxious to condemn her in his own mind, he mistook her calm demeanour as efforts to mask her guilt. With rising anger he watched her acknowledge the combatants in the celebration joust as they filed in front of the dais; he saw her raise her hand in greeting to her brother and watched her mouth curve into a generous smile as her eyes rested upon Weston, Brereton and Norris.

Once the joust was ready to begin, Henry got to his feet and gave the signal which sent the opening pair thundering down the lists towards each other, then sat down heavily in his chair.

Perceptively sensing the King's tension Anne looked at him fearfully, her hard-won composure stretched to breaking point. He was wearing, she noted, a similar expression to that he had assumed when facing Catherine across the court at Greyfriars; an expression of open dislike coupled with resentment and intense anger.

Biting her lip, Anne once more turned her attention towards the joust, although she could not but fear that at last he was planning to take his revenge upon her for not only thwarting his ambitions for a son, but also for holding out against him in the first place and wasting so many years.

Eventually the joust culminated in a thrilling battle between Sir Henry Norris and a lesser gentleman of the court, a battle from which Norris emerged the victor. As he approached the dais to claim his prize, Anne rose to her feet, applauding enthusiastically. Henry Norris bowed three times before finally standing in front of his sovereigns and removing his helm.

Deprived of the stimulating conversation and interaction which she usually shared with the King, Anne, on seeing the knight's face drenched with perspiration, playfully threw him her handkerchief. Gallantly Norris made the courtly gesture of wiping his brow with the scrap of silk before handing it back to her. At the very same moment as their eyes met and their hands touched, the King stood up abruptly, scraping his chair noisily across the boards. Then he turned on his heel and strode off in the direction of the palace without a backward glance. Anne had not been quick enough to see the King's expression, but she knew by the set of his shoulders as he walked away and by the ugly purple patches on the back of his neck that he was in a high temper over something.

Shaking her head in disbelief, she met Norris's concerned gaze before shrugging her shoulders in a gesture displaying utter incredulity and confusion.

With the King gone, the celebrations immediately

ceased. Anne and her ladies made tracks towards the palace whilst those of the King's gentlemen who had completed their rides hurried to get changed in order that they might rejoin their monarch.

Anne had barely arrived in her apartments before she heard a great clatter of hooves in the courtyard below. Moving quickly to the window and looking down, she saw the King and a small party making off towards London. For the very first time in her brief marriage, Henry had left her behind.

Mystified by the events of the day, Anne called for her musicians to play for her. "Perhaps the King is upset because since his accident he can no longer ride in the lists" suggested Margaret Lee as she settled on a cushion at her mistress's feet. But Anne had not heard; she was looking about her. "Where is Smeaton?" she demanded. "I did not raise him from choirboy to personal musician only for him to be absent when needed".

There was an uncomfortable silence. "He was last seen yesterday evening when he set out to dine with my lord Cromwell …" began one of the musicians awkwardly. "It seems he never returned from this engagement for when he was not present at last night's music rehearsal, I sent a page for him…"

"And?" Anne prompted.

"The boy returned much later and informed me that Smeaton was not in the palace".

In a flash, all the puzzle pieces fell into place. The many occasions upon which Smeaton had shown his devotion to her in public; Henry's reaction when she had smiled at Norris during the joust; Cromwell's smugness of the last few days; even the reason for Jane Rochford's air of sly triumph. All was revealed to her in that moment. Anne gasped "Oh dear Lord!" and covered her face with her hands.

Showing the presence of mind that had so endeared her to Anne over the years, Margaret Lee instantly dismissed the onlookers and led her Queen firmly to the seclusion of her bedchamber.

Raising fearful eyes to Margaret's, Anne blurted "He means to get rid of me, Meg. He wants me imprisoned for the rest of my life on some trumped up charge so that he can marry that Seymour slut!"

"And bastardise Elizabeth" Margaret reminded her gently.

Anne's expression of fear turned to one of sheer horror "My baby" she moaned, then steeling herself declared firmly "My position as Queen means nothing to me but I shall fight every inch of the way for my daughter!"

Leaping to her feet Anne paced agitatedly around the small room. "So this is how poor Catherine felt" she said at last. "Now I am a mother I can understand so well why Catherine refused to stand down. She devoted the rest if her life to fighting for her daughter's rights and I shall do the same for Elizabeth".

"Sit down Nan" Margaret soothed. "You are jumping at shadows; it will never come to that".

"But it will!" Anne gripped Margaret's shoulders urgently. "It will, Meg". Then naturally having no idea that she was virtually repeating her royal

husband's words of a few days earlier, went on "He will not dare divorce me, not so soon after the matter with Catherine. It will have to be something more".
"Pre-contract?" suggested Margaret hopefully.
Anne waved her hand in dismissal of that idea. "Too simple, Meg. He hates me now. He is desperate to take his revenge on me for stringing him along for all those years. It will be something more serious than a paltry pre-contract. Treason perhaps, or maybe even adultery!"
"Adultery!" exclaimed Margaret fearfully. "Do you think that is why they have taken Smeaton?"
Anne laughed scornfully. "Adultery with him?" she scoffed. "I would need to have taken leave of my senses before I would stoop to bedding with him!"

Margaret made for the door. "Tom is here in the palace" she said. "I shall ask him to ride to London and see if he can find out what is happening".
"Oh yes" Anne breathed in relief. "Bid him go at once Meg. Not knowing is driving me half mad".
After a fearful glance at Anne's face, Margaret needed no second bidding and not many minutes passed before a cloaked figure galloped away from the palace. However Anne was surprised when Margaret did not return to her at once, although grateful in a way for the rare opportunity of being completely alone. It was nearly three hours later when the door opened at last to admit Margaret.

"You have been an age, Meg" Anne complained, patting the edge of the bed beside her, inviting her friend to sit down.
"I had to go myself" gasped Margaret, evidently

short of breath. "The King is at Westminster".
"But why did Tom not go?"
"He was taken to the Tower yesterday".
Anne sprang to her feet in alarm. "On what charge? Surely he is not implicated in this ghastly affair?"
Margaret shook her head decisively. "It seems not, praise God. He is imprisoned in comfortable quarters on a trivial charge – something to do with the management of his estates, I believe".

Anne breathed an audible sigh of relief then hugged the pensive Meg, who despite her brave words was obviously concerned for her brother's safety. "It may be as well that Tom is safely out of the way, Meg" Anne said softly. At Meg's questioning face, she continued. "If the King is looking for someone to accuse of adultery with me, Tom would be the obvious choice for it is no secret that we grew up together and have always been close".
Realisation was dawning on Margaret's face. "You mean, out of sight …"
"Out of mind" Anne finished for her. "But also the King loves him and would surely never harm him". If both women also thought of Thomas More, whom the King had also dearly loved but still executed, neither voiced their thoughts.
"Did you find out anything else?" Anne asked anxiously.
Margaret sighed and evaded Anne's eyes before answering shortly "Yes". She went on, wishing she could spare Anne the agony. "Smeaton is in the Tower and so are Will Brereton, Francis Weston and Hal Norris …"
"He is trying for the adultery clause then" hooted

Anne triumphantly. "Well, he hasn't a leg to stand on; there is no evidence!"

"George is also taken" Margaret murmured, then before her horrified friend could speak, went on. "And whilst at Westminster I heard one of Cromwell's men say that Jane Rochford's evidence is proving invaluable".

Instead of the outburst Margaret expected, Anne merely sat down heavily on the bed musing "Ah yes, dear Jane. It is her golden opportunity to get back at me for all the wrongs she imagines I have done to her. It seems my life is cursed with Janes – first Seymour, now Rochford!"

Both women passed an uneasy night, each locked in their own thoughts and saying little. Anne refused to go to bed.

When at last another beautiful day dawned, Meg helped Anne to change her crumpled gown before the two women emerged into the Queen's presence chamber. It was completely, utterly deserted. If Anne had been trying to persuade herself that nothing was really wrong then here was the unpalatable truth that something was most definitely amiss, for even since her January miscarriage there had been some hangers on.

Anne paced up and down before the windows overlooking the courtyard whilst Margaret sent for bread, beef and ale so that they could both break their fast. "But I'm really not hungry, Meg" Anne protested, as she was steered towards the laden side table.

"Rubbish!" scoffed her friend, for a moment quite forgetting that she was not just talking to stubborn Anne Boleyn but to the Queen of England. "You have not eaten for hours".

"You must join me then" Anne ordered.

Margaret, who had by now remembered her station, looked shocked at the suggestion. "I cannot eat at the same table as a Queen ..." she began.

"I may not be Queen for much longer" Anne reminded her gently. "This may be the last meal we ever share together in such sumptuous surroundings". She gestured around the room as she spoke. "Just to please me, Meg".

Blinking away tears, Margaret obediently sat down.

Their stomachs satisfied, Anne pushed her plate away and rested her elbows on the table. "I am the last piece of the puzzle" she mused, pushing a few stray breadcrumbs across the table with her fingernail. "Sooner or later they will come and take me too".

There was not long to wait. High above the palace courtyard the great clock struck eleven and as the last chimes died away, Anne's chamber door was unceremoniously flung open to admit the entire privy council with Cromwell and the Duke of Norfolk at the head of the throng.

Without any of the usual or expected niceties, Norfolk walked straight up to Anne and shook her hard by the shoulders. "Bring the Howard name into disrepute, would you?" he snarled.

Angrily Anne shook herself free. "Kindly keep your paws off me!" she stormed. "And as for your accusation, I have done nothing to bring any name dishonour; for any degradation of the Howard name, I suggest you look around your own house before you barge into mine!" Head held high, she faced her accusers.

Ignoring her thinly veiled poke at the well-publicised behaviour of his son and heir, Norfolk fixed her with his most baleful glare. "Then why is it", he sneered, "that we are here on the King's express orders to convey you under heavy guard to the Tower of London?"

Anne stared back at him, speechless, unwelcome tears springing into her eyes. So it had come at last; that which she had been dreading for weeks had finally come to pass. Horrified though she was, there was almost some relief in being finally able to confront her fears.

"You are under arrest, niece" Norfolk said, with such vitriolic emphasis that his spittle hit her cheek.

"I wish to speak with the King" Anne replied haughtily, refusing to meet Norfolk's gaze. "You have no right to treat your Queen in this manner!"

Cromwell stepped forward, his manner humble as always. "I regret that it is quite impossible for Your Grace to speak with the King" he began. "The charges which have been brought against you constitute high treason and as you know Madam, no person accused of such a serious crime may be admitted into the sovereign's presence until proved innocent. Therefore I must ask you Madam, to make ready to leave for the Tower on the afternoon tide".

Chapter 34

Trial by Peers

As she rode in a swift moving barge down the river Thames towards the Tower, surrounded by six burly men at arms, Anne knew that she may well be experiencing her final ride as Queen.

A country girl, although admittedly well-born; her whole nature cried out against the thought of imprisonment. Her conscience was clear; she knew she was totally innocent of the charges brought against her and she had every confidence that the court she would have to face would find for her cause in the end.

However, who but the most sainted could suppress a shudder of fear as they approached the grim portals of that which had become known as traitor's gate, beneath St Thomas's tower? Whatever she was, Anne was no saint.

With sinister creaks, the great oaken and iron gates swung wide to admit its latest victim to the moat. As her barge glided silently through, Anne looked over her shoulder, beyond the gates, out on to the sunlit stretch of river down which she had travelled so many times as Henry's petted sweetheart. By straining her eyes she thought she could see the ordinary people going about their business on the far side of the bank, unaware that at that moment their Queen was landing at the Tower; not in state but as a traitor.

With groans and judders, the mighty gates, their spiked iron bars dripping with slimy river weed, shut firmly behind her. Reluctantly she dragged her thoughts away from freedom and back to her unenviable predicament; she would need all her wits and courage to see her through whatever lay ahead.

Her barge was moored to a rusty iron ring protruding from the outer wall of the flight of steps up which she was expected to walk to be taken into custody by the Lieutenant of the Tower, Sir William Kingston. He stood, along with yet more guards, at the top of the steps looking down on her.

There was nothing else to do then; carefully she stood up, taking care not to rock the narrow vessel, and then stepped daintily on to the first of the landing steps, holding her skirts above the lapping waters of the oncoming tide. She looked so disdainfully upon the helping hand proffered by Kingston that he withdrew it hastily and allowed her to proceed alone.

Momentarily Anne paused on the top step, looking

down at the dark waters of the moat and at her barge and the pitying face of her regular boatman. Would it be better to jump into the water and drown now, she wondered. Then she reasoned that such action would be construed as an admission of guilt and that would never do. Besides which they would surely fish her out before she had a chance to drown with dignity.

Gathering her skirts and her determination, she stepped up on to the stone walkway and stood almost eye to eye with Kingston; she was tall for a woman and he only of an average height which belied his powerful position.

He made a peremptory bow. "Please follow me Madam" he said stiffly.

"Kingston .." she extended her hand and gripped his sleeve as he made to move away. Surprised, he stopped.

"Madam?"

"Do I go to a dungeon?" she asked, her voice betraying her inner panic.

Kingston allowed himself a half smile. "Indeed not. You are to be confined within the rooms you used at the time of your coronation. This way, Madam".

Without further speech, Anne obediently followed him to the aforementioned apartments. Only when she finally stood in those chambers of happy memory did she say "Before you go, Sir William, I would ask one more thing. I was allowed to bring no waiting women with me; will you send for Lady Lee and Lady Berkeley?"

"Four ladies have been chosen to attend you" Kingston informed her. "I will send them to you presently".

Later, when the women entered her chamber, she stared from face to face blankly. "I find all but one of you unknown to me" she said coldly. "Kindly make yourselves known".

They were a Mrs Shelton, Mrs Cousins, Mrs Stonor and, the one she did know, an aunt by marriage, Lady Boleyn, for whom she had long fostered an intense dislike. By their shifty demeanours Anne was in no doubt as to their true purpose. "You are evidently chosen to spy upon me" she said in a sarcastic tone. "Much good may it do you". With that, and much to their consternation, she threw her head back and began to sing one of her favourite lyrics at the top of her voice.

For ten long days she saw no-one but her spies, Kingston, Lady Kingston and Cranmer, the latter also being her confessor. The only information she could glean was that there was much activity at Westminster whilst informants were interviewed and the evidence gathered.

On 12th May Kingston came to her and read aloud the crimes of which she was accused. She gazed at him remotely, as though he were talking about some other woman, not herself. With her hand on her heart she said clearly "I am innocent".
"That may well be, Madam" said Kingston in an awkward tone as he rolled the charge sheet and slipped it into his doublet. "But I am bound to inform you that this day, four of the men accused with you

go to trial in Westminster Hall".
Anne nodded her head thoughtfully. "And will I be informed of the verdict?"
"Indeed" Kingston assured her.

She spent a restless afternoon, jumping at every little sound, alert at the echo of every footstep on the stair. "Her Grace seems most concerned as to the fate of her lovers" Mrs Cousins remarked slyly, hoping to provoke Anne into some indiscreet retort.

Anne regarded the woman through expressionless half closed eyes, deeming such obvious prying unworthy of wasting breath on an answer. However, finally weary footsteps were heard climbing the stair treads to her chamber and soon Kingston stood before her.

Every inch a Queen, Anne drew herself up haughtily and stared him full in the face. "An account of the happenings" she demanded.
As though he were reciting a passage committed parrot-like to memory, Kingston replied in a monotone. "The four were accused of adultery with the Queen and of conspiring to murder the King". As Anne's brow creased in consternation, Kingston continued. "Norris, Weston and Brereton pleaded not guilty to both charges. Smeaton pleaded not guilty to the conspiracy charge …." The Lieutenant paused for breath and Anne broke in.
"You are saying that Smeaton admitted to adultery with me?"
"He did not refute his previous statement in which he admitted having known and violated the Queen"

Kingston confirmed.

"They cannot take his word against mine!" Anne burst out. "He is but a humble musician and I am the Queen; surely in a court of law my words would carry more weight than stories from his imagination? Dear God!" With her head bowed and her hands over her ears as if to fend off the words of Smeaton's betrayal which still seemed to hang in the air, Anne turned her back on Kingston and slowly walked to the window. After some moments, she dropped her arms to her sides and raised her head. Without turning round she addressed Kingston. "And the court's verdict?"

"All were found guilty of the charges as read and are sentenced to die a traitor's death within the week" Kingston replied with obvious distaste.

Anne whirled around. "Then it is plain that the court was informed of the verdict it should return before the trials even began!" she spat. "And worst of all I find it a gross travesty of justice that four innocent men – three of them the King's close friends – are condemned to die in order that the King may be rid of me and free to vent his evil lusts elsewhere! Justice? Ha! No such thing in this land!"

And she would say no more.

On the next day, she received an abrupt dispatch from Cromwell stating that her household had been broken up and her servants either employed elsewhere or retired with pensions.

After flicking thoughtfully at the parchment with her

finger and thumb for some minutes, Anne tore the dispatch in half, then in half again and again until it was nothing but a pile of tiny pieces in her lap. And only then, for the first time since her imprisonment, did she give vent to the hysterical ravings she had suppressed for so long. For a time she plummeted to the darkest depths of despair and only afterwards did she think ruefully that she had no doubt inadvertently given her spies plenty of trivial information which their twisted minds would likely formulate into yet more evidence against her.

May 15th was the date set for her trial and her brother's. At the appointed time Anne, who was to appear first, walked regally into the King's hall, which adjoined the royal apartments within the precincts of the Tower. She mounted the low platform made for the occasion, curtseyed to the rank of assembled peers as court etiquette demanded then seated herself carefully in the chair of state provided and faced her judges. She had dressed elegantly and conservatively for this occasion which could decide whether she would live or die. The severely cut black velvet gown was relieved by a vivid crimson petticoat, around her neck she wore her favourite pearls and her neatly arranged hair was topped by a black velvet hat with a discreet feather ornament.

The jury was composed of her peers; twenty six of them had assembled to judge whether her actions had been treasonable or no, headed by the Duke of Norfolk sitting under the cloth of state with the lord chancellor to his right and the Duke of Suffolk to his left. Just in front of Norfolk sat his son the Earl of

Surrey, the Earl Marshall of England.

Anne looked searchingly at each face in turn and felt her spirits sink as she read their hostile expressions. Only one showed compassion for her plight, and that was the man she had once hoped to marry, Henry Percy, now Earl of Northumberland. She had guessed he would be there but found herself shocked by his appearance. From being a handsome, strapping young man he had become shrunken; his skin wore a deathly grey pallor and his hair was sparse. He was barely thirty and looked sixty.

Percy himself was aware of conflicting feelings as he found himself close to the person of Anne Boleyn for the first time in more than a decade. He had seen her since their courtship of course, but only fleetingly and from a distance. Did he love her still? He could not say, but certainly there still remained within him some spark of feeling for the King's wife. He was astonished at how little she herself had altered. Gone of course was that adorable softness he had first recognised in her, but those great eyes still glittered and provoked and her skin remained as smooth and clear as it had been in her teenaged years. As to her figure, no-one would ever guess that she was mother to one living daughter and three dead boys. Looking down at his own wasted frame, Percy thought sadly how revolted she would be by his appearance. Racked by the cough as he was, he did not expect to see another Christmas and he realised with a sinking heart that if the jury passed the required verdict, neither would she.

As he watched her, holding herself so proudly despite her apprehension, he again cursed his inability to stand by her all those years ago. If they had married, they would each have kept the other safe, and then neither of them would have ever had to face the ordeal before them. His head dropped and in his frailty his eyes filled with tears for the life they might have shared together.

The Duke of Norfolk opened the proceedings. Like the others, Anne was charged with conspiracy against the life of the King and adultery, but an additional indictment accused her of incest with her own brother and of procuring the King's affections by the use of witchcraft.

She jumped to her feet and firmly declared her innocence, gripping the rail before her for support as the first of the evidence was read aloud to the court.
"It is hereby stated that Anne, Queen of England procured for her own lustful pleasures a certain Henry Norris on the dates here given below. Also that she invited a certain Francis Weston, William Brereton and Mark Smeaton to visit her for carnal purposes within her state bedchamber. Later, additional evidence shall be produced containing the details of her incestuous union with Lord George Rochford, her own natural brother".

They dealt with the alleged witchcraft first. She was accused of having used a 'familiar' to do her devil's work and draw the King to her. When they finally allowed her to speak, Anne stated in a resigned voice that she had never looked for the King's attentions and had only taken the usual steps to ensure the safety of her virtue by refusing to live at court unchaperoned and returning the King's 'bed bribes'.

Then the dates upon which all her supposed adulterous acts had taken place were revealed to the court. For every date and time given, Anne had a ready answer; indeed the majority of them were so obviously fabricated that they turned the trial into a farce.

"What do you say to the charge that on October 4th 1533 you did procure Henry Norris to have illicit intercourse with you at Greenwich palace?" droned Norfolk.

"Not guilty" said Anne firmly. "As my physicians will testify, I was still confined to bed following the birth of my daughter Elizabeth and in no fit state to entertain any man".

"On 10th February 1534 did you or did you not invite Sir Francis Weston to know you carnally?" Norfolk continued.

"Not guilty! On that date I was carrying the King's child and would in no way have desired to endanger the birth of a future heir".

And so it continued; for each date stated, Anne truthfully told the court that she was either not at the alleged place of the crime or that she was either carrying, or had hopes of carrying the King's heir on those dates.

For the incest charge, Jane Rochford was called as prime witness and in contrived halting tones, informed the court of the times when brother and sister had been alone for lengthy periods for possible 'unnatural activities'. Having finished her testimony, Jane could not help throwing a deprecating half smile in the direction of her once much envied sister in law.

Refusing to look at her and keeping her eyes on her judges, Anne stated simply and honestly that Jane's evidence was but the rampant imagination and jealousy of a scorned wife and that although her relationship with her brother was close – he being one of her most trusted advisors – they had never in any way overstepped the bounds of natural law.

The most damaging part of Jane's evidence, and that which drew most gasps from the public gallery, was the statement regarding two incidences in November 1535. On 2nd November Anne was said to have lured George with her tongue in his mouth, culminating in carnal knowledge between the two on November 5th.

Anne again stood before the rail and gazed around the court in disbelief before answering that in November 1535 she was again in the early stages of pregnancy and vomiting with monotonous frequency. The onlookers in the galleries began muttering, prompting Norfolk to look up sharply; he sensed public opinion was swinging towards the Queen for every mother present knew that she could not be guilty of that which she was accused.

In reply to the conspiracy charge, Anne laughed briefly and said again. "Not guilty. For what would I be without the protection of my sovereign lord, hated by the people as I have been?"

Then the trial was over and a hubbub broke out in the courtroom that was barely silenced by Norfolk tapping his staff of office repeatedly on the floor. Anne was removed from the courtroom whilst the peers discussed their verdict and was confined under guard in a small chamber close to the royal apartments. She sat quietly, her hands clasped in her lap, staring dully before her. She did not have to wait long; only a very short time elapsed before she was called back and as she rose and smoothed her gown, she feared the worst.

Thankful that the fullness of her skirts masked the shaking of her legs, Anne walked slowly and with great dignity to the prisoner's bar and stood in front of her judges; her upper body craned forward slightly as though she were about to watch a play and did not wish to miss a single word.

"Gentlemen, state your verdicts!" Norfolk commanded.

One by one, each rose to his feet and said loudly and firmly "Guilty as charged" oblivious to the by now obvious unrest in the public galleries and the frequent cries of "Shame!" directed at them. When it came to Henry Percy, so overcome was he by both the knowledge that her eyes were upon him and the effects of his illness, that he could neither rise nor formulate an answer. He was carried swiftly from the courtroom, a shaking, snivelling wreck.

Anne's head bowed and her eyes filled with hot tears at the memory of their brief, sweet love, then as Norfolk addressed her, she raised her head and looked him full in the face, betraying no emotion. "You have been found guilty as charged and the sentence of this court is that you shall be executed within the precincts of these buildings, either burned or beheaded according to the King's pleasure".

She was unaware of the gasps of the onlookers and the jeers of derision aimed at Norfolk. Based on the defence she had made for herself, the verdict should have been acquittal and not a single onlooker doubted that the verdict had been decided before the prisoner even appeared.

Anne's legs almost buckled beneath her and her senses swam, then somehow she pulled herself together. She had lost; there was no going back now. This was real. Looking around the courtroom she said "My Lords, you have done your work well and your sovereign will no doubt reward you for granting his whim so readily. I will not pronounce your sentence unjust or presume that my defence should alter your convictions for I believe that you have sufficient reasons for what you have done, although they must be other than those which have been produced in court today. I am innocent of all those offences you have laid before me and have always been a faithful wife to the King. Perhaps I have not always shown the humility towards him that I should and of late I confess that I have nurtured jealous feelings and suspicions of him which I did not have the wisdom or discretion to conceal. However as God is my witness, I have not sinned against the King in any other way". She paused and looked around the courtroom; at her judges and at the avid spectators in the public galleries, before continuing. "I do not say this in a hope that it may prolong my life because I am not afraid to die. I have protected the honour of my chastity for my whole life and am now not about to admit myself false. I know these words will avail me nothing but I believe that all in this court should hear from my lips my justification of my chastity and honour. As for my brother and those others who are unjustly condemned, I would willingly suffer many deaths if they could be saved, but since it so evidently pleases the King, I will happily accompany them in death and am assured that I shall lead an endless life with them in peace and joy. I would have you remember, my Lords, that there is a King in heaven far greater than Henry Tudor, before whom I and the others shall shortly stand. When you too take your leave of this earth, for it will come to you all in various guises, I pray that you will not suffer for placing your earthly King's wishes above God's justice".

As she finished and was led out, a sympathetic ripple of applause sounded from the public galleries which could not be silenced no matter how many times Norfolk irritably pounded on the floor with his staff. In the passageway she passed her brother, on his way to the courtroom. Only a swift glance passed between them, George's quizzical raised eyebrow clearly expressing his contempt for the charade they were forced to take part in.

As she reached the second floor staircase, Anne automatically turned in the direction of her apartments, only to find her way blocked by Kingston. "I regret Madam that you may no longer reside in the royal apartments ... "Kingston began self-consciously.

Anne understood at once. "Ah yes!" she exclaimed. "I am no longer a Queen, just another condemned prisoner, am I not? So it is to be a dungeon after all?"

"No Madam" the Lieutenant assured her. "Prisoners of rank are confined to the upper rooms of my lodging house on the green".

Chapter 35

Condemned

"Your brother is also to die a traitor's death!" spat Mrs Cousins triumphantly.
Anne feigned indifference; the only sign of her having heard was the raising of her chin a fraction higher than normal. Disappointed that her spiteful words had provided no outburst from the prisoner, Mrs Cousins slunk back to her companions seated comfortably around the hearth.

Alone again, Anne closed her eyes and pressed her fists to her temples. She had guessed of course that George would not, could not be spared. As she had been found guilty of incest it was a foregone conclusion that her brother too would be condemned. However the prior knowledge did not in any way blunt the pain of hearing the actual confirmation.

On the early evening high tide, Archbishop Cranmer rode down the Thames from Westminster to speak with her. Since he was her confessor, she was allowed to be completely alone with him and anything she revealed to him would go no further.

Watching her compassionately as she sat before him, twisting a handkerchief in her hands, Cranmer said softly "His Grace the King offers you an alternative course".

Her hands ceased their activity and she raised hopeful eyes to his face. "An alternative to death?"

Cranmer sighed. "Regrettably, no. But the King does not wish to send you to your Maker shamed by divorce; he wishes you to admit a pre-contract with Henry Percy".

Anne laughed mockingly. "Shamed by divorce indeed!" Why should I care? Whichever way, I shall die and my daughter be declared a bastard. Why should I make the way easier for him? Apart from which, my dear Archbishop, if I was never married to the King, how could I have committed adultery?"

"The other charges upon which you were convicted also carry the death penalty" Cranmer reminded her sadly, for in his heart he thought much of her.

"There is nothing more to say" Anne stated firmly. "He can do what he will to me, I am past caring, but it is better for my daughter to be the child of a divorced wife rather than of a woman who never married".

Cranmer was perplexed by her reasoning. "How so?"

Anne leaned closer to him, her manner confidential. "Because the mere fact of her mother being divorced will not bar Elizabeth from the succession, dear Cranmer. If I were to declare myself unmarried by reason of pre-contract, Elizabeth would have no more right to the throne than my sister Mary's boy".

"But the King will surely have more heirs?" Cranmer questioned.

Anne's eyes sparkled mischievously. "Will he? I think not. That ulcer on his leg was not just caused by his fall, you know. No. It has been present in a minor form these many years. I tell you, it is an outward manifestation of the rot within him. If he gets any more children it will be surprising; if they live to succeed him, it will be a miracle!"

"You speak treason!" Cranmer was shocked, looking about himself as though he expected the King's spies to emerge from every nook and cranny.

"What if I do?" she hissed. "Henry cannot kill me more than once; besides, you are my confessor and bound by God to tell no man what passes between us".

Nevertheless, Cranmer was not happy with the subject matter of their conversation, although he respected Anne's continued efforts to protect the future of her child. He sighed again, his mission today was highly distasteful to him, but he had to carry out his orders.

"Madam, it is not a case of whether you wish to admit a pre-contract or not; His Grace commands that you do so, and in return he guarantees that Elizabeth will remain in the succession, after, of course, any future legitimate child he may have, and the Lady Mary".

Anne looked at him sharply. "You believe he speaks the truth?"

Cranmer spread his hands and shrugged apologetically. "These are the words he spoke to me before I left and the words he wished me to convey to you".

Anne sat back in her chair and looked into the empty hearth, considering all she had heard. "I suppose it could be true" she said at last. "Especially in that the Lady Mary is also the child of a mother whose marriage was annulled and was then also divorced for good measure. Elizabeth is no different to her in that respect".

Cranmer waited expectantly.

Anne had made up her mind. "Very well" she told him. "Let the King have his way; he can call it pre-contract if it eases his conscience, although I cannot speak for Harry Percy".

"I believe secretary Cromwell is dealing with that part of the matter". Cranmer looked away as he spoke; he had no time for Cromwell's methods of extracting information.

Anne intercepted his expression and spoke with urgent concern "He will not seek to harm Percy?"

"No, I do not believe he could. Percy has done nothing wrong; a pre-contract does not attract the death penalty". His eyes flickered to her face; she was laughing silently, hugging herself.

"I have done nothing wrong either, yet here I sit, a condemned woman".

Cranmer shuffled his feet uneasily for he did not wish for her to upset herself further by railing against the injustice of her situation; instead, he brought her sharply back to the present by asking "Do you wish to make confession now?"

Anne sobered, remembering the perils she had yet to face. She nodded slowly, then folded her hands in prayer, bowed her head and poured out her heart to her confessor for the last time.

Much later, when she had been completely absolved and Cranmer was the only other person living who knew the absolute truth of her innocence, she asked about her brother and his friends.

"Do you know when they are to die?"

"Tomorrow afternoon" he replied, averting his eyes from her pained face.

"And the manner of their deaths? Surely not the full penalty for gentlemen?"

"Rochford, Norris, Brereton and Weston are to be beheaded. Smeaton, being low-born, will suffer the full penalty, God help him, unless the King intercedes". He crossed himself reverently as he spoke.

Anne followed his example and then displaying great self-control, spoke of her own fate. "Has the King made his pleasure known?"

"It is to be the block" replied Cranmer shortly. "He thought it would be the method you yourself would choose".

"It may be the last kindness he ever shows me" she whispered. "Thank him for his mercy, for God knows I have lain awake at night sweating with fear lest he choose the fire".

Cranmer was shocked to his priestly core. "Oh no, my lady. He would never wish to cause you such suffering. The very thought of sending a Queen to the fire …" he shook his head from side to side, unable to contemplate such horror.

"He has not stinted though, in his efforts to be rid of

me" Anne reminded him. "I shall be the first Queen in history to die on the scaffold; the first woman, in fact. But then, I was always one to set the fashion!"

Cranmer crossed himself hurriedly yet again, seeking heavenly guidance to protect himself from her frivolity. Getting awkwardly to his feet, he murmured "I must take my leave now, my lady. May God protect you now and in your hour".

Anne looked up at him. "I have one last request to make. Will you convey it to the King?"

"Willingly".

"Good". She smiled with satisfaction. "As you know, I was brought up in France, I speak the language fluently; my dress and manners are all French". She paused, seeking the words with which to frame her final request. "I have lived in the French manner and I wish to die likewise. Beseech His Grace to spare me the butchery of the English axe and allow me to die by the French sword!"

"I will do my best" he promised, his voice thick with emotion.

She knelt before him to receive his final blessing, and then as he left her said softly "Farewell dear Cranmer. If we do not meet again on this earth, then we shall in the hereafter. God keep you".

Finality

It was over; everything was done. Nothing remained but for the final scene to be played. Her death.

With fortitude and from a distance, she had witnessed the butchery of her brother and the others, but to her remote gaze it had seemed that with each fall of the axe, a tangible entity rose heavenwards from the decapitated trunks. It was a sign that God was comforting her; underlining her belief that although their lives on earth were done, their spirits awaited hers in the hereafter. Absently her lips formed the words "We shall be together soon, very soon". She was no longer afraid of death because she was sure that a better existence awaited her on the other side.

It was 6 o'clock on the morning of May 18th 1536; the day was hazy, with the promise of bright sunshine to come. She looked round to where her dear friend Margaret Wyatt Lee lay sleeping; it was due to Meg's arrival the previous night that she had remained calm and been happy for perhaps the last time, recalling happier days with her childhood friend.

Anne was about to wake Meg and ask her to assist her robing when she was startled by the sound of her door being unlocked. Immediately she was afraid that maybe she had mistaken the hour and that it was already time for her death. Frantically she looked from her window and saw that the scaffold was incomplete; there were workman's tools scattered across the platform and the straw was yet to be spread.

Lady Kingston let herself quietly into the room.
"What is it?" Anne hissed fearfully. "It is not already time?"
Lady Kingston raised her hand to still Anne's anxious questions. "There is to be a slight delay Madam; the swordsman is not expected to arrive before eleven, so it will be nearer noon before you are called".
"Then that is the cruellest blow of all" Anne replied bleakly. "I had hoped to be long gone by noon and past my pain".
"Oh there is no pain" the Lieutenant's wife assured her quickly. "They say it is quick and painless, the sensation like a fingernail running quickly and firmly across the neck".

Intrigued, Anne lifted her heavy hair and ran her own fingernail across her neck. "Then it is almost like a caress?" she whispered. "And I have only a little neck!"

Once Margaret was awake and acquainted with news

of the delay, there was little for the two friends to do except wait and pray. Occasionally Anne rose to her feet and walked slowly about the room; not from any agitation, more to exercise stiff muscles. Gazing through her window at the lush grass and trees, she realised that for most of her life her eyes had been half closed to the beauties of the world; she had been too busy running the race that was life. She wondered if such revelations came to all condemned prisoners; that nothing was ever truly appreciated until there was danger of losing it. And she was soon to be deprived of that most precious commodity of all; life.

Between 10 and the half hour, Anne dressed carefully for her last public appearance. She chose a dark grey damask gown with white trimming to the neckline and sleeves, and a crimson underskirt. She had Margaret coil her long hair about her head, then covered it with a plain linen cap which in turn was hidden by a wide brimmed black velvet hat, pinned at a jaunty angle. With her body dressed to her satisfaction and her mind calm, she knelt in prayer to make her peace with the world. That done, she sat close to the meagre fire Margaret had coaxed into life, to warm her cold hands. "How do you feel Anne?" Margaret ventured at last.

After a moment's thought, Anne replied "Strange … more as though I am ready to go to a court function rather than the scaffold. It may sound macabre, but I am looking forward to noon, for already I look towards eternity.

"It is so quiet" wondered Margaret. "Almost as though the whole world is holding its breath". Then into the silence came the harsh chiming of the Tower clock. It was eleven o'clock.

Weary footsteps were heard mounting the oaken stairwell and both women turned expectantly to the door as William Kingston opened it. Always perceptive to others' moods even when under extreme duress, Anne was at once puzzled by the expression Kingston wore. Slowly she walked towards him, her brow creased in consternation. "Mr Kingston?"

William Kingston bowed and then raised troubled eyes to hers. "Madam" he began. "I scarcely know how to tell you this …" His glance flickered across to Margaret, whose eager expression told him that she was hoping to hear news of a reprieve for Anne. Reluctantly he dragged his gaze back to the former Queen, and continued. "The gentleman from Calais still has not arrived, so it has been decided that your appointment must be postponed until the morrow".

Anne bowed her head, closed her eyes and shook her head slowly from side to side. Kingston watched her anxiously, afraid that the delay would cause another bout of the unstable behaviour which was so prevalent during the early days of her incarceration. He was however greatly relieved when Anne raised first her eyes, and then her arms, before proceeding to unpin her hat. "I confess I am disappointed" she told him, occupied with spearing the two hatpins into the hat she now held in her hands. "However, God will help me through these hours and I shall use them to prepare myself all the more diligently for the hour of my death.

Saying nothing, Kingston bowed and left the room. As the sound of his footsteps died away, Margaret's soft sobbing broke the silence. At once Anne dropped her hat to the floor and crossed the floor to take Meg into her arms. "It should be I who comforts you!" Margaret blurted tearfully. "How can you take such news so calmly?"

After a final hug, Anne stood away from her friend and shrugged her shoulders. "I feel I am fully prepared for death" she told her. "If God sees fit to delay the hour, who am I to question his judgement?"

Once Anne was changed back into the faded black velvet, the two knelt in prayer and remained at their devotions until Lady Kingston brought in their supper. Later, Anne's Almoner was allowed to join them, and it was with him that Anne prayed throughout the night whilst Margaret withdrew to sit and gaze thoughtfully into the depths of the meagre flames in the hearth.

As she bade her Almoner farewell soon after dawn, Anne felt rested and calm, almost as though she had enjoyed a long restful sleep. As she and Margaret sat down to a light breakfast at 6am, she found that she had a good appetite whereas Margaret could force very little down, her red eyes proclaiming how she had spent the previous night.

Yet again, Margaret helped Anne don her outfit of choice, reverently kissing the discarded black velvet gown as she lifted it from the floor. Her final task was to dress Anne's hair for the last time, brushing the luxuriant locks until smooth, then twisting and pinning them high on Anne's head. If Anne felt the hot tears Margaret shed as she lovingly performed this last favour, she made no mention of it, only reaching up to squeeze Meg's shaking hand momentarily, causing their eyes to meet in the small mirror set on the table in front of them. Anne smiled; Meg could not persuade her anguished features to form even the semblance of a response.

Once all was done, Meg busied herself tidying the chamber before pulling a chair close to Anne's and taking her hands in hers. "Thank you Meg" Anne told her.
"For what?"
"For being here".

The last minutes ticked resolutely away then suddenly Kingston was at the door and soon the sad procession was making its way down the staircase and out of the front door. On the threshold Anne paused for a second and breathed deeply of the fresh May air, then with great dignity walked slowly along the path to the low scaffold. The spectators, few in number but specially chosen to witness her death, turned to watch her as she mounted the four shallow steps to the platform.

With horror, she felt her carefully mustered courage slipping away from her as she looked down on the small gathering; each face wearing an expression either of triumph or pity. The sly triumph she could face, it was the pity which so nearly broke her. Then

Kingston touched her elbow. "You are expected to say a few words, Madam" he reminded her.
She swallowed hard and nodded "I have prepared a short speech" she told him, in a faint voice.

Turning again to the spectators, she took a deep breath and began. "Good people, I am here to die; for according to the laws of this country I am judged to die and therefore will not speak against it". She paused, looking about her again before continuing, her voice growing in strength with every sentence. "I am here to accuse no man, or to speak of that which I have been accused and thus condemned. I pray God save the King and grant him long to reign over this land, for to me he was ever a good and gentle sovereign lord. If any person seeks to meddle with my cause, I pray them to judge their best". Again she paused and out of the corner of her eye, saw Margaret sink to her knees in misery. She continued. "Thus I take my leave of this world and of you all and I heartily desire you all to pray for me".

Her speech finished, she backed away from the wooden rail and stood, her feet amongst the straw, taking in the last essences of the life she loved so dearly. For the last time she heard the birdsong, saw the bright beauty of the grass and flowers. Tilting her head slightly to one side she fancied she could hear the tramp of horses feet through the golden russet carpet of autumn along the paths of the Kentish woods near Hever. She would never see another autumn; she would never see Hever again.

Kingston touched her again. "Madam, I beg you. It is

time".

"One moment more, Kingston" she begged. "So many thoughts and so little time in which to think them".

With a last look at the bright sky and the shifting clouds, she retraced her steps to where Margaret stood and gave her a tremulous smile. As she reached up to unpin her hat, she could not disguise the trembling of her hands however hard she tried. Turning again to Margaret she gently refused the proffered binding for the eyes and into her hands delivered her hat and a small book of hours she had carried at her girdle since childhood. "Give it to Tom when you see him" she urged. "And tell him … tell him I was grateful to see his dear face in these my last moments".

Margaret gasped. "But where is he?"

"In the Beauchamp Tower, behind me and to my left". Anne replied quietly. "But now I must say goodbye to you and thank you most gratefully for your love and friendship all these years. Give my love to my family and to yours. Watch over my baby. Be brave Meg, for I am glad to die".

Squeezing Margaret's hands in a final farewell, Anne moved away from her and stood tall as her executioner knelt at her feet and with bowed head begged her forgiveness for the task he must undertake. Lapsing into the French tongue, Anne delivered the required forgiveness before handing him a leather purse containing the fee for his grisly work. Turning away, she knelt carefully in the straw at the centre of the platform, for there was no block for this French-style execution. After fastidiously arranging her skirts to cover her feet, she raised her head and boldly and for the first time, looked fully at her executioner; his sinister duty greatly enhanced by the severe mask of his trade which covered the head entirely apart from slits for the eyes and mouth. For the last time, Anne smiled, a beautiful, grateful smile solely for him, for she realised that to spare her further agony he had hidden his sword from her sight amongst the straw.

Before she took up her final position, she looked away to her left and focused her gaze upon the solitary face at the barred window high in the Beauchamp tower, then raised her hand in a silent, poignant farewell to Thomas Wyatt.

Her earthly duties done, she bowed her head and said her last prayers; she knew the swordsman would not strike until she gave the required signal. She could feel her heart pounding, yet felt a strange sense of disembodiment; almost as though she was moving through a dream and watching another preparing to die, not suffering the fate herself.

She murmured "To Jesus Christ I commend my soul", then lifted her head for the last time and held her arms away from her sides in mute signal of her readiness. Her senses as sharp as ever, she heard the rustling as the sword was drawn from its hiding place, thought she heard the soft approach of her executioner. Her eyes wide open, she stared towards the blue horizon of paradise and thought of her family, Tom Wyatt, Meg, the friends who had gone before, and, as the sword swished through the air, Elizabeth.

THE END

Author's Note

In compiling this fictionalized account of Anne's life, I have done my best to weave my story around the real historical events through which she lived without burying her personality under mounds of Tudor politics.

However, the woman who looks out from these pages is the woman I always believed Anne to be; strong, determined, witty, intelligent, forthright and honest. On the negative side, there is no doubt that she was sometimes arrogant, haughty, grasping, indiscreet and thoroughly unpleasant. In short, she was a human being!!

Much of Anne's personal history is unknown, apart from her times in royal service and as Queen. Even her year of birth is a hotly disputed topic amongst historians, some claiming as early as 1501, others 1507.

In this story, I have gone with a 1507 birth mainly because I have always felt that this was so but also because when her remains were examined in 1876 during the restoration of St Peter Ad Vincula, her bones indicated that she was aged between 25 and 30 when she died.

It was also noted during that examination that she was of slender and perfect proportions and that her vertebrae were particularly small especially the atlas joint next to the skull. So she indeed had a "little neck".

The bones of the skull indicated a well-formed and round head with a straight and ample forehead denoting considerable intelligence, large eyes, and oval face. She was of middle height with a short and slender neck; her hands and feet were delicate and well-shaped with tapering fingers and a narrow foot.

There was nothing on the bones of her hands to indicate the fabled "sixth finger" – this was indeed a fabrication of her enemies based upon a slight malformation of the nail on her little finger.

Her limbs were judged to be in proportion to the rest of her body; delicate and slender. The curvature of her ribs indicated a deep and well-formed chest.

Her teeth were found to be in a good state of preservation and it was noted that one molar on the left side was slightly decayed. I do hope that with all she had to bear towards the end of her life, she wasn't also afflicted with toothache.

There have been many excellent accounts written about Anne's life and I have dipped into just a selection whilst researching this novel. I would recommend them all to anyone interested in finding out more about this fascinating, complex woman.

Also listed are a number of books about Henry VIII and the residences associated with the Tudor period. There are many more out there, but the books named in the list are those which have been on my bookshelves for a good many years and have helped me shape the content of this novel.

BIBLIOGRAPHY

ANNE BOLEYN - Marie Louise Bruce

ANNE BOLEYN - Hester W. Chapman

ANNE BOLEYN - Norah Lofts

THE RISE AND FALL OF ANNE BOLEYN - Retha M. Warnicke

ANNE BOLEYN IN HER OWN WORDS & THE WORDS OF THOSE WHO KNEW HER - Elizabeth Norton

ANNE BOLEYN - Carolly Erickson

THE ANNE BOLEYN COLLECTION - Claire Ridgway

THE MAKING OF HENRY VIII - Marie Louise Bruce

THE SIX WIVES OF HENRY VIII - Paul Rival

SISTERS TO THE KING - Maria Perry

GREAT HARRY - Carolly Erickson

HENRY VIII - Jasper Ridley

THE SIX WIVES OF HENRY VIII - Alison Weir

THE SIX WIVES OF HENRY VIII - Antonia Fraser

THE REIGN OF HENRY VIII – David Starkey

LETTERS OF THE QUEENS OF ENGLAND 1100-1547 – edited by Anne Crawford

THE HOUSE OF TUDOR – Alison Plowden

TUDOR WOMEN – Alison Plowden

THE LIVES OF THE KINGS AND QUEENS OF ENGLAND – edited by Antonia Fraser

THE COURT AT WINDSOR – Christopher Hibbert

THE LIVES OF THE KINGS AND QUEENS OF FRANCE – Duc de Castries

NOTICES OF THE HISTORIC PERSONS BURIED IN THE CHAPEL OF ST PETER AD VINCULA – Doyne Courtenay Bell

THE TOWER OF LONDON IN THE HISTORY OF THE NATION – A.L. Rowse

THE ROYAL PALACES OF TUDOR ENGLAND – Simon Thurley

COBBETT'S COMPLETE COLLECTION OF STATE TRIALS VOLUME 1 (1163-1600)

Printed in Poland
by Amazon Fulfillment
Poland Sp. z o.o., Wrocław